# THE WITCH'S SEASON

## The Novel: A Team, A Town, A Campus, The Times

# TERRY FREI

ISBN: 1-4392-3463-9
EAN13: 9781439234631

Visit www.terryfrei.com.to order additional copies.

# PRAISE FOR TERRY FREI'S PREVIOUS BOOKS

## HORNS, HOGS, AND NIXON COMING

"The game and its cultural contexts have been beautifully chronicled by Terry Frei." – Bill Clinton in *My Life*

"One of the better – and most readable – books of social history published in recent years." – Pulitzer Prize-winning editorial writer Paul Greenberg, *Arkansas Democrat Gazette*

"...a superb blending of sports, history, and politics." – Si Dunn, *Dallas Morning News*

## THIRD DOWN AND A WAR TO GO

"Impressively researched and reported and powerfully written, *Third Down and a War To Go* will put you in the huddle, in the front lines and in a state of profound gratitude – not only to the Badgers and the hundreds of thousands of men like them, but to Terry Frei." – Neal Rubin, *Detroit News*

"*Third Down and a War to Go* tells the story of one University of Wisconsin football team during World War II. But to limit the tale to that is like saying *Angela's Ashes* is about Ireland. This book brings to life, in shades of black and blue and blood red, the idea that certain things are worth fighting for." – Rick Morrissey, *Chicago Tribune*

"Here's a book written with love and passion...What began as a sports book comes to resemble something akin to *Band of Brothers*, by the late Stephen Ambrose (who played for the Badgers more than a decade later)...This is an inspiring book, full of fun and pathos and heroism." –Dave Wood, past vice-president of the National Book Critics Circle and former book review editor of the *Minneapolis Star Tribune*.

## '77

"This is more than a football book: With all due respect to those who lived in Denver prior to '77, this is about a birth of a city." – Dave Logan, former U. of Colorado All-American, NFL player, voice of the Denver Broncos, and co-host of KOA Radio's "The Ride Home"

"The games, the politics and the culture with which Frei deals here unfolded 30 years ago, but they're brought to life again in this book with a clarity and a luster that makes the story of Denver and the Broncos seem as fresh as the upcoming football season...Frei has written Denver's version of `Ladies and Gentlemen, the Bronx is Burning.'"

−Michael Knisley, Senior Deputy Editor, *ESPN.com*

"No one knows more about Denver and its sports than Terry Frei does, and here in '77, he describes nothing less than the transformation of a city with a special focus on Denver's most magical team. To know why and how the Mile High City exists as it does today, this is essential history." − Sandy Clough, Denver FM Sports Radio 104.3, The Fan

This novel is dedicated to those who see even a bit of themselves in it.

"Oh, no, must be the season of the witch..."
– Donovan P. Leitch, 1968

# ONE:

## "WAITING FOR THE SUN"

*(Cascade, Oregon; Monday, August 26, 1968)*

Jake Powell's "studio apartment" was a crudely converted attic. The sink, toilet, and bathtub all were within ten feet from the tiny twin bed. His banged-up Schwinn bicycle lay flat in one corner. A clothesline was his closet and the floor was his dresser. His stereo, a tiny box with a turntable and built-in speakers, cost him $7.50 at the Salvation Army store, and the records he played on it were haphazardly piled in a corner – some even in album covers. Small posters of Robert Kennedy, Jimi Hendrix, Jim Morrison, Donovan P. Leitch, and Mohandas Gandhi were taped to the angled walls, and one of a menacing Chicago Bears linebacker Dick Butkus was tacked to the door. To the side of it, a cardboard box overflowed with mimeographed sheets, headlined, "THE CASCADE MANIFESTO."

After fifteen seconds of twisting and rattling at the door, Annie Laughlin managed to get her key and the ancient lock to cooperate and let herself in. Jake was asleep, in only his jockey shorts, with a single sheet strewn over him. Annie nudged aside books and papers from the card table that doubled as his dining table and his desk, put down the bag marked The People's Bakery, and shook him.

"We're going to be late!"

Shoving back his mop of hair and then rubbing his eyes, Jake said, "Good morning to you, too." He looked at his alarm clock, which said 8:32 and was at least close. Sliding out of bed, he shed his jockey shorts and took a step toward the bathtub. Spotting the paper bag, he detoured to snatch a bear claw and took one bite before putting it down and stepping into the bathtub. He closed the wraparound curtain, turned on the shower spray, and was lathering up when Annie cracked open the curtain.

"I'm going ahead," she said. "Don't forget the petitions."

Annie was aggravated, yet unembarrassed. By now, nothing she saw when she barged into Jake's apartment embarrassed her – not Jake asleep, not Jake stepping out of the shower, not Jake on the toilet, not even him in bed with the girl who gave him a dollar off the record-player needle at the record store and then came home with him to make sure it fit the Salvation Army stereo.

After grabbing a donut, Annie hurried out the door and ran down the stairs.

☙

Many seeing Neal Hassler for the first time wondered if he was ill or reached his goals on a successful diet and kept going. Most of his friends noticed his pallor and didn't have to guess. They knew his job was making him sick.

The Cascade University president stepped out of his blue compact car behind Franklin Hall, the ivy-draped administration building. He began his daily brisk walk down 23rd Avenue, the tree-lined main street through the university. For eighteen years at CU, as a professor, as a dean, and finally as president, Hassler had luxuriated in the campus' greenery.

Outside the CU Bookstore on the corner, a sandwich board sign announced: "AVOID THE RUSH, BUY YOUR TEXTBOOKS NOW!" On the side facing the street, someone had drawn a line through "RUSH" and written "DRAFT" over it.

The shop next door opened during World War II as Dottie's Donuts, and Dottie's family still owned it. A year earlier, the shop shut down for remodeling at the behest of Dottie's bookkeeping son, a 27-year-old who preached Marxism yet maneuvered for maximum profit. A week later, it reopened as The People's Bakery.

The young woman with red, frizzy hair behind the counter spotted him and, without asking, retrieved a single maple bar, dropped it in a bag, and put it on the counter. As she poured his cup of coffee, she didn't raise her eyes. "Can't you get the murderers off campus?" she asked.

"Excuse me?"

She gave Hassler a piercing look. "ROTC. The murderers."

Hassler thanked her as he turned away from the counter, hoping she knew the gratitude was for the maple bar and coffee, and not the question.

# ONE: WAITING FOR THE SUN

As he did a couple of mornings a month, he stopped on the stone stairs outside the administration building and gazed at the message carved into the facade.

**FRANKIN HALL**
**"The noblest question in the world is,**
**'What good can I do in it?'"**
**– Benjamin Franklin**

His secretary, silver-haired and plump Diana Gray, had served more presidents than a White House steward. Her frosty professionalism was impenetrable on the job, even for her boss, but he had heard of Diana's vehement loyalty off-duty, including when her Lutheran choir leader tried to console her for having to work for "Hassler, the new idiot" and the choir had to go without a soprano for two Sundays until he apologized.

In the foyer, Diana reminded Hassler that Jake Powell and Annie Laughlin had the first appointment, at 9, "to drop off their petitions."

Hassler had spotted copies of *The Cascade Manifesto* petition around campus during the summer-school session. It was a laundry list; he doubted that many students who signed it had read it, and organizers said they considered this an ongoing drive that would continue through the early weeks of the fall semester. They were dropping off the first wave of signed petitions because the Number One demand – that the CU food service to stop buying West Coast grapes and strawberries – hoped to influence the fall food orders. The petitions also called for a ban on Army, Navy, Air Force, and Marine recruiters from periodically setting up tables, handing out literature, and speaking with students in the Student Union; prohibiting "war profiteers," such as the Dow Chemical Company, the manufacturer of napalm, from conducting job interviews on campus as scheduled in early 1969; and not allowing City of Cascade police officers on university property.

When there was turmoil on campus, Jake and Annie most likely were part of it.

∽

"NO GRAPES...NO STRAWBERRIES...NO EXPLOITA-TION!"

Five minutes into the protest and the chants, Annie already was hoarse. She looked down at the crowd of about a hundred students, gathered below her on the Franklin Hall steps.

Most Students for a Democratic Society firebrands were on the six-year track to graduation, but Annie – the SDS state chairman – not only had enough credits to be considered a full-time student, her transcript also was all A's. She was short of stunning, yet cute – and, again unlike so many of her contemporaries in radical student politics, she didn't try to hide it. Her button-down white blouse with nothing underneath and her jeans adhered to the rebellious conformity, but her short and wavy blond hair was carefully brushed.

She raised her hands to stop the chanting. "I've visited these camps!" she hollered. "They're getting worse, not better! Every grape and strawberry this university orders condones the horrible treatment of the migrant workers! It must stop!"

With his hair flying, Jake charged up the stairs. He wore a beat-up pair of corduroys and a plaid sport shirt he had tucked in, and then purposefully untucked to avoid the impression he was dressing up to see the president. The petition boxes were under one arm, and he used the other to wedge his way through the crowd, up the stairs and to Annie's side.

Annie reached across Jake, into the box, and lifted a stabled set of sheets. "These petitions and all these signatures speak volumes, and the university must pay attention!"

"Must we?"

Annie and Jake turned to see President Hassler. "Your appointment was for a meeting in the office, not a show on the steps," he said. "If you're sincere about this, you – just you two – will come in now, and we will talk about this. And you'll tell these people to leave."

Annie was indignant. "I–"

"Let's go," Jake said.

Still carrying the box, Jake started to follow Hassler, and then stopped. "Everybody!" he yelled, waving. "That's enough...for now!"

Taking a couple of strides back and, putting an arm around Annie's shoulder, Jake gently nudged her toward the big double doors of Franklin Hall. Annie swatted away Jake's arm, but followed, and a few moments later, they were in the conference room adjacent to Hassler's office.

Hassler nodded at Annie and gestured at a chair. Glaring, Annie walked past that chair, to another nearby, but didn't sit.

Jake slid the box on the table, pulled out one stapled petition set, and handed it to Hassler. Both of them sat down – Hassler to read, Jake to wait. The president had gotten to the bottom of the first page when Annie finally alighted in yet another chair, but perched on the end. Jake absent-mindedly touched the MORSE FOR SENATE button pinned to his shirt, and then fingered aside the hair that had fallen over his wire-rimmed glasses.

Annie waved at the box. "It wasn't easy to get that many signatures during summer term, but look at that! Over three thousand so far!"

"Most of them legitimate," Jake added, slyly.

Annie didn't notice the attempt to lighten the atmosphere. Jake caught the curl of acknowledgment at the corner of Hassler's mouth.

"There will be a lot more this fall," Annie said.

"For a start," Jake said, "we're asking you to have the university stop purchasing grapes and strawberries."

Hassler leaned back, crossing his arms. "I won't order a boycott."

Annie exploded. "Are you that powerless?"

Jake pleaded, "Sir, please reconsider! If the university keeps buying grapes and strawberries, it's condoning the exploitation of those workers."

Hassler clasped his hands. "You seem to forget that students already have a voice in what the university orders. If nobody eats something, we don't order it! It's the same with your other issues. No matter how many signatures you get, the military recruiters will be on campus, like other corporate recruiters. Nobody forces anyone to join or even listen. And Dow Chemical? How can you in good conscience deny students the chance to interview with a major company that wants to hire our graduates?"

"Conscience?" Annie snapped. "Dow has none!"

"Then don't apply for a job with them," Hassler said. As he continued, his voice softened. "I need the right to call the Cascade

Police on this campus at any time. It's for your protection. You know how small the campus force is."

"You saw what happened on the Wisconsin campus last year at the Dow protests," Annie said. "The Madison cops clubbed and gassed everyone in sight. It can happen here, too."

"There needs to be restraint on both sides," Hassler said.

Annie jumped out of her chair and started toward the door, then did a sudden pivot.

"They say you're different." She angrily hooked a thumb at Jake. "He keeps saying you're different. You're not."

She was gone.

"Is that your last word on this?" Jake asked Hassler.

"At least for the grapes and strawberries, I will consider whether there's a way to further recognize that individual students believe strongly about this."

Jake stood. "Sir," he said, "thanks for meeting with us, but we won't just give up."

"I know that," Hassler said.

As they shook hands, Jake said, "I hope you understand Annie's heart is in the right place."

Hassler sighed. "I'm not sure I know what that means any more." He nodded at the wall clock, which showed 9:40. "Don't you have to be at practice?"

"Shit!" Jake exclaimed. Catching himself, he said, "Sorry, sir. Is that the right time?"

"Five minutes fast."

Walking backwards, Jake said, "If I'm late, could you put in a word for me with Coach Benson?"

Hassler smiled. "Sure. But I'm not sure you'd like the word."

Outside, at the top of the stairway, Kit Dunleavy, the Campus Daily reporter who covered campus politics, waited. She had a slight frame and long, straight brown hair. As now, Kit usually wore jeans tight enough to leave little to Jake's imagination, but baggy shirts over T-shirts that made Jake wonder.

"What happened in there?" she asked, her pen poised at her notebook.

"Sorry, Kit," Jake said, continuing to walk. "I'll have to let Annie speak for us this time."

# ONE: WAITING FOR THE SUN

Kit followed him. "You sure you want to do that?"

"Hell, no. I said I *had* to."

He broke into a jog.

# TWO:
## "JUMPIN' JACK FLASH"

After trotting the quarter-mile from the president's office to the Cascade football team's dressing room in the basement of Hobson Court, the ivy-draped basketball arena, senior linebacker Jake Powell tossed his glasses onto the top shelf of his locker and hurriedly changed into shorts, T-shirt, and football shoes. Deciding he didn't have time to put in his contact lenses, he raced down the hill to the grass practice field next to Burleson Field, the track team's stadium.

He was five minutes early, but on the first day of fall college football practices, that's late, and he was the last of the eighty-six varsity players to show up.

As Jake scrambled to join his teammates, Alex Tolliver, the Fishermen's star middle linebacker and team captain, waved him over.

"Good start," Alex said dryly. "Before practice even starts, they're asking me where you are."

"I was at the principal's office."

Whistles sounded, and Jake and his teammates soon were going through the first-day regimen of running, agility drills and other physical tests.

Timmy Hilton, Cascade's star junior tailback, outran everyone, although his huge Afro might have cost him a tenth of a second in the sprints. Jake and Alex were at the front in the linebackers' races, playfully leaning into an invisible finish "tape."

Larry Benson, the Fishermen's hawk-nosed head coach, watched most of the workout from the middle of the practice field, making occasional exhorting visits into the positional groups. At forty-four, he still could remember those opening-day workouts when he was a guard playing both offense and defense at the University of Minnesota in the World War II era. As a coach, the first day invigorated him and his staff more than their group two-week fishing trip to Central Oregon's Diamond Lake, when the coaches trolled around the lake in the rented boats, played poker, and took turns gutting the fish. At times, the on-field work seemed the easiest part of his job.

Much of Benson's off-season was spent trying to convince anxious parents, alumni and other fans that the entire student body wasn't stoned, that Freshman Copulation and Public Utility Bombing were not required first-term courses, and that just because a few zealots waved the North Vietnamese and Viet Cong banners outside the CU Student Union, the path across campus was not the Ho Chi Minh Trail.

Finally, he blew his whistle.

"Bring it in!" he hollered, and the players and coaches formed a semi-circle around him.

"Good work!" he said, sweeping his gaze along the rows of players. "It looks as if most of you are in shape."

A sophomore offensive guard broke ranks, moved faster than he had in the sprints, and threw up in the garbage can where the players tossed used adhesive tape.

Benson gestured toward the guard.

"And those of you who aren't, will get there soon – one way or another! Is that clear?"

Heads nodded.

"Now, I think most of you have met Bill Wyden, our athletic director," Benson said slowly, nodding toward the lanky man wearing a coat and tie who was walking from the sideline to join them. "He's asked to speak to you."

Wyden strode in front of the players and nervously cleared his throat.

"I'm looking forward to great things from you this season," he said. "That would be a huge boost to the athletic department. Booster contributions are up thirty-five percent this year after we tied for second in the conference last season!"

"Where's *our* cut?" Jake said softly, but not softly enough. Several players laughed.

"Excuse me?" Wyden asked, looking at Jake.

"Well, you made all that money and..."

"Powell!" Benson hollered.

Alex Tolliver tried to muzzle Jake with a hand on his elbow. It didn't work.

Jake said, "But it's only fair that—"

# TWO: JUMPIN' JACK FLASH

"Back on the line!" barked Benson.

Grumbling and glaring at Jake, the players trotted back to the goal line. The coaches followed.

Special-teams coach Rex Gamberg, in his first season on the staff, rushed over to act as the starting-line supervisor. "Be sure to let Powell know how much you appreciate this!" Gamberg yelled.

As the players sprinted toward the other end of the field, Benson's frown quickly changed into a wry smile. He noticed that Wyden hadn't moved and seemed to be assuming the players would regroup around him when they were done. Instead, when all had made it across the finish line on the return sprint down the field, Benson yelled, "That's it for the group! Powell, be in my office in a half-hour!"

In the end zone, Jake was in a group of players that included Alex Tolliver, Timmy Hilton, senior split end Keith Oldham, and offensive tackle Todd Hendricks. Although he was only a sophomore on the roster, Todd was one of the oldest players on the team, nicknamed "Sarge" because he spent three years in the Army after high school.

Alex Tolliver not only was the team captain, he also was its spiritual, Bible-toting leader. He was raised in the rough projects of Los Angeles, but his faith – thanks to the influence of his strict mother – never had wavered. "Ecclesiastes says there's a time and a purpose for everything," Alex told Jake.

Todd said, "He means shut the fuck up sometimes."

Timmy lifted a hand off one hip and waved it. "Aw, Coach was just trying to cut off Wyden's speech."

Keith Oldham, whose hair was long enough to qualify him for a bass-guitarist role in any rock group, was a member of the student senate and had joined Jake at some of the anti-Vietnam War protests. He also was the best shape of anyone on the team, so he talked as effortlessly as if he hadn't run a step all day. "I bet he was about to tell us to get haircuts, stay out of campus politics, and maybe even beat up some hippies," Keith said.

"I'll trade two more sprints for listening to that shit any day," Timmy said as he and Keith trotted back on the field to catch passes.

$\backsim$

*Portland Herald* sportswriter Dusty Harris tried to catch up with the roster sheet he dropped when he put his cigarettes back into his overcoat pocket and began walking toward the coaches. After a couple of swipes at the grass, Harris gave up on the roster, but continued across the field. He pulled a notebook out of his back pocket, though his note taking while interviewing amounted to scribbling down one word for every response. He regularly had Benson making pronouncements in print along the lines of, "Their gridders are noble as well." Benson hadn't used the word "gridders" in his life.

Harris was fifty-six, but he looked old and sick enough to have been gassed in the World War I trenches, and his rasp added to the impression. His frozen squint gave him the look of a man poring over the *Daily Racing Form* in bad light, trying to find the dollar sign on the old Royal typewriter, or playing coy over a full house. He joined Benson and the coaches as they watched the informal passing-game work.

"So how many showed up with the clap?" he growled.

"Results aren't in yet," Benson said.

Benson started to walk toward the trainers to ask for the updated odds on whether Tom Davis, their gimpy-kneed All-Coast quarterback, could make it through the season. His backup was going to be the rail-thin sophomore Rick Winslow, who had shown a strong arm but was untested. The goal would be for Davis to take all the meaningful snaps and to work Winslow in just enough to get him ready to start the next season.

"How's Khrushchev?" Harris asked.

Over his shoulder, Benson said, "I assume you mean Powell."

"Shit, he is the head of the Young Communists."

"Campus Coalition against the War," Benson corrected.

Harris waved his notebook. "Same thing! Christ, Larry, how do you put up with Powell's shit? You of all people? How many missions you fly?"

"Everybody who came back flew the same number."

"Huh?"

"Not one too many."

❦

# TWO: JUMPIN' JACK FLASH

Benson's office was nothing fancy, as was the case about almost everything tied to the Cascade football program. Even Potestio Stadium, across the Astor River footbridge from the CU campus, was an economic bargain. The earthen concrete bowl replaced the ancient Burleson Field, which remained renowned worldwide as a cozy venue for track meets, yet in its final years of use as a football stadium increasingly had turned off high school prospects and hampered the Fishermen's recruiting efforts. Potestio Stadium opened in 1964, Benson's first season as head coach after twelve years as an assistant under the legendary Hank Gardenia, but the football offices remained in a ramshackle office wing connected to Hobson Court.

As Benson waited for Jake, he looked at the magnetic board behind him that listed the current roster and depth chart, as well as the season schedule on one side, and mused about the Fishermen's '68 chances.

Street and Smith, the preview magazine, had the Fishermen picked to again finish second to Southern California in the Pacific 8, this time alone. In the months since the writer from California turned in his copy for the magazine – it was due roughly an hour after the Rose Bowl ended – Benson had taken down the nameplates for three significant players. A tackle and a quarterback flunked out, not believing until the last second that the coaches couldn't fix it with professors when players didn't show up for classes. The tackle was at Fort Ord, hoping he wouldn't end up in Vietnam. The quarterback had been ticketed to back up the gimpy Tom Davis while Rick Winslow red-shirted. Now he was learning to play hockey in Red Deer, Alberta, and trying to grasp the concept of icing. Also, Tony Brantley, the Fisherman's projected starter at defensive end, left campus to campaign in New Hampshire for Senator Eugene McCarthy, in advance of the presidential primary, and hadn't made it back. Also, Timmy Hilton had been switched from flanker to tailback, where the staff hoped he would be a game-breaker. It was a risky move, but the Fishermen had a handful of high-quality receivers and the hope was to get the ball in the hands of their most talented player more often.

Despite all the changes and uncertainty, Benson was convinced the Fishermen had a bona fide chance to win the league title this season – with a little good fortune...and not too many distractions.

The key conference game, against USC, was in the third week of the season. The good news was that it was at home; the bad news was that the Fishermen would be coming off a road game at powerful Nebraska in the second week.

When Jake dropped into a chair opposite his coach, the linebacker's hair still was wet.

"So you know," Benson said, "President Hassler just called and asked if you got to practice on time. Then he gave me the full report."

"Oh, oh," Jake said.

"Actually, there still are a lot of people around here who think that without you to control Annie Laughlin, the SDS might have blown up the chemistry building by now."

"Nobody controls Annie, coach."

"Regardless, I'm not going to sit here and tell you what you can and can't do outside of football – within reason and within the rules everyone else has to live under on this campus. Fair enough?"

"That's why a lot of us are here."

"But when you're with us, we can and will tell you what to do. This is not a rally. This is a football team. When you pop off like you did with Wyden, you make me wonder if I'm being naïve."

"He was just so–"

"I'm not telling you to make football your life. Make it your focus for part of the day. Timmy could have said that and even Wyden might have laughed. But you can't be a smart-ass with the athletic director, so he comes in here and says that kind of disrespect from a campus troublemaker shows why I need to tighten the reins on everyone in the program."

"Sorry. What did you say to that?"

"That sometimes I wanted to take those reins and strangle you myself. I said you're too small and too slow. I said I wished that Dusty Harris could stop calling you 'rebel linebacker Jake Powell' on first reference. I also said you were an academic All-American, you were fourth on the team in tackles last season, and as hard as we've tried, we can't find anyone to beat you out."

"Gee, thanks."

"And I said your dad would be proud of you."

Jake looked down and said, "Well, at least in football."

"I bet he could have handled it," Benson said. "My sons and I debate this war sometimes and I haven't disowned them."

"Are you coming around?" Jake asked with a tight smile.

"Oh, I wonder about it. But I also wonder what would have happened if we didn't trust our leaders when we were your age."

"That war was different."

"Beside the point! And what happened with Wyden isn't really that important on its own. It's the overall issue. We've shown a lot of faith in you as young men, and I'm telling you again not to abuse it. That's not a request."

"I know," Jake said.

"Then act like you know it from now on."

Gluepots, carbon paper, copy paper, and used-up typewriter ribbons were strewn all over the *Campus Daily* office in the basement of the Student Union. Kit Dunleavy already was enough of a journalist to feel at home among the rubble. She was satisfied with her story, but she had placed the carbon paper backwards for the third page and thus had blue carbon on the back of the story's final sheet. This would have to do.

By Kit Dunleavy

*Campus Daily Staff*

Student activists Monday delivered the first batch of "Cascade Manifesto" petitions to President Neal Hassler, saying over 3,000 students had agreed that the university should cease purchasing strawberries and table grapes to protest treatment of migrant workers in the California fields.

The petitions also asked that military recruiters and Cascade police be banned from campus.

Students Jake Powell, the CU football team linebacker who serves as chairman of the Campus Coalition Against the War, and Annie Laughlin, state chair of the Students for a Democratic Society, also known on campus as the "Roseburg radicals," met with Hassler at Franklin Hall.

The two CU seniors emphasized that the petitions will continue to be circulated during the fall semester, and said they considered the grapes and strawberry issue to be the most pressing because of the imminent beginning of the fall semester and the return of many students to the residence halls.

Laughlin said that the university president rejected the students' argument that the administration should order an immediate boycott of strawberries and grapes. "He needs to wake up and give students voices in what products the university purchases," Laughlin said.

When told of Laughlin's comments about the produce purchases, President Hassler responded: "I have been taking the petition's sentiment under advisement for weeks and I expect to make an announcement on the issue soon, but what everyone seems to forget is that students already have those voices – in the cafeteria lines."

# THREE:
## "BORN TO BE WILD"

*(Wednesday, August 28, 1968)*
 Neal Hassler wrote out his policy statement on grapes and strawberries, grimly considering it a prelude for a contentious fall on campus – and in a state often seemingly caught up in a political identity crisis.

 Oregon's Republican governor, Tim McMichael, was a former television commentator, and his political leanings were unclassifiable and unpredictable. Longtime U.S. Senator Wayne Morse, a cantankerous Democrat from the Willamette Valley, was one of the first on Capitol Hill to publicly oppose the Vietnam War. However, if you believed the polls, Morse's Republican opponent was going to beat him in the upcoming election with a strategy of mild dissent to the war, while mainly implying that Morse was over the hill. Richard Nixon was projected to carry the state in the presidential race, just as he had against John Kennedy in 1960. Especially outside of the Willamette Valley, Oregon could be as redneck as any stretch of Alabama.

 The public affairs office announced Hassler's plan in the afternoon. For the first two weeks of classes, "opt-out" grape and strawberry forms would be available at the registrar's office. Each student could fill out one, and only one, and if it were confirmed to come from a legitimate student, it would count. The university would cut the grape and strawberry purchase compared to a year ago accordingly. If 6,000 of the 15,000 students made the effort to fill out the form, the university would buy forty percent fewer grapes and strawberries for the dormitory cafeterias and other food-service facilities, including the Student Union, as soon as it was feasible. And if it became necessary for the university to cease using grapes and strawberries as automatic accompaniments on some plates because of shortages, so be it.

 Hassler made no direct reference to the "Cascade Manifesto," saying only that he was responding to "student concerns." He also didn't mention that he and his wife, Eleanor, had decided that they wouldn't buy or eat grapes or strawberries in the foreseeable future.

The calls began almost immediately.

Governor McMichael bellowed, "What kind of dim-bulb scheme is that, Neal? Jesus, what did you do, sit down and try to decide what you could do to piss off everyone in the state? And how goddamn much is all that paperwork going to cost?"

A state senator screamed to Hassler that he was surprised that Hassler wasn't in Chicago with the other "nut cases, throwing shit at the police."

The state chancellor of higher education ranted, "Half the students never eat in the Student Union or a dorm anyway!"

Annie Laughlin met with a small group of reporters, including a writer from the Cascade *Times-Register* and the *Campus Daily's* Kit Dunleavy. "Hassler's gesture is cynical, heartless, insufficient and unacceptable," Annie said.

While still scribbling in her notebook, Kit asked, "Why?"

"*Why?* Why *what?*"

Kit finished writing. "Why is it..."

She paused and raised her notebook.

"...'cynical, heartless, insufficient and unacceptable'?"

"You can't be half-pregnant and you can't be 37.2 percent behind a principle," Annie said. "This is morally indefensible. In this kind of issue, there is no room for compromise. Don't you agree?"

"It doesn't matter if I agree," Kit said.

Later, Jake Powell also met Kit and the other reporters outside Hobson Court. The quote the *Times-Register* later selected later was, "I respect President Hassler's attempt to take the students' wishes into consideration, and that he did it early in the petition drive. I don't believe this goes far enough, but I hope the students will speak decisively."

"It sounds like you're agreeing there at least might be room for compromise," Kit said during the group session.

"Compromise is better than nothing," Jake said.

"Annie Laughlin doesn't agree."

"Compromise is better than nothing."

# THREE: "BORN TO BE WILD"

Chicago was a mess, both live and on film, and on all three networks. Rioters swarmed in Grant Park. Excrement, billy clubs, urine-filled balloons, mace, eggs, tear gas, bricks, and epithets flew. Police arrested Abbie Hoffman for having "FUCK" on his forehead. The peace plank was defeated in platform debate. Folk singer Theo Bikel led thousands in the park in "We Shall Overcome."

Senator Abraham Ribicoff, from Connecticut, gave the nominating speech for one of the contenders. "With George McGovern as president, we would not have to have such Gestapo tactics in the streets of Chicago," Ribicoff said.

From the floor, Mayor Richard Daley mouthed an unmistakable, "Fuck you!"

"How hard it is to accept the truth," Ribicoff responded. "How hard."

With 103 3/4 votes from Pennsylvania, Vice President Hubert Humphrey clinched the nomination.

"I want to pack my bags and get out of this city," CBS anchor Walter Cronkite told America.

In his den, Hassler spoke softly to Cronkite's black-and-white image. "I know how you feel. You just wonder what's next."

Eleanor called out from the living room, "What'd you say?"

Hassler rocked his reclining chair forward, walked to the TV set and flicked it off with a turn of the dial. On the move, he said, louder, "You just wonder what's next!"

"President Humphrey!"

"Besides that."

In front of the family's other TV in the living room, Eleanor was working the crossword puzzle from the *Times-Register*, peering over the top of her reading glasses. As her husband joined her, she put down the page. "But I don't know why anyone would want that job – or yours."

"Good point."

Hassler pointed to the *Times-Register*, piled next to Eleanor. "Throw me the sports section, will you? Maybe the football team can take my mind off this. As long as they don't mention Powell."

"Or Annie Laughlin?" Eleanor asked.

Hassler sat down with the sports section. "Not much chance of that," he said. "I'm not even sure she can tell a basketball and a football apart."

∾

Jake and Annie met as high school classmates in Roseburg, seventy miles south of Cascade. Many residents there cut down trees outside town or worked in the mills in town; either way, they came home smelling like wet bark or sawdust. Many of their children, including Annie and Jake's classmates, would follow them into the lumber industry.

When Jake was taking a speech class in his junior year, the teacher, Mrs. Schuler, asked him after football season ended to join the debate team for a tournament at Southern Oregon College.

"Who'd my partner be?" Jake asked warily.

"Annie Laughlin."

Jake didn't know Annie, but he knew enough about her.

"No way!" he said.

Annie's father was a pediatrician and her mother an operating-room nurse. She never made it through a high school period without arguing with a teacher or fellow students. During lunch, she tried to draw the ladies behind the counter into a debate about milk price supports. She was intimidating and brilliant – and knew it. She wasn't too pretty to tie high school boys' tongues, but intriguing enough to be featured in more male fantasies and locker-room banter at Roseburg High than either Miss October or the homecoming queen.

Against his better judgment, Jake agreed to give it a try with Annie for one tournament. That year, the national high school debate topic was, "Resolved: That the grand jury system should be abolished." Jake managed to avoid saying anything stupid enough to make the judges forget that Annie tore apart the opposing team. They debated kids who entered the room with two file folders of cards, filled with evidence lifted from scholarly journals. Annie arrived with two-dozen cards, held together by a rubber band. Jake read aloud the ones Annie thrust at him. Jake didn't even think to look at the cards Annie used until after their third debate on the first day, when Annie had just read four cards that cited studies on the grand jury system. Jake stared at Annie's typewritten messages, faint and gray products of an overused ribbon. The real "evidence" on her cards were the fence-painting scene from Tom Sawyer, the cherry-tree legend of George Washington, a set of bicycle assembly directions, and a limerick that made Jake blush.

"You have to have something on the card, just so they can see the typing," she explained, then noted Jake's incredulous look. "Come on," she said, "you've seen the judges. They're math teachers or somebody's uncle. You can bluff them."

Jake was so numb the rest of the weekend, he wasn't shocked when fellow debater Nadine Hershey – slightly chunky senior straight-A student, Lutheran minister's daughter, and Annie's competition for valedictorian – whispered that Jake should meet her at the school district's van in the hotel parking lot at 11. They didn't discuss the grand jury system. How she got the keys from Mrs. Schuler, Jake never knew.

For the rest of the Southern Oregon tournament, including the championship in a crowded auditorium, Jake's biggest worries were that Annie would decide it would be hilarious to hand him the limerick card and that Nadine would try to hold his hand in public. Annie never stooped that low, and Nadine tried only once.

When he and Annie were introduced as the champions at the awards ceremony, Annie leaned over to him as they held the trophy for Mrs. Schuler and her camera.

"Congratulations," Annie whispered.

"Thanks," Jake said.

"But I hope you used a rubber."

Jake dropped the trophy.

Nadine finally stopped baking him cookies six months later.

Annie showed Jake aspects of her life she hid from others. Jake watched Annie read aloud to the bed-bound at the Veterans Administration Hospital, where she paused between chapters to clean out urine bags. He went with Annie to the recreation center on the wrong side of the tracks in Roseburg and saw her counsel children of the poor and the migrant workers. He already was wondering where she found all the time before she took him to Children's Hospital, where she tutored kids – terminally ill kids, outpatients with hopeful prognoses, or handicapped children there for therapy.

They made their decisions to go to CU independently, but Jake knew that many misunderstood their relationship. In Cascade, Annie's spacious apartment was in one of the more upscale student-oriented buildings near campus. It was a short walk from Jake's apartment, and she had both a key to and the run of Jake's place. Many involved in campus politics believed she had a hypnotic and one-sided hold on him, but they hadn't heard Jake and Annie's frequent arguments. Jake noticed that with her friends, Annie had the ability to forget acrid exchanges; with her enemies, she remembered every word.

∾

Jake and Annie watched the Democratic convention in Annie's apartment.

During a commercial, Jake didn't bother to turn from his prone position on the floor in front of the television.

"Coach Benson wants to know why you're not under arrest in Chicago," he said.

Annie was stretched out on the overstuffed chair, with her legs draped over one armrest.

"What'd you tell him?"

"Your car broke down in Wyoming."

# FOUR:
## "MACARTHUR PARK"

*(Thursday, September 12, 1968)*

 In the back row of the small, musty classroom in the arts and sciences building, Jake rested his right elbow on his desk and cradled the side of his face in one palm. He was waiting for everyone in the Short Story Writing class – including offensive tackle Todd Hendricks and Kit Dunleavy – to turn and look at him, wordlessly asking: *It's yours, isn't it?*

 At the beginning of the period, Peter Nicholson, a Cascade grad, former member of the wrestling team, novelist, and professor who always dressed with the goal of looking like a best-selling author who didn't give a shit, passed out copies of Jake's short story to the class. Nicholson wrote novels and received royalties, but his big killing – enabling him to buy a huge farm to the east of Cascade – was the sale of the movie rights to his best novel, *The Eagle's Lair.* That had been in 1959, and nine years later, the movie still hadn't been made – but Nicholson didn't mind, in part because when the producers showed him the first draft of the adapted screenplay by an Oscar-winning writer, Nicholson was appalled to discover that the story had become more about an irascible secondary character in the book, rather than focusing on the book's narrator, a giant of an American Indian. The word had gotten around that at least once a semester, he told his classes, "Leave it to Hollywood to fuck up a good story," and a fellow professor regularly brought down the house at parties with his impression of Nicholson's anti-filmmaker rant.

 On the first day of the term, Nicholson assigned his students to turn in pieces of their own short fiction – a thousand or fewer words – within a week. His student assistant typed them onto mimeograph master sheets and ran them off, minus the names of the writers. Nicholson's plan was to pass one out each day halfway near the end of the hour, allow time for reading, and close the period with discussion.

 The first story was Jake's: *The Body Count.*

# THE WITCH'S SEASON

*"A-ten-shun."*

*It was the last day of training. Soon they would be shipped to Vietnam. The principles were hammered into them. Counterinsurgency, pacification, free-fire zones, harassment-interdiction fire.*

*The Sergeant made his inspection run down the line. A rabbit was tucked under his arm.*

*"What's this in my hands, McKay?"*

*"Sir, it's a rabbit, sir."*

*"It's cute, isn't it, McKay?"*

*"Yes, sir," he said.*

*"Well, then, why don't you pet it? Go ahead, pet it!"*

*McKay ran his hand over the fur.*

*The Sergeant noticed the next man in line smiling. "Ah, Mr. King," he said sarcastically. "You think it's cute, too?"*

*The man next to McKay pulled his head back and stared straight ahead.*

*"No, sir."*

*"Pet it!"*

*King did.*

*The Sergeant stepped back.*

*With a sudden twist, The Sergeant broke the animal's neck and tore at the body. He hurled the severed head into the lines of men, blood and brains flying. The men scrambled to evade the mess.*

*"Damn it, you're at attention. Attention!"*

*Freezing them with a glare, The Sergeant turned his attention to the remains. Part of the mess hit McKay in the face. He quickly wiped to try to rid himself of the muck on his chin and cheek, but returned to attention.*

*Smiling now, The Sergeant scattered the innards among the men, making sure as few as possible were left clean.*

*He reddened as he surveyed the mess. "Over there, you'd better not let your guard down for a second. Not even if something looks 'cute.'"*

*He let that sink in.*

*"The V.C. don't wear uniforms or look any different from any other gook."*

*Eighty young men got the message.*

*Four months later, at the end of another day of trooping through jungles, Charlie Company's men lounged around their makeshift camp. McKay was in a subdued foursome of card players.*

*The radio gave off static. "Charlie Company, this is Bravo Company. We have a body count of 14 to confirm."*

*McKay groaned, too. Confirming a body count after a long day of combing a free-fire zone was not a task for which anyone volunteered.*

*The Company Commander barked orders to four men.*

*McKay, relieved at not being picked, fell into a light sleep. An hour passed. Despite McKay's dream, the war was still there when the radio barked again.*

*"This is special detail from Charlie Company. We can confirm Bravo Company's body count of 14." There was a silence, but no one was listening. "There are ten children, three women, and one rabbit."*

After allowing them to read, Nicholson asked, "Comments?"

A girl in the front row said, "The war stinks. But isn't that far-fetched?"

"You tell me. Or more important, tell me if that matters."

From the second row, Todd Hendricks said, "Well, I was in the Army..."

The students already had become accustomed to hearing him preface every comment with that, so several of them muttered, "We *know*."

Todd continued, unfazed. "Any D.I. who did that in training would be in deep trouble. That couldn't happen."

From the corner, a lanky guy with short, oily hair and thick horn-rimmed glasses piped in.

"It's ridiculous," he said. "That's not how they confirm body counts. That's not how they use the radio. They are not massacring women and children. Other than that, it's very plausible."

A friend in Roseburg, a Marine, told Jake that during his basic training, the instructor tore apart a live rabbit and lectured the Marines about not trusting anyone. That part was real. Jake was certain that the mentality – a mix of fear, anger and hate – was prevalent when the poor guys went to Vietnam.

He didn't say that in class.

Kit was two rows to his right. "I don't think how you feel about the war really matters when you're evaluating the impact of the story," she said.

Jake slid slightly out of his slouch.

"The point this makes is about the way it's being fought," she continued. "The old viewpoints don't apply, and the confusion can make men – good men, bad men, scared kids – go over the edge."

"War never has been pretty," the guy said. "Kit, your story is naive fantasy."

"I didn't write it," Kit said. "But–"

"Then it must have been..."

He paused to heighten the sarcastic effect.

"...the *rebel linebacker.*"

Jake's anger overwhelmed his embarrassment. "Good guess, dickhead," he snapped.

Amid the laughter, Nicholson lifted his hands.

"All right, all right," Nicholson said. "Mr. Powell, if you're thinking of being a writer, you need to develop a thicker skin. If you don't think so, I'll read you some of the reviews of my novels. I didn't take the bad ones personally." He smiled wickedly. "Those assholes."

After additional mild discussion, the bell rang. Todd headed to the back of the room. As Jake gathered up his books, Todd told him, "Well, you told him. But he's right, you know. That shit doesn't happen."

Todd took off, in a hurry.

As Jake walked up the aisle, Nicholson smiled and asked, "Do we have a little dissension on the football team?"

"Does everyone on the faculty agree about everything?"

"Oh, God, no."

"Do we have a little dissension on the faculty?"

"Oh, God, yes."

"Then I guess we do, too."

Jake caught Kit just outside the door and thanked her.

"Sure," she said. "It was good. How come when I interviewed you, you never said you liked to write?"

"You never asked."

They walked down the hall, but Jake couldn't manage to say anything else until they parted at the bottom of the stairs outside.

"How come you've never gone out with me," he said, trying to make it come off as just enough of a joke.

"You never asked."

"Want to see *2001*?"

# FOUR: "MACARTHUR PARK"

"Sure," she said. "But what about Annie?"

Jake smiled. "She can get her own date."

Kit was left trying to decide which rumor to believe.

❧

Portland, the largest city in the state, was important to the Cascade athletic program. About half the in-state alumni lived in the metropolitan area, and many traveled to Cascade for the home games. The Fishermen also played one home game a year in Portland. Every Thursday during the season, Larry Benson and one of his assistants attended the luncheon meeting of the Fishermen's Booster Club at the Portland Athletic Club, adjacent to Burnside Stadium. Partially because he started his coaching career in the Portland high school system and knew some of these men from those days, Benson didn't mind the drive. But he also knew that some of these men – and they were all men – loved to brag about being an "influential booster." There were three hundred men in this room, Benson thought, and a hundred of them will return to work and talk as if they could call Neal Hassler or Bill Wyden and get me fired tomorrow.

One or two probably could.

The Cascade chapter was more loyal and unconditionally supportive, and many of the members there were Benson's friends. The Cascade boosters tended to be men Benson ran into at the kids' summer baseball games and PTA meetings, when he could get to PTA meetings. The members included his minister, his barber, and his insurance agent.

In Portland, Benson got a standing ovation. "Thanks," he said at the podium. "I can tell we're still undefeated." He quickly moved on to making sure everyone understood that California's star running back, Curtis Lane, was the next Jim Brown.

Questions?

A former regional drugstore owner, who had sold out to a national chain and split his time between Portland and Palm Springs, stood. "Coach, don't get me wrong," he said, "but I saw the television film of practice last night, and I see all that hair hanging out of the helmets. I see Powell is one of the radicals on campus. Are you a rock band, the SDS or a football team?"

The reaction was a mixture of laughter and groans.

Benson was livid, but tried not to show it.

"First of all," he said, "I think you'll notice I never call them 'kids.' And I won't treat them like that." Benson ran a hand over his own short hair, which could have passed a military inspection. "I don't like the new styles. But I am *not* going to tell nineteen- or twenty-two-year-old young men what to think, how to dress, or how to look. That isn't my definition of discipline."

"What is?" asked the booster.

"It's being on time, it's working hard, it's going to class, it's showing you deserve to be treated like an adult."

Some applauded, a few grumbled, most were silent.

Benson didn't see his new special-teams coach, Rex Gamberg, who was sitting at the same table with the questioning booster. Gamberg gave the booster a thumbs-up sign.

A hustling thirty-something insurance salesman waved and stood when Benson pointed at him.

"That's all okay," said the insurance man. "But you need to have fire to be a good football team. Your guys are too much into this peace and love crap. They have to be thinking this is war!"

Benson glared at him.

"My sophomore football season at Minnesota was 1942," the coach said. "My junior season was in 1946. I know the difference between war and football."

After a few moments of awkward silence, a golf course pro quickly jumped up.

"Uh...how's the punting game shaping up?"

❧

*2001: A Space Odyssey* was playing at the Orpheum Theater in downtown Cascade. Jake was self-conscious about asking Kit if she minded walking a mile, but she didn't flinch, and the weather was pleasant. On the way from campus to the theater, they walked past street preachers ("Repent, all ye fornicators!"), street panhandlers ("Bus fare, please?"), street musicians ("Where have all the flowers gone?"), and even a street performance of Hamlet's soliloquy at the fountain in the middle of downtown.

# FOUR: "MACARTHUR PARK"

As they passed the cavernous Millett's Hardware, Jake confessed that he often went into the store to buy something small just to see the little old lady at the counter send the money up to the second floor in the tube that slid along a cable.

"That's what I like about Cascade," Kit said. "You can go from the revolution to the '40s and to the future in the same block."

She pointed to the window of the Blue Crystal, the small store next door to Millett's. The Crystal had been on the agenda at every City Council meeting for eighteen months. The window was almost covered with psychedelic watercolor expressions, and many Cascade residents were convinced it was because the proprietors didn't want the sex on the counters and the sale of LSD to be visible to the passing police on the street. In fact, the Crystal sold records and bongs and cigarette papers for joints, but if anyone had been having sex on the counters, Jake hadn't been in the store at the time.

And *2001: A Space Odyssey*? Jake didn't mind fantasy films, but two hours and forty minutes of man trying to figure out his theoretical role in the universe and beyond didn't do much for him. He would have gone to the mother planet in the first fifteen minutes and then gotten back to the problems of earth. He could tell Kit sensed his uneasiness, but they stuck it out.

They ended up at Terwilliger's, the tavern at the edge of campus where bartenders were cavalier about checking IDs or willingly "gullible" about accepting copies of older sisters' drivers' licenses. The menu was scribbled onto chalkboards around the room, and the posted price of the cheeseburger varied by ten cents from the front to the back. Kit was twenty in a state that officially didn't allow anyone under twenty-one to be served, but she had a twenty-two-year-old sister. "One of these days," Kit said, "they're going to put pictures on these licenses, and we'll all be out of luck."

Annie Laughlin was sitting at the bar with another girl. Jake waved, and then went over to a corner booth with Kit. Kit slid in one side, and then Jake made the decision on the spot, trying to be casual: He sat on the same side. They ordered a pitcher from a waitress who called Jake by name, but at least to Kit seemed to be having a bad day. Jake still was pouring into Kit's glass when Annie dropped into the booth on the opposite side.

"It's on for the twenty-sixth...two weeks from today," Annie said as she refilled her glass from the pitcher.

Jake ignored her. "The other thing about Annie," he said to Kit, "is that she has this aggravating tendency to interrupt conversations and act like nobody else is there. And to mooch beer, even though she's got a trust fund."

He took a sip and turned to Annie. "You know Kit, right?"

"She's quoted me semi-accurately several times."

After an awkward pause, Kit asked, "So what's happening on the twenty-sixth?"

"Something you'll probably want to cover," Annie said. "But you'll have to torture Jake to get it out of him."

"And what's the best way to do that?"

"He's ticklish."

Annie jumped up and went back to the bar.

Kit picked up her mug. She looked down and tried to sound casual. "Ticklish, huh?"

"No comment."

"Really, what's the story with you and Annie? I mean, I don't think I'd want her mad at me."

Resting his glass on the table, Jake cradled it with both hands. Finally, he said slowly, "You don't need to worry about that. Okay?"

"But..."

"You *don't* need to worry about that."

Jake picked up his glass and emptied it with a long swig.

"Be right back," he said, and took off for the bathroom.

While he was gone, the waitress came to the booth, reached for the empty pitcher and knocked over Kit's glass. Kit had to scramble to avoid the beer and the waitress' apology – and a quick handoff of a couple of napkins – seemed half-hearted. Kit had just finished the cleanup when Jake returned.

"Accident?" he asked.

"I don't think so," Kit said. "I'm going to take a wild guess here. I'm guessing you've gone out with the waitress."

"Well," said Jake, self-conscious, "I don't know if you could call it that, but..."

"Whatever you call it, she's jealous."

"Her? Naw. And it *was* a long time ago."

# FOUR: "MACARTHUR PARK"

Kit decided to leave it there. But she did notice that the waitress went off duty and another girl brought the next pitcher.

After Jake filled her in about his family, he learned that Kit's presence on this campus was part of her occasional rebellion. Kit was a junior. Her father was a lumber broker in Medford, a hundred miles south of Jake's hometown of Roseburg and almost to the California border. Kit would have made him happier by choosing Tillamook State, the state's agriculture-oriented school, over CU. "He thought you had to be smoking a joint to be allowed in the registration line here," Kit said.

"Didn't you tell him that's only for the electives?"

When she came home the summer after her freshman year and started talking about Vietnam, her father was incensed. It got worse when her mother found birth control pills in Kit's room and told her father. "He wanted to barricade me in my room or make me go to community college," she said.

Her parents acquiesced to her return to campus, in part because her boyfriend, Christopher, a drama major from Cascade, moved to New York. Chris, she said, was the son of one of the more notorious professors on campus, Sam Reynolds, who taught political science. That caught Jake's attention; he had taken a class from Reynolds and liked him. Chris, she said, transferred to Fordham to retain his student deferment, but spent most of his time trying to land a breakthrough role on Broadway, off-Broadway or anywhere in the same time zone as Broadway, and his relationship with Kit was in the unscripted no-commitment, maybe-we'll-pick-it-up-later stage. It had been over a year since Chris had moved to New York, and their contact was sporadic.

She told Jake that when she announced that she would join a sorority for her sophomore year, her parents were breathing easier. They weren't thrilled that she had joined the staff of the *Campus Daily*, but she assured them that not every story in the student paper was full of four-letter words and calls to revolution.

A *sorority* girl? Jake wouldn't have guessed. And she never had mentioned that, either, when they talked.

"Do you think we wear badges or something?" she asked, laughing. "Besides, the girl at the end of the hall has the best grass connection on campus."

Jake admitted he had believed sorority girls were all Tricia Nixon.

Kit said, "Just like football players are all Cro-Magnon?"

"Just the ones blocking me."

"Speaking of that," she said, gesturing at the pitcher, "I'm surprised they let you drink during the season."

"As long as we don't embarrass ourselves or the program in public, a beer or two is okay. They get wind of us screwing up, we're on probation."

"What's that mean?"

"Coach Hallstrom – he runs the offense – is the probation coordinator. He makes sure someone makes you run a lap, or one trip up and down the stadium stairs, for every beer over two."

"How does he know?"

"We're not sure, but he always seems to be pretty close. He played here and I think he's young enough to remember. But he's also the guy everybody goes to. You can tell him anything, and he'll help you – and not tell Coach Benson if you've really been an ass."

"You know that firsthand?"

"Of course not," Jake said, smiling.

Kit was alternately combative, coaxing and coquettish. She was strident about the war, heating up her views from Fiction Writing class, so suddenly venomous that even Jake was taken aback – especially because she hadn't been visible in the movement as she covered it. Then she got even more wound up, talking about her hopes to begin her writing career in magazines, and then move on to books.

Finally, she caught herself.

"Geez, I'm sorry," she said, reaching for her glass. She drank the last of her beer, and then smiled at him. "I haven't felt like talking like this to anybody in a long time." She scrambled out of the booth. "Let's go."

She was halfway to the door before Jake even could get up, decide how much of the change to leave and follow her. She was waiting for him outside, grinning and leaning against a parking meter, with her arms folded.

# FIVE:
## "HEY JUDE"

*(Saturday, September 14, 1968)*

Annie Laughlin looked forward to long drives. Behind the wheel, she dreamed of missions accomplished and causes rendered obsolete, or of being able to step back and let others step to the forefront. As she looked to the future, she became a special education teacher, a passionate firebrand on behalf of handicapped, with children of her own.

As she sped down Interstate 5 and then U.S. Highway 101, she couldn't get her mind off the imminent SDS meeting at the house in Berkeley. The summons had gone out to campus and state organization leaders. They would go over the events in Chicago and how to respond on the West Coast, and also discuss the proposal from the Magicians, the ultra-radical group with overlapping membership with the SDS.

The Magicians proposed to set off bombs in buildings on major campuses with ROTC units around the country. It wouldn't happen on all campuses, or even most, but enough to make the point a national phenomenon. The bombs would be explosive enough to do damage, but not enough to bring down complete walls. Detonations would be timed to avoid hurting anyone, if at all possible. They would be spaced out, in terms of both time and geography. The Magicians said the targets wouldn't always be the ROTC buildings, as a practical matter – those buildings would be guarded and watched – and also as a means of emphasizing the linkage of the academic structure with the military-industrial complex.

Annie knew more about the budding plot than many of the other SDS leaders because Peter Shapiro, one of the Magician leaders, outlined it all in a letter to her from Los Angeles. She wasn't very far into the handwritten missive before deciding that Shapiro was an idiot to have put it on paper.

Annie thought blowing up buildings wouldn't accomplish anything. She was willing to risk backlash and antagonizing the public to protest the outrage being perpetrated on the American people and on the Vietnamese, and to galvanize dissent, but there were limits.

She decided she didn't have time to stop in Roseburg to see her parents.

⁕

"Damn!"

Offensive coach Howie Hallstrom's voice blasted through the coaches' headsets in the press box booth and on the sideline of Portland's Burnside Stadium. Hallstrom and Larry Benson dropped their headsets and ran onto the field.

Their quarterback, Tom Davis, wasn't getting up.

When California came at Tom with an all-out blitz on second down, he scrambled out of the pocket. Tom's spikes caught in the artificial turf as a tackler twisted him to the ground, and he let loose of the ball, grabbing his knee and rocking in agony.

While coaches and medical staff gathered around Tom, untested sophomore Rick Winslow hurriedly threw warm-up passes.

When Hallstrom returned to the sideline, he called over Rick. The kid is nervous as hell, thought Hallstrom. Why shouldn't he be? Rick and the freshman team played in front of tiny crowds the previous year.

Placing a hand on each of Rick's shoulder pads, Hallstrom looked through the facemask, into the widened eyes. "You're on and you'll do great," Hallstrom said. "First play, run the 28-toss sweep. Make sure you get the snap first. Got it?"

Rick nodded.

The call was a pitchout to Timmy Hilton. Hallstrom didn't want to ask Rick to do too much on his first varsity play. Get the yips out of his system.

Standing with the defensive team on the sideline, Jake was close enough to hear Hallstrom's play call. Yet the delay before the snap was ominous. Rick was changing the play, leaning to one side, and then the other, calling out the new play in the numeric code, making sure his teammates heard.

Rick dropped back, looked to the sideline away from the CU bench, pump-faked once, and finally threw the ball as far as he could. Keith Oldham was a step in front of the defender, running past the Cal bench.

Oldham reached and got his fingertips on the ball, but couldn't hold it.

Hallstrom yanked off his headset and leaned over to Benson's ear. "Well, we know the kid's got balls," Hallstrom said. "Even if he doesn't follow orders."

෴

Neal Hassler didn't completely understand football, so he couldn't love it. If he became interested in anything, he treated it as curriculum to be mastered. Thus it had been with Beethoven and Bach, with Lerner and Loewe, with bridge and gin rummy. He couldn't picture himself becoming fascinated with this game, but he also had come to understand that dealing with the football program was part of his job. Want to talk about an endowed scholarship for the engineering department? Before getting to the engineering scholarship, the benefactor wanted to discuss the Fishermen's chances of winning eight games next season – and beating his asshole brother-in-law's alma mater.

As the first half ended with CU leading 10-7, Clifford Carlson, from the public affairs office, was at the end of Hassler's aisle. "You're on," he called down.

Carlson led him toward the skywalk that would take them to the press box on the rickety wooden stadium's roof, where he would be a halftime guest on the Fishermen's radio broadcast. Hassler had decided there was a 50-50 chance the roof would collapse or he would slide over the edge. Great headline, he thought: "CU PRESIDENT JUMPS OFF STADIUM ROOF"

"Hassler!"

The husky, but seemingly friendly, voice came from a few rows down. Hassler slowed and looked back. The man threw something, not as hard as he could, but in a half-speed, overhand motion, and Hassler felt something hit his shoulder.

The man bellowed again, this time not bothering to hide his contempt.

"Catch!"

As a couple of ushers were hustling down the aisle, a woman was trying to restrain the man, but he wouldn't be quieted.

"Catch!"

He reached into his bag and quickly made another toss, this one softer, underhanded. Carlson, who had turned around and moved to shield Hassler, reached out and made the catch.

"Hey, President," the man said, sneering, "have those for dessert before you give the freaks the keys to the school."

Carlson held several bunches of grapes.

❧

As the fourth quarter wound down, Carlson and Hassler – without his grapes – walked down through the stadium and showed his "OFFICIALS ALL-ACCESS" pass to the guard at the entrance to the field. They were on the sideline, just outside the 35-yard-line bench boundary, when Jake made the game-clinching interception across the middle in the final seconds, and they celebrated as if they were sophomore backup linebackers – and not forty-something university executives.

At the final gun, Hassler walked toward Benson, who was accepting congratulations. Rick Winslow, whose quarterback sneak had run out the clock, trotted over with the game ball and handed it to Tom Davis, in street clothes and balanced on crutches. Because of all his knee problems, Tom was an old hand on crutches, but not even he was adept enough to use them to get across the field while holding a football. Rick took it back and began escorting Tom across the field, toward the tunnel that led to the dressing rooms underneath the stands. Benson put one hand on each of their shoulders and gave a little pinch, then spotted Hassler and angled over to the CU president.

As Benson and Hassler huddled, Jake and Alex Tolliver looked for the blue 28 on a white jersey. As players from both teams walked toward the tunnel, Jake tapped California's Curtis Lane on his shoulder pad. He shook Curtis' hand and said, "Great game."

"I'm glad I won't have to chase you again," Alex told Curtis.

Curtis said thanks.

As Alex stopped to talk with a harried writer, trying to gather quotes before the deadline, the voice came from the kid, just a kid, leaning over from the first row above the portal.

"We kicked your ass, nigger!"

The kid's father was behind him — and smiling. Curtis kept walking, but he looked up and glared.

Jake didn't take it as quietly. "Hey, kid," he hollered, "knock that shit off!"

The kid was surprised, not by the reaction, but by whom had reacted.

"You heard me, kid," Jake said.

The kid's father stopped smiling. "Get your hair cut and then pop off, Sally."

A buddy tapped the kid's father on the shoulder. "Hey, that's Powell!" He turned toward Jake. "Why don't you just move to Russia, anyway?"

As a couple of Jake's teammates started to shove him through the portal, he got in the last words.

"Go fuck yourselves!"

∽

This was progress, Dusty Harris realized. Yet he still missed something about being able to dictate his story over the phone, hearing the fellow back at the office following him with the staccato striking of keys, hearing the bell at the end of the line and then the carriage return, and even hearing the cussing from the guy at the office when "the" kept coming out "hte."

Last year, the *Herald* bought the latest innovations — telecopiers — and he was making use of them after the opener. He yanked his first page out of his typewriter. As Dusty got started on page two, a press-box clerk loaded page one onto a telecopier's cylinder, called the *Herald* sports department, announced he had a page of telecopy from Dusty, wedged the phone handset into two rubber cups, and marveled at the wonders of modern technology as the cylinder began twirling. Six minutes later, the newspaper's own telecopier would have a smelly copy of the page, burned onto the paper.

By DUSTY HARRIS, Herald Staff

He's not ready for Heisman Trophy consideration, but spindly-legged sophomore Rick Winslow on Saturday night threw for two second-half touchdowns and a total of 314 yards as the Cascade Fishermen upended California 34-27 in the season opener for both gridiron squads at Burnside Stadium.

A thrilled crowd of 28,211 watched as a 32-yard aerial from Winslow to fullback Stevie Toland with 1:44 remaining broke a 27-27 deadlock and gave Cascade's green-garbed forces the Pacific 8 Conference win over the Golden Bears.

There were plenty of other offensive heroes for the Fishermen, including Timmy Hilton, the erstwhile flanker who ran for 106 yards on 22 carries in his first game as a tailback, and also caught a touchdown pass. The bad news for the Fishermen was that Winslow had to catapult off the bench in the second quarter because veteran signal caller Tom Davis, who has been plagued by physical mishaps throughout his career, suffered another knee injury.

The Fishermen's brain trust, including head coach Larry Benson, will be anxiously awaiting the verdict from the medicos Sunday, but Davis might be sidelined for the season.

☙

It was nearly 2 a.m. when Timmy Hilton drove into the Cascade apartment building's lot. He reached out the car window and opened the door from the outside, which was the only way the door on this '59 Plymouth would open. It had 96,321 miles on the odometer and eleven Coke bottles on the back floor.

Jake, along for the short ride from the parking lot at Hobson Court after the bus ride from Portland, noticed Timmy's roommate first.

David Armstrong, the 6-foot-8 basketball player whose curly blond hair could be spotted above the heads on campus, was finishing up a piss on the bushes.

"Couldn't get in the bathroom," David called over his shoulder. "Think somebody's screwin' right in the bathtub!"

Judging from the blasting stereos and the crowds on the landings, the party in Timmy and David's apartment wasn't the only one still going in the building.

When Timmy cranked up the driver's side window, each twist sounded as if it might be the last before the handle broke off. He needed three tries to turn the key just right and lock the door.

David fought with his zipper as he walked toward the car. He wavered as if he had taken an opposing forward's elbow to his head. "Who's going to steal anything from that piece of shit?" he asked, and then quickly changed the subject. "Hey, guys, good game! I might get laid tonight just for being your roommate."

"You're underestimating your charm," Timmy said dryly. He smiled at Jake. "I think we're way behind everyone else."

"We can rally," Jake said. "Actually, all I want is two for the road before I go home. If there's any beer left."

David laughed and gave Jake a thumbs-up.

Jake charged up the stairs, toward the second-level apartment with the outside door. Timmy couldn't have kept up with his line-backer teammate, even if he had wanted to. He couldn't remember ever feeling this bruised after a game when he played flanker. Now he was trying to run over defensive tackles, not away from defensive backs.

Timmy didn't mind having a chance to wind down with some socializing after the games, but he knew he was going to have little choice in the matter all fall – if he wanted to sleep in his own apartment. When he agreed to share an apartment with the basketball player, Timmy had known of David's preference to be not just the life of the party, but also the host of it.

During the first week of their freshman year, they always seemed to be the last two at the unofficial jocks' table in the corner of the dormitory cafeteria: David, the flaky white basketball player, and Timmy, then a still-shy football player. David could make Timmy laugh, but then listen five minutes later to Timmy's confessions about home-sickness without making Timmy feel as if he were a wimp. Timmy missed his parents, and he missed fighting with them. He missed his old room in the house and his friends in Olympia, Washington. He hated his dorm room, and their friendship crossed a threshold when David said he knew what Timmy meant. David said he hated the damn acoustic tile on the ceiling because he'd counted every one of those little holes – and counted them both in the daylight and in the dark. One thousand, four hundred, twenty-eight.

They seemed to have closer friends than each other and were far from inseparable, yet they talked with each other as they talked with nobody else. So when David announced late in their freshman year that he was going to line them up an apartment for the next fall, Timmy didn't object. He found he liked not living with another football player and enjoyed sharing the place with someone who had a different circle of friends. When David pulled stunts like missing the potentially game-winning shot at the buzzer for the Fishermen against whoever the hell that was last season, then running out the side door of Hobson Court and not stopping until he got home, where he immediately grabbed a beer and watched television in his uniform, that enhanced his image as a flake.

Now this was Timmy's season and David's party.

Jesus, Timmy thought as he and David walked up the stairs, they probably could smell the marijuana smoke in Albany.

"Hey, I thought we were gonna keep that out of here," Timmy said. "The coaches will hear about this by morning. If they don't smell it first."

The music was drowning out Timmy.

"What?" David hollered.

"I thought we..."

"What?"

"We agreed..."

David waved him off and kept walking, so Timmy gave up. Timmy didn't want any grass, but he didn't want to preach about it, either.

Walking into the apartment first, David turned and wordlessly bowed at Timmy, the conquering hero. The living-room guests in condition or positions to pay attention clapped and cheered. On the ripped black vinyl couch and brown loveseat, though, couples were preoccupied.

Jake was leaning against the refrigerator, with an opened beer of his own and one waiting for Timmy. He handed over the extra and said, "I really am taking off. I'm beat."

As Jake went out the door, Timmy headed toward his bedroom, hoping it was either empty or occupied by someone he could chase out quickly.

☙

# FIVE: "HEY JUDE"

They started talking when there were about ten SDS leaders in the house, a cavernous Victorian in the Berkeley hills. They reached a consensus by the time about three-dozen were present. They agreed the SDS wouldn't be a direct participant in the Magician bombing plot, but also not attempt to discourage or derail it. Peter Shapiro, looking Annie in the eyes, said how disappointed he was that the two groups couldn't get together on this. Annie also knew from past experience that when he gave her that look, "get together" had a double meaning.

During one bathroom break, Annie found a radio, searched on the dial, found the post-game show and listened long enough to find out that the local team — the California Golden Bears — lost to the Cascade Fishermen. She even heard one broadcaster say that Jake Powell, "perhaps better known for his activism off the field than his play on it," made the crucial late interception.

# SIX:
## "BOOKENDS"

*(Monday, September 16, 1968)*

Because she was doing a student-teaching stint at South Cascade High School, Annie Laughlin this semester made her deliveries of coffee, donuts, newspapers and a monologue to Jake Powell's place earlier in the morning than in the past.

Halfway through their breakfast, Annie laughed and read aloud the item from the man-about-town columnist in the *Portland Herald* about a football fan throwing grapes at President Hassler at the game on Saturday night to protest "his concession to the radicals."

"That guy probably was an idiot," she said, "but that was a great touch."

∽

The twenty-six drama students, sitting cross-legged on Neal Hassler's office floor, said they wouldn't leave until the university president dictated that the university granted full tenure to a drama department assistant professor, Reynaldo Archuleta.

Hassler knew that his department superiors had decided that Archuleta didn't even deserve to be an instructor. Archuleta showed up only about two-thirds of the time, often leaving his students on their own to "improvise" or to take off. When he did show up, he did very little teaching. The department chairman admitted to the tenure committee that once his antenna was raised, he and others did more checking around. Among other things, they discovered that Archuleta's claim to be an American Indian – which counted in his favor in the hiring process – was at least dubious and most likely a complete joke. "Goddamn guy would have said he was Pakistani if he needed to," said one of those who had done some checking.

Because Archuleta had been arrested at an antiwar rally in San Francisco for throwing smoke-bombs at police, and his declarations that the Joint Chiefs of Staff were "worse than the Nazis" made the papers, some of his students – including, apparently, those now camped in Hassler's office – tried to portray him as a victim of anti-free speech oppression. The department chairman scoffed at that, saying the lesson should be that if you're a fraud, you should keep your mouth shut and don't call attention to yourself. Hassler agreed with that.

To the students, he said, "It's not my place to unilaterally decide on tenure, and even if it were, from what I've heard, Mr. Archuleta doesn't deserve it. So you're going to be here a long time. The bathroom's over there, the janitor comes at seven, but you can't make long-distance calls unless you know the code."

"So you think we're bluffing," a guy said.

"I think you're sincere. But Mr. Archuleta has been judged not to have earned the right to continue on the tenure track."

"Bullshit," another guy said.

The others were extolling Archuleta's virtues when Archuleta walked into the office.

"Thanks for your support," he said with a majestic flourish, "but I'd be grateful if you leave with me now."

Hassler had never seen him before. To the president, this seemed as much of a staged drama as if they all were reading from paperback editions of *Much Ado About Nothing*. As the students filed out, Hassler decided that Archuleta probably hoped this could win him sympathy and renewed consideration.

"Can I come back and talk about this sometime soon?" Archuleta asked as he lingered in the doorway.

"I'll listen," Hassler said. "But if we talk, you can drop the drama, please."

❧

Rod Smith, the *Campus Daily* editor, was in the habit of talking as if he were writing a rough draft of an editorial, trying out each line. That wasn't just in the office, either; he sounded that way over cereal in the cafeteria. He almost always wore wild pants and a white shirt – white T-shirt, or white button-down dress shirt, or white shirt with a huge collar. His friends told him it looked as if he couldn't decide whether he wanted to work for the *San Francisco Examiner* or the *Berkeley Barb* after graduation.

Sitting against the end of one of the typewriter desks, he looked up from the typewritten list of story ideas Kit submitted.

"'Campus marijuana use?' Isn't that kind of 'No shit, Sherlock'?"

"Well, it could be," Kit said. "But I want it to be more than that. I want to get a campus supplier or two to talk. How they grow it. Who buys it. People say, 'Everybody smokes pot,' but nobody has tried to document it in an anecdotal way. It won't be numbers, it'll be people."

"Well, give it a shot," Rod said. "But you're going to have to promise 'em anonymity, aren't you?"

"If there's no other way, yeah."

"I don't want a whole story where it reads like you made it up, okay? I want real scenes people here recognize, even if you don't name names. Tell me something I don't know. If it's just, 'Gee, a lot of students smoke pot,' I don't want it."

Rod nodded toward the photo lab at the back of the office.

"You could start there," he said.

The smoke, wafting from the lab, had reached them.

It wasn't from tobacco.

# SEVEN:
## "CLASSICAL GAS"

*(Friday, September 20, 1968)*

The hotel operator was too cheery for Howie Hallstrom's early-morning tastes. She should have been soothingly apologizing for ending his dream of a 99-yard, game-winning drive. Instead, the operator sounded to the Cascade offensive backfield coach as if she thought Hallstrom was showered, dressed, on his fourth cup of black coffee, and deliriously happy to be in Nebraska.

"Good morning, this is your wakeup call. It's seven o'clock and forty-two degrees. Go Big Red!"

Hallstrom slammed down the receiver, telling himself he hoped the corn crop died on the vine. Or wherever corn dies.

The night before, when they were on the four-lane Cornhusker Highway, heading from the Lincoln airport to the downtown Cornhusker Hotel, the marquees outside Cornhusker Equipment, Cornhusker Cleaners, Cornhusker Dairy, and Cornhusker Methodist Church had predicted scores posted. They all were similar to the one outside Cornhusker Truck Wash: "BIG RED 56, CASCADE 10."

The red was everywhere. Nebraska red. Cornhusker Red. Obnoxious Red. When the bus driver pointed at the lighted State Capitol dome in downtown Lincoln, Hallstrom snorted. "The hayseeds should paint *that* red, too."

After that, Hallstrom noticed that the bus driver hit every red light.

It had been a staff consensus to get to Lincoln on Thursday night, get acclimated Friday, and get the hell out of town as fast as possible after the Saturday afternoon game. This wasn't a brilliant move, Hallstrom told himself as he started to get out of bed and the phone was ringing again. Where the hell was Carl Steele, his roommate on this trip? Out jogging already?

Steele, the young linebackers coach, was another victim of the running craze in the state of Oregon. Bill Manchester, the famous coach of the Fishermen's track team, was the guru. His campaign to take running to the masses was taking hold nationwide, and his best-selling book on citizen running was in its seventeenth printing. Hallstrom routinely argued that the Oregon driver's test should include not only parallel parking, but also braking for nutty joggers who step off the curb without looking.

Thanks to Manchester and friends, typical Cascade residents' routines often included arising early, going out for a run, and then making sure the whole world knew how far they ran that morning, right down to the tenth of a mile. Plus, an aggravated Hallstrom thought, they never were around to answer the phone when you needed them.

Hallstrom got to Larry Benson's call on the fifth ring. "Dusty Harris woke me up at one," Benson said, "and told me that his paper would be running a letter to the editor this morning about Powell cussing out a kid in the crowd at the Cal game."

"He read it to you?"

"Yeah. The kid was crying, all that."

A key rattled in the door. Steele came in, dripping with sweat. Knowing how much it infuriated Hallstrom, Steele said with a smile, "Six-point-two miles."

"Hey, Jim Ryun," Hallstrom said, holding the receiver out for Steele, "this one's on your side of the ball."

∽

Steele found Benson in the meeting room where the team was going to have breakfast. Benson was standing along one wall, talking with Rex Gamberg, the special teams coach, who didn't notice Steele's approach.

"We have to tell him he's got to decide between football and politics!" Gamberg said.

Before Steele could jump in, Jake cruised through the door, oblivious.

"Jake!" Benson barked, then motioned over the befuddled linebacker. With a nod in the direction of the door, Benson banished Gamberg. "Just me and Carl," he told Gamberg. It was in line with coaching protocol to make it the head coach and Jake's position coach double-teaming the player, so it wasn't necessarily a slight of Gamberg. Yet the other coaches had concluded that Gamberg, previously an assistant at a California junior college who was hired at a rock-bottom salary as an "extra" assistant to help out mainly with administrative details, had jumped at the chance to curry favor by serving as Bill Wyden's "insider."

Benson told Jake about the letter in the Portland paper. "It says you cussed out a kid in the crowd, crushed him, sent him home bawling because he said something about your hair. It said this is a bunch of undisciplined renegades, so maybe it should have been expected."

"That's—"

Benson cut him off. "It said this team looks like a sleazy rock band, so you think you have to talk and act like one."

Jake didn't know where to direct his anger — at the coaches confronting him, or the world.

"But he called Curtis Lane a nigger!"

"Who did?" Benson asked.

"The little shit called Curtis Lane a nigger, so I told him to knock that shit off. Then his dad and his buddies started screaming at me about my politics."

"What exactly did you say?"

"To go fuck themselves."

"Great."

"But I didn't say that to the kid!"

"I'm not sure that matters."

Jake was incredulous. "You're not saying you don't believe me, do you?"

Benson shook his head. "First, you need to be more careful than that with a twelve-year-old kid. Even if that's what he said—"

"Coach, I'm telling you, that's what he said."

"I'm just telling you this is the kind of thing that gets blown out of proportion. Especially now."

"That's what you're doing! Blowing it out of proportion!"

Steele turned over his palms as a calm-down signal. "Look," he said, "all we're saying is—" Suddenly, he was looking beyond the group.

Wyden was approaching.

"Good morning, gentlemen," the athletic director said as he joined Jake and the coaches. He was greeted with nods and mumbles. "Mr. Powell," Wyden said to Jake, "as you might have heard, we have a problem."

"Mr. Wyden," Jake said, "we're not talking about the weath–"

Benson started talking over Jake about halfway through the sentence and got Jake to stop, but not in time.

"We're taking care of it, Bill," Benson said. His tone clearly was saying to get the hell out of the way so they could finish taking care of it, but Wyden was impervious as he pressed on with Jake.

"You're going to call that kid and apologize."

"You don't know what happened!" Jake said, leaning forward and angrily waving one hand. "Don't you *care* what happened?"

Wyden held up a page from a hotel notepad with a phone number scribbled on it. "I am going over to that phone and calling the kid's father, and you are going to apologize to him. Then we're going to set up a time when you can apologize to the kid himself."

"I will *not* apologize."

"Then you will *not* play."

Steele tried to divert Wyden. "Bill, we've been going over all of this."

"Bill, please, let us handle it," Benson said. He was not pleading, but making a statement. "It isn't as simple as they're making it out to be. Jake says he was responding to a racial slur at Curtis Lane."

"I don't care," Wyden said, holding out a piece of paper. "Here's the phone number." He handed it to Benson. "You talk it out all you want, but if he hasn't called the father and kid and apologized for cussing at him by tomorrow morning, he doesn't play. I'll go to the president on this, if I have to. And *you*," he said, glaring at Jake, "have to learn that you're representing this entire athletic department, not just yourself. You need to think about choosing between football and politics."

"Gee, that sounds familiar," Steele said dryly.

"Bill, please don't go too far," Benson said. He was looking not at Wyden, but at Jake, ordering Jake's silence with his eyes.

Wyden stared at Benson again. "I'm sorry, but I think once you think this through, you'll see that I'm right. I don't think you understand how big they're making this in Portland. Especially because it's Powell."

He walked away, toward the front door and what the coaches guessed was a rough morning of golf with the Nebraska A.D.

"Doubleheader," Jake mumbled.

Wyden stopped, then turned. "What's that?"

"Make all the putts," Benson said quickly, while wondering how the hell Jake knew that nickname. "We'll talk about this later."

Wyden stared, more intently than Benson ever had seen him stare. This was ominous, and not because of the one incident. This was about more than whether his rebel, too-smart-for-his-own-good linebacker had to apologize to some dumb-ass kid. This was about a detail-oriented accountant type who had been promoted from assistant athletic director to replace Hank Gardenia, the former head coach and Benson mentor who decided he didn't like the desk job and abruptly retired. Wyden had been called "Doubleheader" behind his back ever since he fouled up and signed contracts for road games on the same day in 1977 against Oklahoma and Texas.

"And by the way, Larry," Wyden said, "it's getting to the point where you might want to talk to some of the guys about getting haircuts." He hooked a thumb at Jake. "Like this kid, for example." He stormed off.

Benson turned to Jake. "Now, you. You can't tell every idiot you run into in life to get screwed. You'll be spending all your time doing that because there are just too many idiots out there."

Jake asked, "Like *that* one?"

Benson and Steele laughed, caught themselves, and tried to look somber. It was too late to fool Jake.

"We call the kid's father," Benson said. "You admit you shouldn't have lost your temper. You say there are certain words that shouldn't be used in situations like that, and the kid used one, and you used one, and you regret that. When you're on the phone, you don't use the word, 'sorry.' If anybody – like a reporter – asks, we say you were responding to what you felt was an inappropriate comment, but you regret your language. We'll finesse it with Doub – with Wyden."

Jake was wavering. "So I don't really have to apologize?"

"Nah. Just fake him out."

"Matter of fact," Hallstrom said, "he can go fuck himself."

They all laughed.

Sensing the heavy conversation was over, a grim-faced Timmy Hilton joined them. "Coach," he said to Benson, "I just want to tell you that whatever Powell's done now, we've taken a vote and we're behind him."

"Oh, yeah?"

"Sure." Timmy grinned. "The vote was twenty-eight to twenty-seven."

༄

Neal Hassler was in his office for five minutes when Clifford Carlson called from public affairs.

"See the letter on the editorial page of the *Herald?*" Carlson asked.

"Yes," Hassler said, "and there's already a message here from Bill Wyden saying he's handling it, whatever that means. And another one from the governor, saying he hopes I'm going to look into it."

"I'm getting calls here, too," Carlson said, "both from reporters and from people who want the football player thrown out of school."

"Tell 'em I'm in a meeting. Until Tuesday."

༄

After the Fishermen's light game-eve practice in Lincoln's Memorial Stadium, Timmy and Jake were among the first group of players walking from the locker room to the buses when a Nebraska student who looked like a Future Farmers of America chapter chairman spoke up.

"Hey, any of you Timmy Hilton?" he asked.

"Timmy Hilton missed the plane," Timmy Hilton said.

"Thanks, asshole," the student said.

Timmy trotted ahead and put his arm on Jake's shoulder.

"Hey," Timmy said, "will you please tell that guy back there what he can do to himself?"

"Ohhhhhh, no," Jake said, throwing up his hands.

They got on the nearly deserted bus and took seats across the aisle from each other, near the back.

"All right," Timmy said. "You can tell me. How much trouble you in? Stairs until you throw up?"

"Worse."

"Yeah?"

"Howie just told me he was going to make me go to the Students for Nixon rally."

"Shit, I'd think you'd like that. You'd get to argue with 'em."

"I'm turning over a new leaf. I'm going to smile and say, 'Jesus loves you.'"

"Yeah, sure."

Jake bounced out of his seat, quickly unlatched the window, slid it down, and yelled at the still-gathered Nebraska students, "Hey, Jesus loves you!" He slid back into his seat, smiling smugly at Timmy.

"I think I liked you better the other way," Timmy said. "Now you sound like my dad."

Teammates were filing onto the bus, but Timmy and Jake still had a little privacy.

"My dad tells me three things," Timmy said. "Jesus loves me. Root for Humphrey. And get a haircut."

"In that order?"

"Well, he's been big on Humphrey lately. I think he's given up on Jesus and the haircut."

"At least he talks to you," Jake said.

"Your dad doesn't?"

"My real dad died in the Korean War when I was a little kid."

"Sorry."

"My stepdad's good to my mom and for a long time he was great to me. Little League coach, catch, ballgames, father-son banquets. But when I started trying to find things out about my dad and started asking questions about Vietnam, my stepdad couldn't take it. We don't scream at each other. It's just a freeze. It's like I'm really somebody else's son now. When I started getting active in the movement, that was it."

"What about your mom?"

"I'm tearing down what my dad died fighting for. I say I'm fighting against what killed him. She says I'm attacking what he was trying to preserve. She says I'm not inspired by my father; I'm pissing on his grave."

"She said 'pissing'?"

"Well, she said, 'Urinating.' Sounded even madder saying it that way."

"My mom's idea of cussing is calling me 'Timothy James!'"

"My stepfather got transferred to Pittsburgh. We weren't talking by then, anyway. My mom and I weren't doing much better. Last time I talked with her was last Christmas. I get cards from her. Chatty stuff. That's it."

The bus was filling up, and Jake suddenly felt as if they were standing in front of microphones, facing the rest of the team.

They sat, silent, for a few moments.

Todd Hendricks stopped at the seat in front of Timmy and, still standing, looked out the window.

"Hey," the big lineman said as he sat down, "check out the tits on that one."

His teammates obliged.

"It's gotta be the corn," Timmy said.

⚭

Father Robert Basinger was the forty-year-old priest assigned to the Catholic archdiocese's Newman Center near campus, and also was the chaplain at Cascade's Saint Vincent Hospital. Annie Laughlin was sipping coffee with him in the hospital cafeteria, and the priest lightly fingered his wispy beard as he listened.

"I can't forgive them," she said bitterly. "I still can't. I'd kill them if I could. Does that make me a hypocrite?"

"You're just *thinking* about it," he said softly.

"I thought the church said thoughts counted, too."

"There's a lot of debate about that."

They sat, silent, for a minute. Basinger put his hand on Annie's.

Finally, Annie said, "Okay, let's move on. The protest. You sure being there won't get you in trouble?"

"The archbishop and I have an arrangement," the priest said. "I can speak out. I can be there. I just can't appear to be leading or egging on the students."

"And if you do?"

"There's a vacant parish in the Mojave Desert."

⚭

## SEVEN: "CLASSICAL GAS"

After the light practice, Benson picked up his phone messages at the front desk. Some were from Oregon television, radio and newspaper reporters. From his room, he made two quick calls to radio stations. To his chagrin, neither interview was about whether CU had a chance against favored Nebraska. Next, although he didn't have a message from him, Benson called the *Herald*'s managing editor. Benson politely asked if the *Herald* always ran letters to the editor without trying to verify whether any incidents described really happened or attempting to get the other side of the story.

❦

The pink message slips were waiting under the door when Alex Tolliver and Jake arrived back at their room after practice.

Alex picked them up, glanced at them and passed them to Jake.

The first was from Annie. The operator hadn't done a good job of spelling in the transcription process, but it still made Jake laugh.

"MESSAGE: You should have just called him a fashist."

The second was from Kit.

"MESSAGE: Seeking comment about Herald letter for Daily story."

Jake wanted to call her, but not for that reason. He tried a collect call to the number Kit left, but there was no answer and the operator insisted that twenty-seven rings were enough.

Jake decided he needed a Coke. After dropping a quarter into the machine, he heard Rex Gamberg's voice behind him.

"Don't screw up the machine, too," Gamberg said.

Jake turned around.

"Excuse me?"

"You're putting yourself and your causes ahead of this team and this program. The shit with the kid is the least of it."

Jake angrily yanked his Coke bottle out of the slot. He reached down and used the bottle opener, then faced Gamberg again. They glared.

Jake took a swig and walked past Gamberg. "It's nice to know you're so supportive of the rest of the staff after Coach Benson gave you a chance," Jake said. "Where were you? Tinker Toy J.C.?"

"They know how I feel," Gamberg said.

"See?" Jake retorted as he walked away. "That proves they can put up with assholes like us on both sides."

∽

Lincoln's Gridiron Lounge featured a football-shaped bar, display cases with a helmet from every college program in the country, generously poured cocktails, cuts of prime rib that overwhelmed anyone except offensive tackles, and raucous Friday night performances by selected seniors from the Nebraska marching band.

The Nebraska A.D. told Wyden he would be right back. He was wearing his red jacket, so he was easy to follow as he glad-handed his way through the room and gave the signal to the band, which had played the Nebraska fight song eleven times since Wyden came in. That was a Friday night tradition; so was the next gesture of hospitality for the visitors. The band tried to make "Mighty Cascade" – more of a ballad than a fight song – sound stirring. The Cascade fans in the bar, all six of them, stood and sang. It was not quite the "La Marseillaise" scene from *Casablanca*.

After the song, Wyden went to the phone, called the hotel, and had the clerk page Benson. The coach was in the meeting room with the team, watching *The Graduate*. The movie was still in theatres after nine months in release, but the players had been all for renting the print. Benson was just close enough to Jake to hear his whispered debate with his defensive teammates. Jake said he would have stayed with Mrs. Robinson and left Elaine alone. The others said he was nuts. Katharine Ross, anytime.

Benson wasn't thrilled to be summoned to the phone. He was even less thrilled when he discovered who was calling.

"Larry, are we all set on Powell and the kid?" Wyden asked.

"Can't this wait?"

"Are we all set on Powell and the kid?"

"Bill, we called the father, and we're all set."

# SEVEN: "CLASSICAL GAS"

The band began another chorus of the Cornhuskers' song, and the diners sang along.

*"There is a place called Nebraska*

*"Good, old Nebraska U..."*

Wyden pressed on. "Did he call the kid, too?"

The band and the singing around the athletic director were loud enough to be excuses.

"I can't really hear you, Bill, but we're all set."

"I said ... did he call the kid, too?"

"Thanks, Bill, talk to you later."

Click.

༄

The phone was ringing when Jake and Alex Tolliver returned to the room after the movie.

Jake grabbed it.

After Jake and Kit had talked for twenty minutes, but showed no signs of stopping soon, Alex told Jake that if he didn't end the conversation within the next eighteen seconds and let them get to sleep, Alex personally would start reading aloud from the Gospels in the background.

After Jake hung up, it hit him.

He never gave Kit, the reporter, an official comment about the post-game incident in Portland.

# EIGHT:
## "I'VE JUST GOTTA GET A MESSAGE TO YOU"

*(Monday, September 23, 1968)*

The grape and strawberry opt-out results were back. Roughly twenty-eight percent of the students had signed the forms, requesting that the university cut the grape and strawberry purchases.

This was a foggy resolution, not a mandate, Neal Hassler decided. At least it was better than the poll that ran in the *Campus Daily,* in which the mutually exclusive responses – respondents were asked to choose either buying at the previous year's levels, cutting back, or completely boycotting – added up to 116.4 percent.

Hassler summoned the food service director and told him to cut the grape and strawberry purchases about thirty percent from a year ago.

The nervous director was acting as if he expected to be asked to account for a missing $176,000 from department funds. "I'll try," he said.

"You will not try. You *will* do it."

"But we already put the orders in for at least the rest of the calendar year. It's probably too late to change the contracts."

"You mean you knew this vote was coming up and you put in the orders for the rest of the year?"

The director nodded.

"How much did *we* order?"

"Same as last fall semester."

"Why?" Hassler spit it out, feeling both powerless and angry.

"I was told to."

"By whom?"

"The chairman of the state board. He said he'd talked to the governor."

"Excuse me," Hassler said, gesturing at his door, "does it or does it not say 'president' there? And why didn't you at least tell me about this, much less ask me? I'll be damned if I'll have you plotting behind my back because the governor doesn't want to lose eleven votes in Hood River."

"What am I supposed to do when the chairman calls? Hang up on him and come tattling to you?"

Hassler was angry with the chairman of the state board. He was even angrier with himself for not picking up the phone and calling the son of a bitch.

"We'll do it next semester," he told the food service director. "Is that clear?"

❧

In Fiction Writing, the Jack Kerouac want-to-be in front of Jake Powell turned around. "My dad almost made me drop out because he bet two-hundred bucks on you."

"How many points was he getting?" Jake asked.

"Sixteen."

"Sorry."

Jake smiled ruefully, thinking the Fishermen played decent football for most of the 31-13 loss at Nebraska, and that he was thankful Todd Hendricks had skipped class that day – because Todd would have punched this kid.

"And then," Kerouac said, "I told my dad that the player who told the twelve-year-old kid to go fuck himself in Portland is in my Fiction Writing class, and he *really* went nuts!"

Kit Dunleavy was grinning. She wondered how her father would take the news. *Hey, Dad, you like sports, so the good news is I'm going out with a football player. But here's what you'll think is bad news: Guess which one.*

Kerouac wasn't going to leave Jake alone. "Now my dad says he hopes O.J. Simpson runs for three hundred yards against you Saturday," he said.

❧

Annie Laughlin loved taking history courses, because she didn't feel as if she was studying. She was a voracious reader with a photographic memory and a natural writing touch, so she could fly through either multiple-choice or essay tests. Carrying a double major in education and history was an easy decision, and she inadvertently triggered a bitter debate within the education department when she was assigned as a student teacher at South Cascade High.

Some of the education department professors argued that as much as they respected Annie's activism and her anti-Vietnam war stand, they were playing with fire – and risking the viability of the student teacher placement program – by dropping one of the state's most notorious rebels into the classroom.

Others said there was no reason to bring that into play, that Annie was the top undergraduate student in both departments and obviously had aptitude as a teacher. She was going to sample working in a mainstream classroom, but she still was thinking that at some point, she would redirect her teaching energies and work with handicapped children.

At South Cascade, which virtually abutted the CU campus and included many faculty offspring among its students, no parents had complained. Even Annie, braced for challenges, was surprised. She was so good in the classroom, her teaching mentor – the beloved Mike Schwartz – let her handle a couple of classes in American History II the first week and decided if he scheduled racquetball matches for third period the rest of the semester, the students wouldn't be cheated at all. So far, Annie's political activism wasn't an issue. She was confident and acerbic, but certainly not revolutionary in her interpretations as she discussed Reconstruction.

Schwartz also got the impression that about half the boys in the class already had crushes on her. They variously tried to hide it or, he assumed, bragged about they'd like to do with her to their buddies after the class.

"Nice job, Annie," he told her after the final student left. "Come on, lunch is my treat in the faculty cafeteria. You don't know what the teaching life is all about until you sample the Swiss steak."

Annie smiled tightly. "Thanks, but I have to get to a planning meeting at the Student Union."

"Planning another protest?"

"No," she said as she gathered up her books, "a mock trial."

Schwartz squinted. "Should I ask?"

"Sure."

"A mock trial for whom?"

Smiling tightly, she responded, "I didn't say I'd answer."

# NINE:
## "HELLO, I LOVE YOU"

*(Thursday, September 26, 1968)*

Clifford Carlson called. "Neal, they're screwing with the recruiters!"

With his heart pounding and his footsteps failing to keep pace, Hassler briskly walked the quarter-mile to the center of campus. God, don't let it be a Grant Park-style melee, he thought. He hoped the two campus police officers assigned to the Student Union, and alerted to pay close attention to the recruiters' tables during their latest scheduled week-long visit, had helped keep everyone under control.

The Union was an L-shaped brick building, home of everything from the *Campus Daily* and the Black Student Organization to the bowling alley. The armed forces' recruiting tables, where one representative from each service handed out literature and answered questions without having the option to sign up students on the spot, were set up in the long lobby outside the Union's ballroom. It amounted to semi-isolation because students needed to know where to look, or be lost in the Union, to come across the recruiters. Only student organizations were allowed to set up tables for sales and information in the high-traffic area adjacent to the cafeteria.

When Hassler arrived and rushed toward the ballroom, he squeezed through an overflow crowd of students milling around the doors that led to the lobby. He almost laughed at the silliness of his reflexive requests to be excused as he slipped between the students, and heard the whispers of recognition in his wake.

In the lobby, the recruiters stood behind their tables. The campus police officers flanked them. The recruiters' looks seemed to be a mixture of amusement and disdain.

Hassler reached a line of students holding a rope, setting off the recruiters and the protest unfolding in front of them. From behind, Hassler tapped the shoulder of one guy holding the rope. To Hassler's relief, the guy stepped slightly aside, lifted the rope and allowed Hassler to duck under it. As he stood back up, he was surprised – briefly – to see Jake Powell and Father Basinger from the Newman

Center standing at the rope, a little farther down, with "front-row" vantage points. Jake's look was almost a wry welcome, even a touch friendly. Basinger, wearing his clerical collar, was as calm as if he were watching parents take a newly baptized infant back to the pew.

Beyond the rope, the protesters had set up two tables of their own in the middle of the lobby, and one plush office chair faced them. A bearded male student sat in the chair, wearing a choir robe and holding a gavel. Hassler's arrival had brought an end to what he presumed to be the "proceedings."

Annie Laughlin faced the "judge," holding one of the recruiters' pamphlets, and it was drenched with what Hassler hoped was red paint. Annie's gaze at Hassler was challenging and angry. Her hands were red, too.

Hassler didn't notice Kit Dunleavy on the periphery, taking notes. He approached the military men first. "You all right?"

"Sure," said the Marine.

"They touch you?"

"Nope. Just this hollering bullshit."

"They were free to leave," Annie said.

The Army man smiled grimly. "We're not deserting our post."

Hassler turned to the students on the other side of the rope, who had quieted, as if they wanted to hear the exchange between the president and the soldiers.

"What's going on here?" he asked loudly, immediately feeling silly. When the protesters' shouting began again, Hassler held up one hand. "No, wait a minute. I can see what's going on."

"They were on trial," Annie said defiantly. "As symbols. Imperialist war. Crimes against civilians."

"They were waging imperialist war at those tables?"

"They're a part of it."

Hassler turned back to the "spectators." He said, "I hear a lot of talk about freedom of speech on this campus."

The "judge" pounded his gavel. "Guilty!" he hollered.

"Guilty!" many in the crowd yelled.

Hassler half-expected the next words to be, "Off with their heads!"

He hollered, "Enough!"

# NINE: "HELLO, I LOVE YOU"

Basinger half-raised his hands, and it was as if he had grabbed all the students at once. They – even Annie – quieted down. Besides, the students were mesmerized, because the former dean, usually mild-mannered in public, was pissed off. For a few seconds, the only sound was Kit's pen scratching on her notepad.

"This isn't right," Hassler said. "What about the freedom to listen and choose? How about the Coalition Against the War? Didn't you have a recruiting table in this same building last week – and right outside the cafeteria, where you had a captive audience? Did anyone try to disrupt that?"

From his vantage point along the rope, Jake shook his head.

Hassler plowed on. "These are the very kind of fascist – yes, fascist! – tactics so many of you seem to deplore! You're trying to deny them the right to talk to students, and deny students the right to talk to them!"

Voices were raised and fingers were pointing, around Hassler, behind Hassler. Now Jake tried to conciliate.

"Sir, it's nothing against them," Jake began. "But allowing recruiters on campus says we have nothing to be ashamed of in this war, and it's even an implied approval of it all. We have no business being in this war, and there are a lot of things that go beyond it, too. Like who's having to fight it!"

"That's completely beside the point here," Hassler said.

"It's always beside the point with you," Annie said.

Jake said, "These people aren't selling magazine subscriptions. They aren't lining us up to work in the accounting department after graduation. We have friends dying over there, and for what? Are we supposed to believe this can end soon?"

"That still is another issue," Hassler said softly. He noticed Carlson walk up to the fringe of the crowd with two more campus police officers. He nodded to Cliff, then looked around and said, louder, "That's another issue altogether!" He glowered at Annie, who looked as if she was about to charge over and spit in Hassler's face. "The issue here is that you made a mockery of the very ideals you want us to acknowledge. You want to protest the war; that is your prerogative, within the limits of decent, human conduct and the rules of this university. But you can't demand to be heard, and then shout down anyone you disagree with."

Basinger called out to Annie. "You've made your point."

The priest walked through parted students and put his hand on the lobby entrance door that part of the milling group was holding open.

"Let's go," he said.

Reluctantly, Annie followed him. So did Jake, again jealous at the power Basinger had to make Annie suddenly reasonable. As the ringleaders and followers started to file out, though, Annie began the chant.

"Guilty! Guilty!"

Hassler stayed until the lobby again was empty of all except the recruiters.

❦

Before practice, Carl Steele leaned over in front of Jake as he was stretching.

"I hear you tried to join the Army this morning," the linebackers coach said.

Jake laughed. "They said I had flat feet."

"Damn," said Steele, "we're stuck with you."

Steele looked down, picked at the grass and tried to be casual. "Be careful," he told Jake.

Larry Benson joined them. The head coach kneeled down, like a catcher, and pulled a blade of grass out of the ground. Without preamble, he said, "Two things, Jake. One, if the recruiters had been physically attacked and you in any way could be connected to it, that would have been it."

"But I was just watching!"

"Don't insult me and say you weren't in on the planning."

"I was in on the planning."

"Two, you need to be thinking about how you'd be letting your teammates down if you screw up. Okay? You're still walking a tightrope, and you're going to fall off the damn thing if you keep this up."

"I'm fine, coach. Besides, we didn't do anything stupid. Nobody touched or threatened them and we told everyone to let them leave if they wanted to."

"You think everyone will do what you tell them to? We can't even do that!"

Abruptly, Benson stood and blew his whistle, signaling the start of practice.

Two hours later, one of the interviewers waiting for Benson after practice was David Burke, the sports reporter from Portland's KPO-TV. It was the rare day when anyone from a Portland station showed up, and Burke closed the interview with something other than football.

"Finally, coach, we have received word that one of your starting linebackers, campus rebel Jake Powell, was involved in another protest today, this one against military recruiting on campus. Some people say he should be dropped from the team. Where do you stand on this?"

"Jake was one of many students there, and he did not directly participate," Benson said. "He was on his own time, he is sincere in his beliefs, and he has a right to express them, as much as I frankly disagree with them. If more details come out that change my opinion, if the university decides to punish any of the students involved, I will back that one hundred percent — even if one of the students is Jake Powell. And I have told Jake that."

Burke turned toward his cameraman.

"There you have it," Burke said. "From Cascade, this is David Burke, Eyewitness News."

After holding his frozen smile for a moment, he put down his microphone and turned to Benson.

"Sorry," he said, "I had to ask."

"I understand," Benson said. "But how come you people in the press always say 'some people' when you mean 'I'? You want me to toss him, don't you?"

"Absolutely. He's not good enough to get that much rope."

"Ah, the old 'Depends-on-how-good-you-are' standard! Well, that's not the way I operate."

"Well, coach, with all due respect, I'm hearing more and more people saying you're some kind of peacenik, too."

"You're missing the point," Benson said, and started to trot toward the arena.

The grizzled equipment manager, Jim Tunis, a campus institution, heard the last part of the exchange as he gathered up footballs.

"Hey, dipshit," he growled to Burke.

"Me?"

"Yeah, you."

"What?"

"Next time, ask if you can see his medals."

∽

Jake had learned to accept Kit's tendency to nod or say hello, or both, to almost everyone she passed on or near campus, and he had stopped trying to decide who she was seeing for the first time or who had been in her Econ class.

"You know ... Hi ... that you've got to ... Hi ... give me better quotes next time," she said to Jake and the others. "Annie was much better. Don't be mad, but she's in the story a lot more than you."

"I thought I was pretty good," Jake said. "You didn't like the bit about magazine subscriptions?"

"The editor said your stuff sounded like slogans written on the bathroom wall. He said Annie was full of fire—"

"And brimstone," Jake said.

"So most of what you said got cut."

"Overshadowed again. I might need to start writing out my lines first. Or hire a ghostwriter."

Kit laughed, and then turned serious. "You know when you say things like that, people say you treat this like it's a game, too."

Jake couldn't hide his exasperation. "I think you turn people off if you can't at least smile every once in a while," he said. Then he held the door open for Kit, and didn't say another word – except to put in their order – for the next ten minutes.

Halfway through their dinner, Jake put down his burrito and picked up his thought as if he had just paused for an instant. Kit now knew it was one of his quirks. Sometimes, he could resume where he had left off last Tuesday.

"Plus," he said, "whenever someone calls me a radical leader or a rebel linebacker, I look around to see who they're talking about."

"Well, you are radical. You are a rebel. You are a leader. And you are a linebacker."

"Jesus, I'm not out there blowing anything up."

"Well, for one thing, from what I can tell of your technical abilities, you'd probably blow yourself up, too."

"Or half the campus."

"Or half the state."

Jake took another bite. "Somebody waves the North Vietnamese flag," he said halfway through the chewing, "I'm there telling him that isn't the answer, either. I'm not into this freedom fighter line of bullshit. Vietnam's just none of our business. Annie knows all that. She knows that if she gets carried away, I might be the one saying, 'Now wait a goddamn minute.' But sometimes I think she goes out of her way to keep me out of the worst of it."

"But what if they kick you off the team, anyway?"

"For this? I don't see how they can. Unless they do something to everyone who was there."

"They might try. Anyone say anything at practice?"

"The coaches did. And Timmy asked me if Annie used real blood."

In the two weeks since *2001*, they had gone to Terwilliger's, eaten lunch together in the Student Union, studied in the library, and even steamed up the corner of the enclosed sorority porch. But she had balked at going to his apartment, although he never had asked directly. She had a test. She was tired. She had to go right back to the sorority.

Tonight, she walked with him from Taco Time to his apartment. He led her in the tenants' entrance, the back door, and followed him up the back stairway. There were two separate apartment doors on each side of the second-floor landing, and then his single door on the third. "They used to keep their grandmother's old trunks here," he said as he fiddled with the lock. "Now it's just me."

"Do you mow the lawn and get free rent?"

"Shut up and don't trip over the bathtub."

Inside, she looked around, wide-eyed and trying not to laugh. "My sister was so jealous when mom told her I'd met a jock. She said you guys drive hot cars and get money in envelopes, so you have the best apartments."

"Tell her they're a little behind in their payments to me. And in case you haven't noticed, I don't have a car. Any car."

"You don't even have a good bike," Kit scoffed, noticing his beat-up Schwinn on the floor. "Who'd steal that? Why do you even bring it up here?"

"For companionship," he said. "I talk, and it listens. Haven't moved it in about a year."

"I almost believe that. Hanging around with Annie long enough could do that to you."

Kit surveyed the mess. "I don't think you expected to get me back here tonight," she said dryly.

"Cleaned for an hour," Jake said. "Before then, you couldn't see the floor."

✑

The blanket and bedspread were on the floor, and a sheet partially covered them as Jake felt Kit's head and soft hair resting on his chest. He traced the small of her back with a single finger. She lightly pulled a tuft of his chest hair, then caressed his chest with all four fingertips. Her eyes rolled up, and she looked at the posters.

"That's quite a mix," she said. "Bobby Kennedy and Bupkis."

"Butkus," Jake said.

"Close enough."

"I was mad when Bobby jumped in," Jake mused. "It was going to screw up McCarthy. But turned out that McCarthy was the one on the cloud. Bobby was with Cesar Chavez, he was with the people, and you could reach him."

Jake gently rolled Kit over, onto her back, kissed her, then put his elbow beside her on the bed and his chin on his hand.

"I went home to Roseburg when he campaigned there," he said. "Annie told me I was wasting my time, but she gave me her car. Bobby looked at all those rednecks in hunting shirts and told them he was for gun control and ending the war. I went up to Portland on primary night and I couldn't believe it when McCarthy won. I hadn't done much for him except wear a button and pass out pamphlets at the Union. When Bobby came through, he stopped right in our group. We told him we were sorry for not doing more. Bobby put his arms around us and said he was sorry he let us down. We were ready to run to the car and drive to California and begin campaigning."

He waved his hand in disgust.

"We should have gone," he said. "I didn't have anything against McCarthy. Still don't. I respect Humphrey more than you do because I think Johnson's held him hostage. I guess I hope he wins. I don't know if he can make a difference, though. I can't bring myself to work for him. Bobby would have made a difference."

Jake took a deep breath, and he was shivering.

"I cried. I got up that morning, and I heard what had happened in L.A. and I cried." He sniffled. "Jesus, I'm sorry. Four months later and..."

"Don't apologize."

He was almost asleep when Kit said, "I stayed with McCarthy."

"Hmmmm?"

"I stayed with McCarthy, and I thought it was great when he beat Bobby in the primary."

He was almost asleep again when she asked, "Why football?"

"What?"

"I've wanted to ask you that for a while."

"What?"

"Weren't you supposed to get up one morning and decide it's ugly and violent, and you don't want any part of it?"

"I've known three − no, four − guys like that. I look at it this way: Number one, I'm getting to go to school for free."

"So you can spend all your money on an apartment," she teased.

He tugged lightly on her hair.

"Number two," he said, "I can't convince myself to despise the game. You've heard all that talk about football camaraderie and learning how to get along? It's not bullshit; it's true. Most of it's true. I'm from a town where the hunting shirts gather at the piddly-ass airport and heckle Bobby Kennedy, and I'm trying to accomplish something with black guys from the ghetto in Los Angeles and guys who think Wallace is right. I'm playing next to Alex Tolliver. He's from the projects in Los Angeles. He's the team captain and got votes from guys whose parents didn't want 'Negroes' in the public schools."

He closed his eyes. "Now maybe we should get some sleep," he said after a few seconds.

"No, we shouldn't," she said, reaching.

# TEN:
## "ALL ALONG THE WATCHTOWER"

*(Monday, September 30, 1968)*

Reading the *Portland Herald* that morning left Neal Hassler with a churning stomach and simmering anger. The editorial made it sound as if Hassler caved in to the students who put the military recruiters on trial. Caved in? No, it's worse than that, he thought bitterly. Readers might infer he handed the protesters the keys to every campus building and promised to have all university officials out of their way by the end of the week. It repeated the error that had been in all the original stories, saying the students had forcibly prevented the military men from leaving the building before Hassler showed up and escorted them out.

The crucial points were that the protesters left the Student Union on their own and the recruiters were untouched. Hassler was convinced that trying to have the demonstration leaders arrested or brought before the Student Conduct Board would have made it worse. The leaders would have been grateful for the martyrdom. They showed some restraint the final day of the recruiters' week-long stint in the Student Union, only picketing outside the building. Area recruiting officials agreed with Hassler, acquiescing in the decision not to punish the protestors. Even the students' radical *Campus Daily* grudgingly praised him. The *Daily* proclaimed that if Hassler let outside cops – and not just the campus police – into the Union, this could have been Chicago all over again, to a lesser, but no less disgraceful, degree.

Yet the *Portland Herald* was indignant.

"By failing to take sufficiently decisive steps to maintain a semblance of order on campus, Cascade University president Neal Hassler is risking the sort of excessive and misguided student and outsider agitator militancy that turned New York City's Columbia University and San Francisco State into armed camps earlier this year," the paper editorialized. "Even more alarming, one of the ringleaders of the recent protest of Army recruiters' appearance on campus was a scholarship football player, tackle Jack Powell, and neither the university president nor the football coach saw fit to hold him accountable. This is permissiveness run wild. Moreover, the university implicitly has endorsed the other ringleader, Students for a Democratic Society state chairman Annette Laughlin. The *Herald* has learned that Miss Laughlin has been placed by the school's education department as a student teacher at South Cascade High School, and that the high school has received complaints that Miss Laughlin encouraged several of her young students to attend and participate in the demonstration."

Hassler didn't even notice that the paper got Powell's name and position wrong. He also hadn't known that Annie Laughlin was serving as a student teacher.

Finally, the editorial brought up Reynaldo Archuleta again, calling him "anarchist drama professor with abhorrent views," but didn't bother to point out that he essentially had been fired.

What of the comparisons to San Francisco State and Columbia? Let's see, Hassler thought. Down in San Francisco over the past year, marauding protesters, ostensibly from the Black Student Organization, torched the bookstore and tore up the cafeteria. After the student newspaper mildly criticized the campus Black Power movement for taking too much direction from outsiders, the editor and the advisor were beaten. The SFSU faculty voted to continue the ROTC program, so the SDS and the Third World Liberation Front occupied the administration building. In a speech on campus, a part-time member of the faculty hinted that the university president and a provost should be "taken out." One San Francisco State president had quit; his interim successor was called down to Los Angeles for a chewing-out from the state system's trustees. At Columbia, demonstrators occupied five buildings in April. When the school finally called in the New York cops, over seven hundred demonstrators were arrested.

Hassler asked himself: Is that what these stupid sons of bitches at the *Herald* wanted here? Because this isn't San Francisco or New York and this is just a college town, they don't think it could happen here? Or do the idiots at the *Herald* think that because we've had a silly mock trial and a lot of yelling with no violence, we're on the verge of a revolution?

Plus, did they really think that all student teaching appointments passed through the president's office for approval? That was between the education department and the public schools involved. He would check out the charge that she had recruited the high school students to attend the demonstration. If she had, she had gone too far, and he would have the education department yank her out of that classroom – for cause.

Damn, Hassler thought, he wished those clowns at the *Herald* had to answer to somebody beside themselves. The notion that they were accountable to the public was a joke; the public seemed malleable and willing to buy it – hook, headline and sinker.

Hassler occasionally went to Portland to meet with the *Herald*'s editorial board. He did it because he was supposed to do it. The governor did it, the leaders of the Legislature did it, mayors did it, and even presidential candidates did it. Hassler wasn't sure he would do it again. Hassler had been in rooms with leading lights of academia, arts, and business, but the newspaper set new standards for so much arrogance backed with so little substance.

Steaming as he looked over the editorial one more time at his desk, Hassler called his wife. Cancel the *Herald* subscription, he told her.

She didn't argue. "The kid always throws it in the bushes, anyway."

&#x2040;

Sophomore quarterback Rick Winslow was raised within a few miles of the Stanford campus. Linebackers coach Carl Steele, who recruited the San Francisco area for Cascade, was raised in San Francisco and worked as an usher at the 49ers' Kezar Stadium. So they had plenty to talk about and notes to compare when Steele tried to convince Rick to attend CU.

During the recruiting period, Stanford said it wanted Rick, but then stalled to see how many players higher on the priority list would accept scholarship offers – a common recruiting maneuver. Stanford finally got a commitment from a high school All-American from Los Angeles, and there wasn't a scholarship left for Rick.

The only times Rick questioned his decision to attend CU were when he called home, collect, and when he walked into the dungeon with chicken-wire stalls that the Fishermen called their football practice locker room in the basement of Hobson Court. But Rick loved the campus and the town. He and Todd Hendricks were thrilled to be in the first year of residence in one of the football team's traditions – a rental house dubbed "The 22nd Avenue Boys Club." For as long as anyone could remember, football players lived in the four-bedroom brick house a block off campus. The previous year, while Rick and Todd played on the freshman team, they agreed they would take over the house's lease when four seniors left, and they now had two other sophomore housemates.

Even the landlord was pleasantly surprised so far this school year. When Rick's friends visited, they asked how they conned the women into staying around to keep it so clean. Rick found it funny, given the reputation of the football program, but there was a touch of military discipline to the place, thanks to Todd.

During his Army stint after high school, "Sarge" defended the country from invasion while stationed at Ft. Lewis, Washington, and he admitted to his friends and teammates – including Jake – that he was relieved to avoid service in Vietnam and he wasn't certain the South Vietnamese cause was worth the loss of American lives. His attitude about the war fluctuated, though, because open challenges tended to bring out the patriot in him.

Every week, the other three players turned money over to Todd, who took it to the store. The agreement was that while he was gone, they cleaned the house, and not just once over lightly, but seriously.

Todd had joined the Army not out of conviction, but because he was an Eastern Oregon farm boy who wanted to buy time, put away some money and get away from the local girl who had him scared she was pregnant. She wasn't, but she wasn't going to let him off easy if he had stayed around Oregon. Rick often asked himself why they put up with Todd's shit around the house, but he always ended up remembering there was a lot to be said for having one of the few homes on the campus fringe that didn't smell like dirty socks, warm beer and potting soil.

Rick and Todd were eating breakfast, getting ready for Political Science 201, taught by the infamous Sam Reynolds, the fiery forty-seven-year-old with a doctorate and a reputation that made him highly sought for comment when reporters needed someone to interpret the political winds of dissent in the country.

# TEN: "ALL ALONG THE WATCHTOWER"

"Come on," Todd said, "Reynolds is a jerk. When he said football was fucked–"

"Aw, he's just trying to stir it up. That's why his classes are so full. He puts on a show. And we've both been part of it."

As they ate, KBON broke up its otherwise steady programming of rock and commercials for the sixty-second hourly news minute at the convenient and regular time of forty-eight minutes past the hour. Hubert Humphrey was going to speak on Vietnam that night in Salt Lake City. The speculation was that he might finally break with President Johnson on the war and at least propose a halt to the bombing of North Vietnam. Meanwhile, perhaps in anticipation, Richard Nixon again dropped some hints that morning.

Nixon hinted he would accelerate the training of the South Vietnamese army as president, and step up the transfer of responsibility from U.S. troops to the South Vietnamese. But in no way would Nixon sanction the abandonment of the South Vietnamese army until it was capable of taking over. The combined forces would not be cut, Nixon insisted, and he said Humphrey would be irresponsible if he raised unrealistic hopes about a quick pullout of American troops.

As they went out the door, Rick couldn't decide if there was any good news in there. He was nineteen, he was planning on being a political science major, but he knew he didn't have many of the answers yet, neither for the midterm nor beyond. He knew he didn't like the war. After watching the clips on the war on the *CBS Evening News*, he was more certain that he didn't want to serve in it. His father had just sent him clippings from the *San Francisco Chronicle* about two of his high school classmates who had been killed in action. Both of them had been nobodies in high school. Samuel R. Califano? Was he the one from shop class? Was he the one always smoking in the bathroom? Or was he the kid who had the fifteen-year-old Plymouth and the thirteen-year-old girlfriend?

When the football players walked into the class, Professor Reynolds was leaning forward, with one arm on the podium, waiting for the top of the hour.

"I'm shocked you're not on crutches," he told Rick.

Reynolds' smartass smile could make him hard to read; he had a smart-ass smile when he ordered toast and coffee. Yet Rick thought he detected some sympathy amid the sarcasm.

Rick was sacked eight times against Southern California. He threw 53 passes, completing 27 for 291 yards. Nice numbers, but not enough, especially because they couldn't get any kind of a running game going. Timmy Hilton scrambled just to gain 36 yards, while USC's O.J. Simpson streaked for 125. Despite all that, the Fishermen and the favored Trojans were tied 17-17 until Southern California scored with 1:12 left.

As Rick and Todd slid into their chairs, Todd called out to Reynolds, "I thought you didn't even read the sports page."

"I was putting it in the bottom of the bird cage."

After the bell rang, Reynolds tossed out the issue of whether it was proper to have ROTC program on campus and whether the prominence of football was another example of misaligned priorities.

"Aren't both players and officer candidates being exploited? Is it fair that a quarterback is going to college for free, when others are either scrambling to pay tuition or having to skip college altogether and risk their lives for a dubious cause in Vietnam?"

When he finished, he was looking at Rick.

The quarterback could feel the other eyes, and the unspoken challenge. Come on jock, defend yourself. So he did. "How come people like you don't bring up anyone on a music scholarship?" he asked. "Or a Regents Scholarship? They aren't marching into the draft board, either."

"Because the music department isn't trying to run the school, like the athletic department is," a guy behind Todd said.

"And half the football team shouldn't even be in college," piped in a girl.

"What do you mean by that?" Rick asked angrily.

"Come on, they pull strings or cheat to get you guys in school. And then to keep you eligible."

"Name me one player they did that for."

Reynolds wasn't even trying to suppress his grin.

The girl shrugged. "I mean in general. They pamper you jocks."

Todd spoke up. "Sorry, sis. You people are full of shit."

That triggered both nervous titters and angry retorts.

Reynolds held up his hand. When it was quiet, he said, "Tell her why."

"I got out of the army fifteen months ago. I've got buddies who've gotten their asses killed in Vietnam and I'm glad I'm not over there now. I'm not going to apologize for that. How can you be against the war, then be mad at me for not being there?"

"Because the system's not fair," the girl said.

"Maybe not. But they have Army nurses over there, too. When're you signing up?"

"Oh, don't be—"

"And this pampered bullshit? I took the entrance exam twice before I could get my scholarship. They're after my ass all the time to be in class. They're checking with the professors all the time. Right?"

He was looking at Reynolds.

"True," Reynolds said, "and duly noted."

The girl was undeterred. "I don't get it," she said to Todd again. "Are you against the war or for it — as long as someone else is doing the fighting?"

"I think we should either fight the damn thing to win or get the hell out," Todd said. "I know we're getting guys killed because we're afraid to fight it the right way — and people like you are part of why we're afraid. Plus, everybody around here's nervous about getting drafted if they flunk or if the government ends student deferments. That's at least half the reason for all this shit around here about the war. If it was an all-volunteer Army fighting this, nobody would give a damn here."

"That's the stupidest thing I've ever heard," the girl responded. "But I guess I shouldn't be surprised to hear that from a jock."

*That* drew Rick back in. He asked, "How come we make such a big deal about individual rights and lack of prejudice and all that around here but you see nothing wrong with grouping all of us together as 'jocks'? Jesus, we're not all alike. We argue about politics and everything else in the locker room."

That intrigued Reynolds. Smirking, he asked, "Can we come and listen sometime?"

"You'll have to ask the coach," Rick said, "but everyone here seems to be forgetting that our linebacker just led the protest against the recruiters."

Todd laughed bitterly. "Powell didn't tackle *them,* either," he said.

❧

When Annie made it to South Cascade High's Room 128 three minutes before the start of the day's third period, five students – three boys and two girls – were waiting outside the door in ambush.

"Sorry, Miss Laughlin," said a floppy-haired boy who, because he still was trying to master the art of shaving, had a bandage on his chin.

"I take it you're the ones who were at the Union."

"Yup."

"How'd it get out? I didn't see you."

Another boy said, "My mom saw our pictures in the *Times-Register.* We were way in the back, but you could see us. She must have called and snitched."

"But the editorial was in the *Portland Herald.*"

"Her brother is a copy editor there."

"How convenient," Annie said. "So how did you hear about the mock trial in the first place?"

The other boy smiled sheepishly. "We didn't," he said. "We were at the Union to buy some pot."

Annie waved both hands. "I didn't hear that!"

A girl interjected, "Oh, oh, this doesn't look good." She nodded down the hall. Cliff Quinn, the principal, was approaching them in lockstep with Mike Schwartz, Annie's supervising teacher.

Quinn asked, "Miss Laughlin, can we talk in my office?"

As Quinn led her away, toward the main office, Annie turned back and looked at Schwartz, who gave her a tight smile and a slight shake of his head.

She wasn't sure how to read that.

❧

# TEN: "ALL ALONG THE WATCHTOWER"

When she left Quinn's office twenty minutes later, she was surprised to see two of the boys from Schwartz's class waiting in the main office lobby.

They stood up, anxiously questioning her with their eyes.

"Do we need to talk with Mr. Quinn?" the floppy-haired junior asked.

"If you want," Annie said softly as they walked into the hall. "But you don't need to. All he asked for was my word that I didn't recruit you to skip your classes and come to the demonstration. I told him I didn't even know you were there."

"Are you still teaching?"

"For now," Annie said. "For now. But he said if I drag you into anything, or campaign on the job, that'll change."

⁓

The Fishermen's record was 1-2. The losses were to two of the best teams in the country, Nebraska and USC. As the director in the Cascade television station's studio barked out that Benson's weekly live television show would begin in a minute, as more lights came on and as Hal Hayes, the KCTV sportscaster, took one more look at himself in the hand mirror, Benson again had the urge to call the long-retired former athletic director of a decade ago – Hank Gardenia's predecessor in the job – to cuss him out for his advance scheduling. Rather than looking for cupcake opponents, that A.D. had scheduled three of the four '68 non-league games against top-flight programs. At the end of the year, was anyone going to care about anything but the record? Would they get extra credit for having played Nebraska, Air Force, and Colorado in the non-league games, and because the only "breather" was against Idaho? Of course, they wouldn't. Benson again promised himself that if he ever became an athletic director, he would schedule the non-league games against not only the Little Sisters of the Poor, but also the Little Brothers of the Poor, and Little Nieces of the Poor.

Five minutes later, Benson found himself saying in response to a question from the sportscaster about the schedule: "No, Hal, we always welcome the challenge of playing the nation's best teams."

Saying anything else, he knew, would sound like an excuse.

༄

"This is the way it started at Columbia, too," Annie heatedly told Jake Powell.

They were in Terwilliger's, where Coach Benson's show flickered on the little television at the end of the bar. Jake pretended to be paying more attention to Annie than the television.

Jake spotted himself making another tackle on the highlights from the USC game. He knew if he was making a tackle, it must have been the first half. Annie had stopped talking, so Jake asked, "What do you mean?" He had no clue what Annie had said.

"Columbia wouldn't ban the recruiters from the campus for good, either," Annie said. "That got us started there."

Jake knew the code. "Us" was the SDS. He knew that Annie's major regret was that she hadn't attended the conference that had produced the Port Huron Statement, the SDS founding manifesto, and she was convinced that if she had been there to help Tom Hayden, it would have been even more insightful.

"Look," Jake told Annie, "sometimes I think you really believe this place is just like New York. You're sitting in some classes next to a farmer's kid, and you think he's going to pick up a picket sign and camp in the administration building just because you say so?"

"Not because I say so," Annie said, "but because it's the right thing to do. We don't need the whole student body, anyway. Just enough. There were only a hundred and thirty in the president's office at Columbia, and they wrote about it like it was the whole world. Hassler can't just walk off and have it end like that."

The football highlights were over, so Jake no longer was distracted. "Hassler handled it pretty well," he said.

"What?"

"You heard me. He handled it pretty well. We had the trial, you made your point, he made his, and he didn't call in the outside police to beat the shit out of us. Or is that what you wanted, a police riot?"

Annie looked away.

"Well," Jake finally said, shaking his head, "at least I'll give you credit for not doing anything stupid enough to bring them in." Jake was tempted to call her gutless for not doing more, but he didn't want that to come off as a challenge. Instead, he said, "Hassler's not one of the assholes, and the sooner you figure that out, the better. I'm still on the football team because we didn't do too much, and because Hassler didn't overreact to what we did."

"If they'd thrown you off the team, we would have had pickets outside the athletic department, too."

"Come on, Annie, I'm still not even home free on this. If I lose my scholarship I'm going to have a hard time staying in school. You know that. And if we do much more, you're risking your student teaching credits, too."

"We won't let that happen."

Jake decided he would try one more time. By now, he had given this speech so often he felt like a candidate on a bus tour.

"You know," Jake began slowly, but loud enough to be heard over the din, "I remember when you would have dazzled Hassler with eight-syllable words and an eight-minute speech."

"You're one to talk," Annie snapped. "At least Hassler's not a twelve-year-old kid at a football game, Mr. Sensitive."

"You know that's not the same thing. I don't think you've changed that much, have you?"

"Jake, this isn't 1965," she pleaded. "This isn't Roseburg anymore. Too many people have tried being polite too long. You can't sit there, raise your hand, and hope they call on you."

Kit Dunleavy slipped into the booth next to Jake. She could tell she was interrupting an argument, and that the best way to end it was to plow right in with something else.

"My dad just said they might come up for the Air Force game," she said. "Would you have a way to get four tickets, or should I just buy some?"

"When's that game again?" Annie asked.

"Second Saturday in November," Kit said. "Right after my parents vote for Nixon."

Jake knew that Annie hadn't needed to be told when Air Force was coming to town.

∞

Bill Wyden hated getting work-related calls at home, but if chatting with Dusty Harris of the *Portland Herald* got his name in the paper – and better yet, if Harris again called him "CU's bright, young athletic director" – it would be worth it.

Harris actually hadn't called for a story, but was in search of twelve tickets for his relatives for the Washington State game. Harris could buy twelve tickets by walking up to the window fifteen minutes before the game, of course, but he hadn't paid for a ticket in his professional life, and he wasn't about to start now. He wanted to go through the motions of talking business before he brought up the tickets, so he asked if it was true that the football staff was catching heat from the boosters. Harris knew this was true, of course, because some of the boosters called him and told him they were damn angry, and they were going to call the A.D. and tell him so.

"I'm concerned, too," Wyden said. "Washington State's not bad, and if we lose this one, we can kiss the rest of the season goodbye, and nobody will come to the last three home games, either. But, Jesus, Dusty, you can't quote me. The entire staff will be evaluated after the season, as usual. Don't quote me on that, either." He paused. "Not yet, anyway."

Harris made a mental note to keep checking back, then said, "Say, Bill, could you do me a favor?"

# ELEVEN:
## "SCARBOROUGH FAIR"

*(Tuesday, October 8, 1968)*

The Tuesday press gathering wasn't the highlight of Timmy Hilton's week. Arthur Feldman of Sports Publicity had trained the players to check the bulletin board outside the locker room every Monday after practice, and every week, Timmy was in demand.

TUESDAY LUNCHEON INTERVIEWS, MEMORIAL UNION, ROOM 206

Rick Winslow – Meet with Blair McCullough of the Times-Register and Dusty Harris of the Portland Herald, 1:30 p.m.

Keith Oldham – Meet with Hal Hayes of KCTV, 1:45 p.m.

Timmy Hilton – Meet with Hal Hayes of KCTV, 1:30 p.m. Meet with David Burke, KPO-TV of Portland, 1:34 p.m. Meet with Tom Gondrezick, KWBA of Portland, 1:38 p.m. Meet with Pete Gonzales, KALB-TV of Portland, 1:42 p.m. Meet with Blair McCullough of the Times-Register and Dusty Harris of the Portland Herald, 1:45 p.m. See Arthur Feldman to call Jim Murray of the Los Angeles Times, 1:50 p.m.

The weekly luncheon made the week easier for the reporters and also kept them out of the way. They showed up at the room in the Student Union, ate a free lunch, interviewed Benson about the upcoming opponent, and then talked to several players. They could stretch out the material through several stories all week and – this was the key – rarely have to attend practice.

Feldman at least always seemed to show up and break up the interviews with Timmy and the other players when the questions were getting repetitive or stupid. Feldman proudly called himself the "designated asshole," and he was so deft at the task, the reporters didn't hold it against him. "It's amazing what they let me get away with when I buy all the drinks," he once told Timmy.

As he did every week, Timmy was shooting to arrive one minute late to the room on the second floor of the Union. He didn't want to seem eager. Killing time before going upstairs, he sat on the stairway and read the *Campus Daily*, oblivious to the other students scrambling past him. Some of the glances back over shoulders involved annoyance; most reflected "Hey, that's..." recognition.

When he saw the *Daily's* lead story, Timmy wished he had checked the speaker's schedule on bulletin board outside the Black Student Organization office. It might have been interesting to hear the director of San Francisco State's Black Studies program declare on campus yesterday that black students must formulate plans to take over or disrupt their schools if racist policies and teaching continued.

Timmy looked at his watch, then got up, climbed the stairs and walked in to face the cameras.

"Congratulations on being named Pac 8 Player of the Week," Hal Hayes of KCTV said at 1:32, then stuck the microphone in his face.

"A tip of the hat to you for being named Pac 8 Player of the Week," David Burke of KPO-TV said at 1:35, then stuck the microphone in his face.

"It must be a thrill for you to be named Pac 8 Player of the Week," Tom Gondrezick of KWBA-TV said at 1:38, then stuck the microphone in his face.

"Congratulations and a tip of the hat to you for being named Pac 8 Player of the Week. It must be a big thrill," Pete Gonzales of KALB-TV said at 1:42, then stuck the microphone in his face.

Each time, Timmy humbly thanked his offensive line for the holes they had opened against Washington State and named all the starters. Timmy tried to do it breathlessly, so the station wouldn't be able to cut off his answer and leave off the names. He also knew the TV types would find a way. When the final TV interviewer, Gonzales, asked his one question and got the rote response, he lowered his microphone, nodded and, as the cameraman heeded the cue to stop filming, said to Timmy, "Thanks."

Timmy responded, "Okay if I ask *you* something?"

"Sure."

Timmy grabbed the microphone out of Gonzales' hand. Holding it up, Timmy asked with mock earnestness, "Is this TV stuff as easy as it looks?"

He thrust the mike in Gonzales' face.

"Well, Timmy," Gonzales said, "maybe *you'll* try it someday."

# ELEVEN: "SCARBOROUGH FAIR"

Timmy feigned horror and handed back the microphone. "No way!"

By then, the *Herald*'s Dusty Harris was waiting to get Timmy's comments – or a facsimile thereof – down in his notebook. "So, Timmy, could you talk about being Pac 8 Player of the Week?" Harris asked.

"Well, most of the credit has to go to the offensive line," Timmy said solemnly.

Ninety minutes later, Dusty finished his story in Feldman's office and a student assistant sent it to the *Herald* on the athletic department's telecopier.

> By DUSTY HARRIS, Herald Staff
>
> CASCADE – Last Saturday against Washington State, Larry Benson showed his faith in both his offensive line and his tailback.
>
> The Cascade University mentor knew it was risky, but he was insistent that he had the offensive weapons in the correct places. That meant he was going to leave Timmy Hilton at tailback, even though the cynics were saying that the former flanker didn't belong in the backfield.
>
> On Tuesday, Benson and Hilton had the last laughs together. Thanks to Hilton's stupendous 183-yard rushing game in the 31-16 conquest of WSU on Saturday at Potestio Stadium that evened the Fishermen's season record at 2-2, he was named the Pacific 8 Conference Player of the Week.
>
> "I would be remiss if I did not pay tribute to the gladiators in the trenches," Hilton, the smooth junior from Olympia, declared Tuesday on campus.
>
> Opined Benson: "You are seeing the genuine Timmy Hilton. He has both pride and courage, and I do not believe that has been sufficiently acknowledged, even by our most faithful followers."

◦‿◦

Carl Steele helped provide emotional balance on the staff, and he was proving to be a bright coach who was able to make the most of the tools he was given on the defensive side of the ball in an offensive-minded program. He worked mostly with the linebackers, but also helped coordinate the defense.

On defense, the Fishermen had a few talented players, including Alex Tolliver, the middle linebacker who seemed to always find the ball, and all the defensive players had heart. Jake Powell, the outside linebacker, was smart and tough, and Steele admired him, but he probably had little business starting for a Pac-8 team.

Steele played as a guard and end at Utah State, did his Army stint, then coached one season at a small college in Montana before taking a temporary assistant's job at Indiana that ended when his predecessor returned from a sabbatical. Finally, he gave up, renting a U-Haul trailer and planning to go into the insurance business back in the Bay area. With twenty minutes of loading help from a buddy, they emptied the Bloomington apartment of all the furniture and Carl and Eva took off for San Francisco.

They stayed overnight with friends in Salt Lake City, and as he and Eva ate breakfast the next morning, Carl saw a small story in the Salt Lake paper about Cascade promoting its offensive line coach, Larry Benson, to head coach after Hank Gardenia became athletic director.

During his brief stint at Indiana, Carl met Benson at the national coach's convention. At one of the cocktail parties, they had ended up talking about fishing and their reactions to attending a lecture session about the power running game conducted by a "genius" offensive mind. They decided the coach wouldn't be such a genius if recruits ever heard that his school was going to crack down on boosters paying the players twenty-five dollars an hour to be on call to shovel snow from automobile dealership lots – in the summers.

Calling from Salt Lake, Carl was shocked when he got through to Benson on the first try and asked if there were any openings on his staff. Feeling comfortable with Benson, Carl confided, "If I don't get a job in a week, I have to start wearing a tie and work with actuarial tables." Benson said he needed a freshman team coach, and that at least would get a young coach's foot in the door. If Carl was interested and he showed up at Cascade, he would get an interview.

On a Saturday in late January, Carl, Eva, and the U-Haul pulled into Benson's driveway. Benson took Carl to Gardenia's home, and the three men talked for an hour. After Benson and Gardenia huddled, they offered Carl the job at a salary that would have insulted the night-shift manager at Burger Chef. He took it, gladly, and Steele coached the freshmen for two seasons before moving up to the varsity.

On this Monday in Cascade, Steele represented the staff in discussing the Washington State game and told the Fishermen's Booster Club it was amazing how much stronger the defense looked when the offense controlled the ball and didn't turn it over. He said it almost tentatively, and he carefully qualified it so nobody would walk away thinking he was criticizing the offensive staff, because he knew as well as anyone that the Fishermen's top talent was on offense and they needed to be wide-open to win.

He was pretty sure one or two men in the room understood his point. Steele had spotted one former CU linebacker sitting in the front row. That's one. Then there was the old guy in the back who played both ways in the 1930s. That's two. If the old guy had his hearing aid turned on.

∽

The knock was Neal Hassler's only advance warning. Governor McMichael, the former television commentator who still had a tendency to act as if the entire world was his private studio, opened the door and was in the office before Hassler could say yes, come in or stay the hell out.

"See what we're in for?" the governor said, flourishing a copy of the *Campus Daily* in one hand.

"Nice to see you, too," Hassler said dryly. "Now what are you talking about? You burst in here – no warning, no call, and not even a buzz from Diana – and expect me to read your mind?"

The governor was shocked. For the first time during their relationship, Neal Hassler wasn't being deferential.

Recovering, McMichael plowed on. "So I come down from Salem and I'm wasting my time at a luncheon and they keep sticking newspapers in my face and saying, 'Look at this!' Jesus Christ, Neal, this is why everybody's so worried about what might happen on this campus. People are scared to death the same kind of thing can happen here that happened in San Francisco—"

"I read that somewhere just the other day."

"Well, damn it, that editorial said what people are thinking, and I'm one of those people. That's all on top of the mess with the recruiters last week. This time, it's not just redneck farmers from Prineville. It's not just the morons in the clouds at the *Herald,* and I'll deny ever saying that, by the way. Christ, here's an article in the student paper with some guy from San Francisco State saying we might be next."

"That's not what he said."

"He sure as hell implied it. He implied it standing at a podium in the Student Union with the university seal staring the photographer right in the goddamn lens. It's a good thing the *Campus Daily* was the only paper there." He pointed at the shot of the speaker, who was pointing in anger. "This picture would have been great in the *Herald* this morning, wouldn't it? This is going to get around, anyway. And I'm telling you, reasonable people are sweating about all of this."

"What do you want me to do?" Hassler asked. "The worst thing we can do is to try and tell the Black Student Organization or anyone else that they can't bring in whoever they want to speak because we don't like what he might say."

The governor sat down opposite Hassler and leaned forward. "All I'm saying is that people are afraid and mad, and I think they have a right to be. You've got to be conscious of that. If it takes putting your foot down heavily a time or two to make it clear we won't put up with that kind of Columbia or San Francisco State crap around here, it's got to be done."

The governor inhaled slowly, exhaled slowly, got up, put his hands in his pockets, and paced.

"I'm not trying to be an asshole," McMichael said. "I know you're caught in the middle. I'm just saying that's the type of shit you've got to keep in mind when other things come up. We both might have to be tougher in the future, or we're going to have the kind of mess that isn't going to do anybody any good. The legislature would cut the budget, the parents would send their kids to junior college instead, and then what would you have?"

"Integrity."

McMichael laughed bitterly. "Well, big fuckin' deal."

# ELEVEN: "SCARBOROUGH FAIR"

❦

"Shut up!"

Much to Jake Powell's surprise, they did.

The leaders of the Campus Coalition Against The War, a coalition so loosely organized Jake wasn't even sure it could lead anyone else, were meeting at two big tables pulled together in a back room of Terwilliger's. In front of them sat pitchers of Hamm's beer and baskets of fries, and a few came back from their visits to the bathrooms smelling like a walking joint.

Several of the coalition members wanted to talk about how they could use the Cascade-Air Force Academy football game in early November to make an anti-war point.

"A protest?" Jake asked. "Fine, I'll go along with that. Count me in. I'll carry a sign until I have to go to the locker room. I'll put a black armband on my uniform. I'll even see what I can do about intercepting a pass, returning it for a touchdown, and telling the quarterback it was my private protest."

Annie, sipping, almost spit out her beer. "Fat chance of that," she said.

"Thanks a lot. Come on, if you think screwing up the football game is going to do any good, you're really off base." That set off clamor. "No! Why'd you make me the chairman if you didn't want to listen to me? Was I just supposed to be the token jock?"

The gay student leader – Jake wasn't all that far removed from considering "gay" a synonym for happy – glowered. "Don't you have to go to practice or something?"

"What are we talking about here?" Jake asked. "A whole bunch of vague shit. Something drastic, you say. Well, what's that? Blowing up their bus? With or without them on it? Blowing up the stadium? With or without people in it? Smoke-bombing their locker room? Kidnapping the starting backfield? Storming the press box and lecturing on the P.A. system? Spray-painting 'Screw the Air Force' or a peace sign on the Astroturf? What?"

"Those are all good ideas," Annie said.

"Except I wouldn't say 'Screw,'" the gay leader said.

Ultimately, they agreed to ponder possibilities and talk more the Sunday before the game. Jake was thankful about that. There wouldn't be enough time between the meeting and the game to be too ambitious. Unless...

"Annie," he said on the sidewalk, "I see those wheels turning. You've got something else going."

"Who, me?"

"If you cross me on this, I'll never forgive you."

Annie was silent, looking down as she walked.

"I mean it," Jake said.

❧

Rick Winslow tried to memorize the facts about the Magna Carta, but his mind wandered. Runnymede, 1215, barons forced King John to sign, showed the stupid son of a bitch that he could be forced to account to the realm, 26-zigout should be open to Keith Oldham if they play man-to-man on second-and-long.

Todd Hendricks burst in, ceremoniously threw Rick's coat on the floor, clicked on the radio on the nightstand, and fiddled with the dial until he found the familiar voice. Rick knew this must be something important to drag the big tackle away from this week's episode of *The Mod Squad* and undercover cop Julie, the woman for whom he would forsake all others.

President Johnson was talking about Hubert Humphrey. Finally. Professor Reynolds had noted many times during the semester that LBJ had remained silent during the campaign. Reynolds said that LBJ seemed to be either: a) indifferent about who won; b) pulling for Nixon; c) pissed off at Humphrey; or, d) certain that if he supported his own vice president, it would hurt more than it helped. Or maybe he was all of those.

"Few men I have ever known have understood our urgent national needs so well," LBJ said. Nixon, he all but said, is an idiot. And, he asked, what do you think of the possibility of Spiro Agnew becoming president of the United States?

Listening at his desk, Rick said, "I'd just make him sign the Magna Carta."

# ELEVEN: "SCARBOROUGH FAIR"

෴

Kit paused on the stairway leading to Jake's apartment.

The door to one of the two apartments on the second floor was open. The music was loud enough to make Kit, who loved to crank her own stereo, feel as if she should cover her ears, and if she stood still for a minute and inhaled, she might be as high as if she had smoked an entire joint.

"Welcome!" a deep voice called.

She walked, tentatively, through the door and stood a step inside, letting her eyes adjust to the dark.

A guy approached out of the dark and reached to Kit with a joint. He was naked. The scene came into focus. Murky focus. Maybe twelve guys, eight girls.

Kit took the joint, though. The guy at least stood at arm's length, waiting. She took a hit, a deep hit, exhaled, and coughed as she handed it back.

"Thanks," she said as she turned to leave.

"Hey!" the guy called. "Come back!"

"Maybe next time," Kit said, not turning back.

Upstairs, when Jake opened the door, she nodded down the stairway. "How often does that go on?"

"How much did you see?"

"Enough."

"Not often," he said, stepping aside to let her in.

"*How* often?"

Jake smiled. "No more than twice a week."

Looking him in the eye as he closed the door and turned, she asked, "You ever joined in?"

"Oh, come on, Kit. That look like my style?"

"No, but that's not what I asked."

"No," he said. "Almost once, but no."

"Do I want know the definition of 'almost'?"

"No. The answer is no. Pretty much."

# TWELVE:
## "MAGIC CARPET RIDE"

*(Saturday, October 12, 1968)*

Kit Dunleavy was on her side, curled up, and staring at the wall next to the bed. She heard the radio knob click, and then the newscaster reading.

"If the Fishermen can pull off the upset in the Los Angeles Coliseum tonight, they'll be 3-1 in the Pacific 8, still have a shot at making the Rose Bowl, and – "

"Earth to Kit."

Chris Reynolds, the blond would-be actor, stood at the dresser mirror with his back to Kit. He wore only a pair of boxers as he brushed his bushy hair. "Hey, come on, I know you're awake," he said. He never looked at her reflection, but only at his own.

Kit rolled over and tried to sit up, and made it about halfway up before she leaned back against the headboard.

ᨀ

The previous night, Kit and her sorority roommate, Lisa Camby, stopped through Terwilliger's. Kit congratulated herself for having the discipline not to order French fries, but then stole half of Lisa's order – and stopped only after Lisa sprayed her hand with ketchup, also getting a bit of her sleeve.

As they approached the sorority, Lisa was talking and preoccupied. For a few steps, she didn't notice that Kit had stopped and was staring at the front porch.

Lisa's voice tailed off and she turned, looking questioningly at Kit. She could see that Kit was stunned by something she saw, so Lisa pivoted and saw the ruggedly handsome Chris Reynolds sitting on the bottom steps of the porch. Lisa immediately knew it was the ex-boyfriend Kit had talked about.

He stood up, and as if he had been away for ten minutes and not over a year, said, "Hi!" He seemed taken aback that Kit, so shocked to see him, didn't squeal and hug him. So he extended his arms. Kit didn't move.

"I take it this is the famous Chris," Lisa said.

"At least I'm still famous," Chris said.

"You didn't even tell me you were coming," Kit said flatly.

"Kit, for Christ's sake," he said, exasperated, "my grandfather had a heart attack. My parents want me to see him."

"You couldn't even call?"

"I tried! Nobody answered!"

That was plausible, considering the sorority phone often rang a hundred times before anyone answered — if anyone answered at all.

"Jesus," Chris said, reaching out for Kit's arm, "somebody stab you?"

"It's just ketchup," Kit said. But she let Chris gently take her arm and look.

Kit nodded to Lisa. "Go ahead."

After Lisa was out of sight, Chris was imploring. "Look, I apologize. But I'm here now and you know how I feel about you."

"I guess I do. When you're here. But a lot has happened, Chris."

"Kit," he said softly, "let's at least go get something to eat and talk about this."

"Just talk," she said.

⁓

Now, on Saturday morning, Chris came back to the bed and, sitting on the edge, reached out and hugged her as she sobbed on his shoulder.

"I love you, you know," he said.

"I know. When you're here, you love me."

After a couple of seconds, Chris said, "There seems to be a significant omission here. Your next line is supposed to be, 'I love you, too, Chris.'"

"I don't know anymore. There's no script here."

Chris stood up. "We don't have to tell each other it's forever or anything, Kit," he said. "We're taking that as it comes, okay?"

"I'm not sure I want that."

"Jesus, we both have friends screwing anything that moves. Even my parents. Neither one of us is like that—" He noticed Kit's twitch. He sat back down on the bed. "I'm not, either," he said. "You're asking me if I've been a monk? No, I haven't been. But I love you, Kit. And notice I'm not telling you to be a nun, either."

"No, Chris, I'm screwing the whole junior class," Kit said sarcastically.

"Oh, don't take it that way." He looked down, for the moment uncharacteristically vulnerable, and then asked quietly, "Love him?"

"Yes."

The vulnerability disappeared. "Doesn't change anything," he said, shrugging. "You go on with him and we'll just take it all as it comes. But don't rule me out, all right?"

"I think I have to."

"You say that, but it doesn't change anything. I'm going back to New York and we'll see what happens. Kit, I have to try seeing what I can do there."

"I know you do. I'm not telling you not to. But I'm not part of that. And I have to say I don't want to be. Not now."

Chris got up, went into the bathroom, and stepped into the shower. Kit pulled her clothes back on and, still barefoot, went downstairs. She went into the kitchen, opened the refrigerator, grabbed a Coke and sat at the kitchen table.

"Damn," she said.

"My sentiments exactly," Naomi Reynolds said as she breezed into the kitchen in her loosely tied bathrobe.

Everywhere Chris' mother went, she breezed. Naomi, who in her theatre world was considered forty-ish, was still alluring enough to play younger women.

"Let me guess," Naomi said, taking stock. "You weren't quite prepared for Chris to reenter your life. You're surprised, confused, distraught..."

"Close enough," Kit said.

Professor Sam Reynolds and his wife, both Cascade natives, had been living for ten years in the huge house on the south edge of town. Naomi still was the charmer of the Cascade parties, even before she sat down at the piano and took them through Eliza's songs in *My Fair Lady*. Chris' parents were infamous for their open marriage: Naomi preferred young actors, drawing the line only at Chris' close friends. Sam, the brilliant political science professor, had no lines at all.

Kit had taken a couple of sips when a young man walked sleepily into the kitchen, wearing a T-shirt and jeans but looking as if he hadn't been coherent enough to do anything but throw on the clothes. He leaned over and kissed Naomi, then said, "I gotta go."

To Kit, Naomi said, "Kit, this is Geoffrey."

To Geoffrey, Naomi said, "Geoffrey, that's Kit, our son's sort-of-former girlfriend."

To Kit, Naomi said, "Geoffrey's playing a German soldier to my Maria in *Sound of Music*."

Geoffrey was gone.

Self-conscious, Kit said, "Sorry about your father-in-law."

"Oh, he's going to be fine," Naomi said. "He's too damn ornery to die."

Sam Reynolds shuffled into the kitchen in a robe and slippers, with a book tucked under his arm. He charged to the refrigerator, opened it, pulled out a carton of eggs, and plopped it on the counter. A young girl, a sophomore perhaps, was behind him. She lingered in the doorway, hesitantly, self-conscious in one of Sam's dress shirts and nothing else.

"So, Kit," Sam said as he opened the cabinet and reached for a frying pan, "still like your eggs over easy?"

Kit said nothing. She was shaking her head, so slightly it was her secret. She told herself: Welcome back to the circus.

༃

An hour later, Chris and Kit pulled up to the front of the sorority. They hugged and Kit quickly broke off the kiss. "Don't get out," she said.

He stepped out of the car, anyway, and followed her to the porch.

"I'm going to see grandpa today, and be back tonight," he said.

"No," Kit said sharply. "Besides, I really have something else I have to do."

"I thought the football player is in Los Angeles."

"He is."

"Kit," Chris said as she stood on the top stair, "don't close the door."

As he reached for her again, she headed to the front door and opened it. She turned around and looked back through it. Then she slammed it, considering the move symbolic. She hoped he did, too.

∽

At the Skyline Nursing Home, Annie Laughlin read aloud two chapters in Louisa May Alcott's *Little Women* to the group of twenty women in the little library who no longer could see well enough to read on their own. Annie knew a few couldn't comprehend the material – any material – but she always was inspired by the smiles of recognition from others at many of the passages.

Pushing a wheelchair, Annie took her favorite, octogenarian Vivian Amacher, back to her room. Vivian had been a high school teacher for forty years and a widow for nearly twenty, and she and Annie often talked about the evolution of education. Vivian's theory was that even as her teaching career was winding down, curriculum had become too specialized, too soon. She argued that it did students a disservice to allow them to make too many elective choices, even in high school. She believed retreating from long lists of mandatory reading, especially the classics, was the first step in the deterioration of the republic.

Today, Annie told Vivian of her continuing angst over trying to balance her love of her student-teaching stint and her appreciation for the South Cascade administration and faculty sticking up for her, with her need to continue fighting for what she believed in – and against what she didn't. Vivian never argued politics with Annie. Mostly, Vivian listened and asked questions. Sometimes, she was challenging; other times, she was trying to take stock and understand.

"You know what I liked about teaching most of all?" Vivian asked.

"What?"

"I never stopped learning about myself."

"So what are you saying?"

"People like you and me find the choices hard. I couldn't compartmentalize my life, because I was a teacher and I thought about it everywhere I was, all the time. I saw excellent teachers who could be passionate in the classroom, and then walk out at the end of the day and turn the switch off. They'd do their work at home, too, but their emotional involvement wasn't there. It always was for me, no matter where I was or when it was. Even when I had my own kids, I wasn't able to treat it like a job. I didn't always put my family first. I know this sounds terrible, but I thought there were some kids I taught who needed me more than my own kids. My husband didn't always understand that."

"Well, I'm a long way from those kinds of choices," Annie said.

"No, you're not," Vivian said. "It'd hard for one person to change the world; it's easier, but maybe no less important, to change a life. I felt as if I was doing that every day."

Annie still was thinking about that long after she got home.

༄

As the party gathered steam, pot smoke drifted through the house. Kit wasn't tempted. Not this time.

One group passed around joints in the middle of the living room. Another, all set with individual supplies, pretended to watch the television in one corner. Five other guys looked through one of the town's most impressive album collection in the "family" room. In the tiny dining room, a few couples sat intertwined on one chair apiece and groped, while others hadn't bothered to close the doors of the two bedrooms down the hallway. In the jammed kitchen, the conversations were about school and who was screwing whom, either at that very moment in another room or in general, and the beer cans in hands seemed incongruous.

In the corner of the living room nearest the front door, Kit leaned against the mushroom cloud "Ban the Bomb" poster. The radio blared out the play-by-play from the Cascade-UCLA game, and Kit and two guys were listening to the unfolding rout in Los Angeles.

The Cascade radio network's play-by-play announcer sounded as if he were trying to remain solemn, so he wouldn't offend the relatives of the dearly departed. His sidekick had all but given up game details and instead kept reminding listeners that the charter flight would return to Cascade in the morning and that next week's game against Idaho would be a chance for recovery.

Somebody hollered from across the room. "What's the score now?"

Kit said, "UCLA 43-24."

"How much time?"

"Four minutes."

Kit took her reporter's notebook out from the back pocket of her jeans and walked away from the radio console. The party's host, a senior business student, Scott Probst, was leaning against the refrigerator, holding court, when Kit interrupted. "Can we talk now?"

"Sure. Step into my office."

Scott led her down the stairs, into the dim and damp basement, reached up, tugged on a little chain and threw light on the subject. The basement was a jungle of marijuana plants.

Kit and Scott already had agreed she wouldn't use his name or say anything about the location of the rented house in her *Campus Daily* story. She was going to use his campus nickname, "Weed." Kit thought he was an idiot for not trying to be more discreet. Kit heard about it before she even joined the newspaper staff, and she knew that some of the pot that passed through the sorority came from this basement.

Scott gave Kit the tour, which didn't take long. There were yells from upstairs, and Weed paused just long enough to decide it wasn't a raid. "Probably just Cathy Whatshername showing off her tits again," he said, laughing.

"How much do you sell?"

"*Mucho.*"

"How much is that."

"That's all I'll say."

"To anybody?"

"Shit, no, have to keep it under control so idiots aren't knocking at the door at four in the morning."

"Feel guilty?"

"Give me a break."

"Ever scared?"

"Do I look scared?"

He offered her the joint.

"No, thanks," she said without looking up, scribbling to catch up.

"On the job, huh?"

She shrugged.

When he led her upstairs, he stopped at the top. Cathy Whatshername was blowing some guy in the middle of the kitchen.

Kit looked for her coat, hoping that nobody was screwing on top of it. She spotted it on top of the television cabinet and momentarily angered the solitary guy watching *Mannix* by getting in his way for about eight-tenths of a second, apparently long enough for the private detective to dodge another bullet. She poured herself a beer for the road from the keg.

"How bad did the game end up?" she asked the guy.

"Didn't you hear us screaming? We won!" By now, he didn't seem to care about *Mannix*. "Let's screw," he said.

"I'll pass," she said as she headed to the door, assuming he'd go back to smoking or taking whatever had been passed around to make him hallucinate about a comeback.

❧

Jake Powell had a hard time believing it. Not long ago, they were getting blown away 43-24. UCLA even put in a few scrubs. Jake had lost one contact lens in the second quarter and didn't have a replacement, so he couldn't read the time on the Coliseum scoreboard. But he knew there wasn't enough left. Get in the locker room, get on the damn plane, and get home. Finally, he asked the trainer. Four minutes, thirty-eight seconds left.

Rick Winslow threw a down and out to Keith Oldham and then a little flare to Timmy Hilton, who did two pirouettes and made it into the end zone. Even the UCLA fans gave him a hand, and Timmy coolly handed the ball to the zebra. After the extra point, UCLA led 43-31, and the trainer told Jake that 4:05 remained in the game.

Jake trotted back on with the onside kick team. A UCLA player jumped, got his hands on the bouncing kick and managed to hold on in the collision. In the pile, Jake clutched and grabbed and tried to steal the ball, but the guy wouldn't let go. UCLA could kill the clock or, even if it had to punt, probably hold on. As the third-and-eight play unfolded a minute later, Jake thought, even as he tried to fight off a blocker: *What idiot called this play?* The quarterback cruised down the line, Alex Tolliver hit him as he was making the pitchout, and the ball bounced far short of the tailback. The Fishermen recovered.

On the next play, Rick tossed to Timmy along the far sideline. Timmy had a step on a linebacker, cut back and turned it into a forty-yard touchdown. After the extra point, it was 43-38, with 2:24 remaining. The Fishermen had only one timeout left, so again there was no debate about kicking it deep and trusting the defense. It had to be another bouncing onside kick. *Don't go for the ball*, Jake decided as he saw the UCLA guy's eyes widen and his hands start to reach. *Hit him so goddamn hard the ball will pop off his hands. Yeah, just like that.* As he ended up beneath a pile, he listened as his teammates' celebratory hollers let him know they had the ball.

Some UCLA fans were returning to the stands. The Fishermen had plenty of time. Timmy gained five yards on two carries. On third down, Rick threw down the near sideline. Keith Oldham and a UCLA defender came down together, fighting for it, and when the official ruled it dual possession, the Fishermen had a first down on the UCLA 11.

Timmy ran for six. Rick was sacked, but on the next play threw to Oldham in the back of the end zone for the touchdown that put the Fishermen ahead 44-43, with thirty seconds left. They failed on the two-point conversion, but that didn't turn out to be a problem because UCLA couldn't get into field-goal range. On the last play, Jake watched the last pass sail over his head and fall incomplete. He heard the gun and leaned over, spent.

In the locker room, Larry Benson told them they'd remember this one for years, and Jake knew he was probably right. Rick's locker was near Jake, so Jake could hear the young quarterback talk with the reporters.

"What'd you say in the huddle when it was 43-24?"

Rick responded, "I said, 'We've got 'em right where we want 'em.' And Timmy told us to pick it up because he could score from anywhere on the field in ten seconds."

Carl Steele appeared at Jake's locker and shook his hand. "Good game," he said.

"Thanks, anyway," Jake said. "Any chance we could burn the defensive films?"

Bill Wyden squeezed through the tiny visiting locker room, congratulating the players. By now, Jake wore only a jock and his sweat-soaked T-shirt. As the athletic director neared him, Jake turned and bent over, pretending to be searching for something in his equipment bag.

It was an effective full mooning.

&#x223D;

Neal Hassler listened to the football game with his wife for a while, until UCLA seemed to have it locked up. He told Eleanor he was going to putter in the garage. As he stacked the old newspapers, he suddenly felt the need to get away, on his own, for no good reason he could think of, just because, so he poked his head back in the door and said he was going for a walk.

"Now?"

"El, this is the first night in a week it hasn't been raining and I feel like taking a walk!"

Eleanor said the kids might be calling long distance at some point, as they often did on Saturday nights. "And have you taken your pills?"

"El, yes, I've taken the darned pills, and yes, I can walk alone." He didn't add what he was thinking: *Get away for a while. Screw the governor. Screw 'em all.* And: *Maybe I should get a dog.*

After two circuitous tours of the neighborhood, the second because he realized he didn't remember many of the details of the first, he ended up at the always-open Payless and bought razor blades. A little later – how much later he wasn't even certain, but his watch said 12:45 – he was startled to realize he was sitting on a bus bench several blocks up Wadsworth Boulevard and hadn't remembered walking there.

Back at home, Eleanor greeted him at the door, and for a second, he thought it was because she was worried he had thrown himself into the Astor River.

# TWELVE: "MAGIC CARPET RIDE"

"You missed the end of the football game!"

"How much did we lose by?"

"We won!"

# THIRTEEN:
## "PEOPLE GOT TO BE FREE"

*(Wednesday, October 16, 1968)*

Neal Hassler humored Eleanor as long as he could stand it. She had been calling four times a day this week, but today she was up to three by 10:30.

First call: "I just noticed the ad for *The Star-Spangled Girl* in Portland," Eleanor said. "Neil Simon – you liked *The Odd Couple* – wrote it, so I think I'll send in for tickets for us. Six dollars for two. That's all right, isn't it?"

Fine, Eleanor.

Second call: "What do you want for dinner?"

Anything, El. *Anything*, okay?

Third call: "Guess who we just got a letter from, after all these months?"

"Come on, El, I know what's going on here! I'm not some little kid you have to check up on! I'm still taking Dr. Hill's pills, too, all right?"

She answered quietly. "If you quit that job before you come home, that would be even better."

Eleanor knew how much he hated giving in to the governor and the chairman of the state board, finally making an official request to the Cascade Police Department to not only be on call to come on campus, but to make regular patrols and supplement the university cops. The *Campus Daily* portrayed the presence of Cascade police on campus as the invasion of the Gestapo, and an overt slap in the face of those circulating and signing the petition to ban Cascade police from the campus. The overreaction almost shoved Hassler into the governor's camp on this one.

Governor McMichael thought the Cascade officers would be deterrents; Hassler believed that after all the fuss over their deployment, regular patrols might cause more trouble than they would prevent. He preferred simply having the right to ask for help in emergencies. He didn't admit that at the Kiwanis Club meeting in the back room at the Mr. Steak that noon. "I'm starting to think we should put a new motto over the doorway at Franklin Hall," he told the Kiwanis. "Change it to 'Everybody calm down!'"

Even the owner of the construction company who lived up the hill from the Hasslers' house in the neighborhood's palace, and so often stopped to talk when he walked the dogs on the weekends, had a vacant stare. Hassler had hoped for at least a nod of sympathy, if not agreement.

"In these times," he continued, "any learning institution is a marketplace of ideas. The fuss over a few malcontents, some well meaning, some intent on nothing but disruption, is unwarranted. A few of the students are overreacting to the presence of the Cascade police on campus. Most of the others understand. It's for their own benefit."

He believed some of it.

෨

Jake Powell finished reading, turned over the final page, put it on the thin stack and looked at Kit Dunleavy, on the other side of the table in the Student Union cafeteria. As he read the story, she twirled the ends of her hair around one index finger, trying to read *him*.

"It's really good," he finally said.

"Really?"

"No, I'm just saying that." Not catching the irony, Kit looked hurt. "It's really good," he said again, quickly, "but it's going to get you in trouble if they run it."

"Oh, they've got better things to do than chase down a few potheads," Kit said.

Her story on marijuana use on and around campus quoted eleven students and two professors, without naming them. She resisted using her own experiences as examples and remained detached. She talked to over twenty-five other students, establishing that grass was all over the place, and that most considered it both quasi-legal and harmless. Yet the ideas that every student had a stash in the bedroom and all used it only to warm up for acid trips were exaggerations. The plan was to run the story in the *Campus Daily* next week.

# THIRTEEN: "PEOPLE GOT TO BE FREE"

❧

Already this week, with a breather against Idaho coming up, Larry Benson had been on three national radio shows and eleven local radio shows. He talked with writers from Los Angeles to Boston, and accepted a call from the sports editor at United Press International in New York, who informed Benson that he was the news service's national coach of the week.

Benson went to the booster clubs in both Cascade and Portland, and, amazingly, nobody asked about hair. So many people told Benson they stopped listening when it was 43-24, he began to wonder if anyone heard the comeback. At practice, standing in the light rain and ignoring the water dripping off the brim of his baseball cap, Benson addressed the players. "We've got something going, so let's build on it," he said. "Now let's go to work!"

As the players broke off to head to group work, players hollered. Jake pitched in with, "Even the rednecks love us again!"

Benson couldn't hear him, but Howie Hallstrom and many of the players did.

"Powell, for chrissakes," Hallstrom said. "Cork it."

"Don't drag that shit into it here," Todd Hendricks said, accidentally brushing Jake in a pack big enough to provide him an excuse. "You can be such an asshole."

Jake stopped in his tracks, and after a couple more steps, so did Hendricks. The face-off caught Alex Tolliver's attention. The team captain grabbed Jake around the shoulders and dragged him toward the end of the field where the linebackers would be doing their work.

After practice, Hallstrom and Carl Steele surprised Jake, chasing him down and flanking him for a few strides before even saying anything. The three of them walked together up the hill, to the dressing room. His teammates peeled off. Jake wondered if they were in on the conspiracy.

Jake was tired, wet and dirty, but he loved practice in this kind of weather, even liked the stench of the swampy and drenched muddy turf on the practice field that smelled as if seven thousand seagulls had just done their business. Steele took stock of his filthy linebacker, smiling at the sight of the anti-war militant who so loved to try to violently bury a ballcarrier's nose in the mud. Jake smiled back, not even turning when Hallstrom started talking as they were halfway up the hill.

"Jake," Hallstrom said, "you're wearing us out. We're trying to give you credit. You hang around with Annie Laughlin. That's your business. Larry's told us a thousand times that without you to keep her from going loony, the SDS nuts might have turned the administration building into their own goddamn Holiday Inn by now – or worse."

"Oh, I wouldn't say that."

"Larry would – and has."

They were coming to the stairway that led downstairs, to the dressing room in the arena basement, and it was Steele's turn. "Here's our question: If you're a voice of reason on campus politics, how come you're such a pain in the ass here?"

"This isn't the real world," Jake said. "When I'm a pain in the ass here, it's usually because I'm joking around. When it comes to the war or something else important, it's different."

They were inside the building doorway, and Jake scraped his shoes against the mat that removed a lot of the mud from between the spikes. Jake knew that the whole team would be asking about his discussion with Hallstrom and Steele the second he walked into the locker room.

"Coach Benson takes more crap about you than anybody on this team," Steele said. "All of us do. I'm not just talking about that little incident with the kid and the stuff with the recruiters."

Steele held up a hand, holding off Jake's protest. Hallstrom jumped in.

"He's right," Hallstrom said. "We get letters from idiots all the time about you guys. You do an interview with a television guy, and you're wearing a Morse button and a peace sign button, and Larry gets questions from the boosters at the luncheon about how he can allow open advocacy in the locker room and how it shows you don't have your mind on the game."

"Coach–"

"That's the kind of shit we get about you. Know what Larry told the booster asshole? He said he didn't want players who had their minds only on the game because there's more to college than that. You think he's just decided to let you go your own way and he's not paying attention? That's bullshit. He's paying attention a lot more than you know. All of us are. You don't seem to have any idea sometimes, because I think if you did, you'd shut your mouth a little more often."

"At least around here," Steele said.

Without another word, Hallstrom and then Steele each patted him on the top of his shoulder pads – Hallstrom on his right shoulder, Steele on his left – and walked away, toward the coaches' locker room at the other end of the hall.

❧

Timmy Hilton broke away from watching television and tried to make progress on his essay about the Munich Conference.

As David Armstrong popped in and out to run off his mouth, Timmy wrote that Neville Chamberlain was naive, gutless, and short-sighted. He used up three-quarters of a page and three-quarters of the pencil's eraser.

"Timmy! Timmy!"

"Whaaat?" What now?

"Gotta see this!"

As the anthem played, Tommie Smith wore the gold medal and a black glove on his upraised, clenched right fist as he stood on the top step of the medal stand at the Olympics in Mexico City. On the step below, John Carlos wore the bronze medal and a black glove on his upraised, clenched left fist. Both had their heads down.

"This is really going to piss people off," David said.

Earlier, they had watched Smith and Carlos run first and third in the 200 meters, but they hadn't dreamed the medal ceremony would be more compelling.

"...and the home of the brave," Timmy mouthed, thinking not about the nation, but the men on the medal stand. He turned to David. "They've got balls, all right, but I hope they didn't just win Wallace another million votes."

# FOURTEEN:
## "ABRAHAM, MARTIN AND JOHN"

*(Thursday, October 24, 1968)*

*Bam, bam, bam.*

Startled by the insistent knock, Kit Dunleavy opened her eyes in Jake Powell's apartment and saw Hubert Humphrey – on an HHH for President poster. She had brought it with her the night before, taped it to the wall and said, "He's starting to speak out."

*Bam, bam, bam.*

Wearing only a pair of sagging briefs, Jake swung out of bed and started to the door. Kit sleepily marveled at how domestic she and Jake had become, with Annie an extension of the relationship. Kit no longer was embarrassed when Jake casually peed with her in the room. When Annie showed up, Kit didn't bother to put anything over the "PROPERTY OF FISHERMEN FOOTBALL" T-shirt and panties. She also had lost the capacity to be jealous of Jake's ability to be so relaxed around Annie in his underwear.

"*Buenos dias,*" said Annie, finally bursting in.

Adjusting her routine, Annie lately had been bringing three coffees. Jake sat in the one chair, Kit lounged on the bed, and Annie sat cross-legged on the floor.

"Listen," Jake said, looking at the front page of the *Times-Register*. "Nixon said that Humphrey, and I quote, 'has the fastest, loosest tongue in American politics. On the great issue of war and peace, on the great issue particularly of whether or not we should have a bombing pause–'"

"Whether alone was enough," Annie said casually.

"What?"

"'Whether or not' is redundant."

"Jesus," Jake snapped, shaking his head. "'On the great issue particularly of whether – or not! – we should have a bombing pause, he's been for it unconditionally, and then he said we should have conditions.' Unquote."

"Humphrey never said he was for an unconditional bombing pause," Kit said.

"That's Nixon for you," Jake said.

Kit was two pages into the *Portland Herald* sports section when she saw Jake's picture next to a column written by another veteran scribe, and not Dusty Harris. "Who's this Marine?" she asked, mocking. On the page, he was fiercely charging the camera. The picture was from press day two years ago, when he still had a regular barber. His "haircuts" since came when he stood in front of the mirror with a pair of scissors about once every six weeks.

"You are, and I quote," Kit said, chortling, "'a gritty senior defender who makes up for a lack of brawn with brains. Just ask the Idaho Vandals, who couldn't score a point against the Fishermen last Saturday until Larry Benson emptied his bench in the fourth quarter of a 49-13 rout that gave the Cascade forces a 4-2 record in the 1968 campaign. Powell, a rebellious sort involved in radical campus politics and off-the-field controversy earlier in the season, is a foursquare team player on the field who had four unassisted tackles and an intercepted pass against the Vandals. He and ace fellow linebacker Alex Tolliver again will anchor the defense this week in the crucial conference matchup against Stanford.'" She paused and rattled the paper for a second, rolling it slightly as if her eyes still were sliding down the page.

She continued, "Powell also is an unrepentant slob who should try doing his laundry once in a while instead of stealing jock straps from the athletic department and wearing them when all his underwear is dirty. Which is about eighty percent of the time."

Kit had him on the hook until about "slob."

Annie wasn't paying any attention. She was looking at the metro page of the *Times-Register*, and for Annie, reading was a complete sensory commitment.

"Kit, heard about this?" Annie asked.

"What?"

"The district attorney says he's probably going to subpoena you."

"I told you!" Jake said.

"About what?" Kit asked, although she already had guessed.

"Come on," Annie said, "your story. Your" – and she, too, was reading from the paper now – "'controversial story on marijuana use at Cascade University.' The grand jury, ahem, 'looking into drug trafficking' is going to order you to tell them what you know. Reveal your sources."

"Aw, they won't push it," Kit said.

"They'll milk this for all it's worth!" Annie said. She asked Kit, "When do you turn 21?"

"Last week. We invited you, remember?"

"Shit."

There was another knock and Lisa Camby, Kit's sorority roommate, rushed in. "Kit, it's been crazy," Lisa said, ignoring Jake and Annie. "Scott showed up at seven, looking for you, and he was scared to death."

Kit remembered Scott Probst – "Weed" – saying so casually asking on the night of the tour: "Do I look scared?" She almost wished she had seen him this morning, shitting his pants. "I promised him, Lisa," Kit said.

"Then your dad called. He heard about it on the radio down there. I said you had just left."

"How'd he sound?"

"I think he's on his way up to kidnap you. I don't think he believed you'd just left."

Kit snatched her jeans off the floor. "I think me sleeping somewhere else probably bugged him more than the story," she said. "I'll go call him from the Union."

"Hold on," Jake said, "I'll go with you."

"That won't do any good. See you in Fiction Writing."

Kit put on her coat and tossed her backpack over her shoulders. On the way down the stairs with Lisa, she managed to laugh. So you're going to wear this football T-shirt to Fiction Writing and look as if you just got out of bed. Jesus. Why don't you just wear a sign? I'M SCREWING THE FOOTBALL PLAYER.

Maybe she'd keep her coat on.

❧

Larry Benson still dreamed. When he was a kid outside Litchfield, the small Minnesota town, he was going to be a cowboy, leaving behind the dairy cows and milk stools to drive cattle. When he was playing at Minnesota, he dreamed of picking up his All-America certificate. When he was flying the P-38 fighter plane over Japanese targets, he was dreaming about returning alive and then drinking that sludge they called coffee during the debriefing. In the P-38, you didn't dream too far ahead.

As a high school coach in Portland, he fantasized about winning a state championship. As a college assistant, he thought of how he would handle the attention as the head coach who took his team to the Rose Bowl and – reaching down from the shoulders of his adoring players – shook hands with the losing coach at midfield. Now that he was a head coach, he still had that Rose Bowl fantasy.

There were other moments when he wondered if he was enjoying himself. A picture from his daughter's latest high school yearbook stayed with him. It was a shot of a blackboard in the section of arty shots about student life. Somebody had written:

> *I wish I was*
> *What I was*
> *When I wished I was*
> *What I am now*

He didn't know if it were lifted from a Greek philosopher or a contemporary long-haired poet, but Benson identified with it, thinking, know how you feel, kid.

Benson loved teaching. He enjoyed the classroom when he was a teacher-coach at the high school and small-college levels. More than that, he found working as an assistant coach with his own pack of guys on the football field – the offensive linemen – rewarding. They were the slugs, the grunts, the overlooked, and the under-appreciated. *Remember, guys, keep your feet moving. They'll call this holding; they'll let you get away with this...at least most of the time. Lower. Higher. Wait half a count. Move out quicker. You'll get over her. Do it again. That professor isn't such a bad guy; try talking to him. Keep your head up. Penicillin. Not everybody can start, but you're important to this team. Everybody has gotten homesick one time or another; it's nothing to be ashamed of.*

He still had some of those relationships as the head coach – his office could be a confessional – but not as many, and some of his friends in head-coaching told him he was crazy to maintain that kind of closeness at all because detachment was more efficient. Still, he felt like a front man. So much of his job was to talk to the reporters, give speeches, delegate authority, and referee the turf battles.

Benson knew he was a good head coach, but he also knew that he got so many more little pleasures out of being an assistant. If he still were the offensive line coach, on nights like this, the Thursday nights, he would be home and not heading to this Homecoming Committee's kickoff reception at the Thunderbird Hotel.

He called it the nametag circuit, and in part because he hated nametags. Wear it, and you look like a buffoon. Don't put it on, and you look like a pompous jerk assuming you don't need a nametag because everybody knows you're the highest-profile man on the university payroll.

"Let's switch nametags," he told Neal Hassler at the door.

"Won't matter," Hassler said wryly. "Even if they think you're me, half the people still will want to talk to you about football."

❦

Jake was barely over the embarrassment he felt in Fiction Writing as Kit took off her coat and everyone in the class saw that T-shirt. Tonight, he was surprised. Kit was standing in the doorway, wearing a prim blue dress. A dress? Kit? Whoa.

"You have to get a phone," she said as she walked in.

"Not until somebody dies and leaves me money."

"Well, my father and I just had a lovely dinner. We agreed on two things: Thousand Island dressing and a baked potato."

"At least you're still here."

"That was touch and go. 'You, young lady,'" she said, imitating her father, "'will promise me to tell them what they want to know. You have no obligation to protect criminals. Either that or we head right back to Medford after dinner. Together.'"

By dessert, she told Jake, her father had agreed to let her stay in Cascade and wait it out. Her dad said of the D.A.: Maybe the man's just blowing campaign hot air. Finally, as Kit was getting out of the car at the sorority, he told her that he would support her no matter what. He wouldn't agree with her, but he'd stand by her. Because he loved her.

"All I said was thanks," she said. "He's sitting there, waiting for more. I say thanks again. That's all. And I let him drive off. He comes two hundred miles to see me, he's driving off to a hotel, and that's all I've told him. Then he was gone, around the corner. I almost cried. He's an ornery, closed-minded, love-it-or-leave guy, and he tells me that. I don't say anything else."

"Come on," Jake said an hour later, handing Kit a sweatshirt this time. They had barely caught their breaths, they both were glistening, and Jake's sudden re-channeling of his energy wounded her.

"Where're we going?" she asked.

"To the phone."

At the corner gas station, he read her the number of her father's hotel, and she dialed.

# FIFTEEN:
## "HUSH"

*(Sunday, October 27, 1968)*

Neal Hassler awakened before his wife, put on his robe and slippers, and wrestled with the percolator for five minutes to get the coffee brewing. Delaying going to the porch after the newspaper, he sat and watched the black liquid – his preference was the darker the better – pop up in the glass window.

Without even seeing it, he knew the gist of what was in the paper. Hell, the whole state did. For days, the *Portland Herald* plugged the Sunday story: "Turmoil on Campus: Cascade University In Upheaval." The other colleges in the state, Oregonians were led to believe, were turmoil-free.

Hassler met twice in three weeks with the *Herald* reporter, Oliver G. Driscoll, who tried to dress like a highest-finance banker, but didn't pull it off because his necktie always looked as if both he and his mother had tried for twenty minutes to get the knot right and never did. Hassler sensed the story in the paper would be a textbook case of a preordained approach. By god, there is trouble on that campus, and they were going to document it, make it sexy, and sell goddamn papers to nervous Oregonians.

Hassler finally exploded at Driscoll during the second session. "You throw me a loaded question. I give you my gut reaction, start to explain the background, explain what might not meet the eye. That's apparently too boring for you because you stop writing."

Driscoll mumbled that the rest of his answer would be captured on the tape recorder running on the table between them, but Hassler didn't believe that mattered. He was being tuned out. Besides, he wouldn't be shocked to find out later that this idiot had threaded the tape onto the reel inside out and nothing had been recorded.

After Driscoll left the second time, Clifford Carlson from the public affairs office dropped in. Carlson was a former reporter, and the Driscoll assholes of the business had helped drive him away, so he already had guessed how it went and Hassler's briefing only confirmed that. "I knew we were in trouble," Carlson said. "I haven't met a reporter yet who put his initial in a byline who wasn't a jerk."

Now, the jerk's story was on Hassler's porch. Eleanor hadn't canceled the *Herald* subscription, after all, and when Hassler figured it out, he decided dodging the news wouldn't help. He was on his second cup of coffee and flipping through the *TV Guide* – the handiest reading material – when Eleanor joined him in the kitchen.

"No paper yet?" she asked, still a little sleepily.

"Oh, I assume it's out there."

"Come on, honey, it can't be that bad."

Eleanor retrieved the paper herself, rolled off the rubber band on the porch and pored over the story just inside the front door. She read the first part on the cover, then flipped and folded, reaching the full-page conclusion on the inside. She considered hiding it from her husband and saying the kid must have forgotten the Hassler house. But he was going to have to see it eventually, and it might as well be now.

It was about rebellion. Rebellion in the classroom. Rebellion against the Greek system. Rebellion against parents. Rebellion by the Black Student Organization, the SDS, the Campus Coalition Against The War, homosexuals, women. Rebellion over the allocation of student fees. Rebellion and turmoil everywhere.

His face-to-face clashes with the firebrands left the impression that the only students who hadn't shown up were the ones who were too busy taking drugs or screwing in the dormitories. The grapes and strawberry confrontation and the furor over the military recruiters came off as Annie Laughlin filibusters, with "football star" Jake Powell and Hassler watching and listening. Driscoll must have listened to all of Annie's answers – a hell of a lot closer than he had listened to Hassler's.

What of Archuleta, the drama instructor? Driscoll hadn't even asked about it. One of the students in the office that day said, "Bullshit." Yet the *Herald* story billed the brief sit-in as an "epithet-filled confrontation over a controversial professor's employment" and again gave no mention that the university had determined Archuleta wasn't qualified and was a fraud.

"This isn't going to let up," Eleanor said. "Quit. Look at what this is doing to you."

"I bail out, admit I'm a failure, walk away, and maybe let somebody else who doesn't know anything about this campus and this faculty and this state come in?"

"Well, if that's what they want..."

Despite this story, he felt he was starting to win back himself and others. The construction company owner from up the street had stopped on one of his walks past the Hassler house. After the small talk, he said he wanted Neal to know that he had been thinking a lot lately, and he had decided that given the circumstances and the times, someone like Hassler, who listened but didn't always give in, was an asset. "You're in the middle," he said, "but you aren't being steamrolled by either side, and I guess I have to respect that."

"You just guess?" Neal asked, smiling.

Hassler decided that giving in on the Cascade police issue hadn't been a total waste; it bought him some breathing room with the governor and the state board. But this newspaper series was going to turn up the heat.

"I'm not quitting," he said to Eleanor. "Nobody's asked me to and–"

"Don't I count?"

"They aren't trying to run me out of here yet, and I think even the governor knows if they put somebody else in my chair, the times aren't going to change. All this crap hasn't prevented the university from continuing to function. I have to get some of the credit for that, don't I?"

"At least you're believing in yourself again."

"I never stopped. I just wondered if others had, the ones who really count, like you."

"Don't be silly."

She picked up the newspaper, pointed to the headline and said, "But you're forgetting that people – the governor, the chancellor – read this and believe it."

"If that happens, that's their problem. Not mine."

❧

Carl Steele was whispering. "Thank God for the rain."

Eva elbowed him. Here in the fourth row of pews at the Newman Center, during the period for individual prayers, you give praise to the Lord for opening the heavens and delivering a game-long drenching the afternoon before? But they both were grinning.

Father Robert Basinger was a brilliant preacher, with a talent for punchy and humorous storytelling to make his point – and brevity. His policy that if Jesus walked in the back door, he could have eight minutes at the pulpit, but that no other sermon should run over five minutes. Many faculty members, and not just students, were drawn to attend the Newman Center masses. Because the turnover among the parishioners at the Newman Center – nearly within a booming punt of the football practice field – was steady, many in his audience hadn't seen the *Times-Register's* story on Basinger shortly after his 1965 arrival in Cascade. Steele was shown a yellowed clipping later, and the word got around; most at least were vaguely aware of his background. Raised on a ranch in Idaho, he was a crack Army sharpshooter in Korea. When he discovered a North Korean sniper he killed couldn't have been more than fourteen, his conversion to passionate Christianity began.

Most agreed Basinger recently was more careful in his pronouncements from the pulpit, or at least wasn't calling attention to his activism in the anti-Vietnam War movement. But even Steele had heard about Basinger's presence at the protest against the military recruiters in the Student Union.

"Great game," Father Basinger said at the door. "Great defense. But when you took the field goal, I was booing, too."

Steele grabbed Basinger's elbow. "I forgive you, Father," he said.

Basinger suddenly became more serious. "How's Jake Powell playing?"

Steele knew the priest and the linebacker had shared the podiums at protest meetings, and that they had talked about Jake losing his father in the same war in which Basinger fought. Steele laughed. "I wish he was as much of a pain for the other team as he is for us."

"Do you know his friend, Annie, too?" Basinger asked.

The parishioners were piling up behind the Steeles, and Carl was becoming conscious of the impatience. A few simply peeled off and walked around; others waited to say hello to Basinger.

# FIFTEEN: "HUSH"

"No, I can't say I know Annie," Carl said. "But I sure know *about* her."

"Well," said Basinger, "if you ever see her with Jake, introduce yourself. And say you know me, too."

"Why?"

"Long story."

The day before, Stanford had taken the opening kickoff, driven 80 yards for a touchdown, and never had come close to scoring again in the driving Oregon rain. Steele's linebackers, including Alex Tolliver and Jake Powell, played well and CU won 10-7. It was a soaking, wet defensive gem.

Rick Winslow completed enough passes with the drenched balls to keep the two key drives going – the ones that led to a third-quarter field goal and a fourth-quarter touchdown. The fans (including at least one clergyman) booed when, on a fourth-and-three from the Stanford five early in the fourth quarter, Benson sent on the field goal team and accepted the three points that cut the deficit to 7-3. They weren't booing later, when Timmy Hilton leaped over the pile for the winning touchdown. Altogether, Timmy ran – actually, hydroplaned – for 168 yards. Southern California won, too, but the Fishermen were in second place in the Pac 8.

After church, he ran Eva home and was looking at film of the Washington offense fifteen minutes later in his darkened office. Howie Hallstrom burst in.

"Nobody said a word about this in the paper," Hallstrom said excitedly. Steele turned around. Howie held a press guide, open to the year-by-year results.

"This is the first time we won three out of four against the California schools since my junior year," Hallstrom said, "And that was the last season we went to the Rose Bowl. This is what you call an omen."

Steele had heard Hallstrom's banquet spiel. Hallstrom poked fun at himself for making it into the Rose Bowl loss to Michigan in Pasadena for the final few plays, and lining up opposite the exhausted Michigan star. When the game ended, the Michigan star mistook Hallstrom for the Fisherman who had been going against him for most of the afternoon, hugged him, and told him he had played "a hell of a game."

Steele smiled as he remembered that, and then moved to the present. He said, "To get to the Rose Bowl again, we're gonna have to get O.J. Simpson hit by a bus."

❧

Father Basinger called the Newman Center a "mini-church," and he couldn't remember from whom he stole the line. After his previous posting at an affluent parish in Beaverton, outside Portland, the Newman Center assignment was a reinvigoration. In the suburbs, his wry humor, whether in homilies or during pancake breakfasts after mass, either offended or sailed over the heads of many parishioners, and many of the older regulars considered him irreverent and sacrilegious.

He also knew that having a young woman visit the parish center in Beaverton would have caused a scandal. Here, in Cascade, Annie had the virtual run of the building, and after he finished the second of the two masses, Basinger wasn't at all surprised to see her in the upstairs living room, waiting and reading.

Annie rarely attended mass herself, which didn't offend Basinger. When she did, she didn't take communion, because she never officially had converted to Catholicism. Still, Basinger considered her both one of his closest friends and a pseudo-parishioner.

Noting his curious look after they exchanged greetings, she held up her book. "I ran some things over to the junior high for Mike Schwartz last week," she said, "and went in the library. They had this." The book was a well-worn, apparently popular copy of the juvenile novel, *Brian Browning, Air Force Cadet.*

"I thought you were a Nancy Drew girl," Basinger said.

Annie shrugged. "Know thine enemy."

She handed Basinger the book, still opened – apparently with a purpose.

"Read this page," she said, tapping the right side. "It gave me an idea."

❧

## FIFTEEN: "HUSH"

Timmy Hilton frequently played basketball on Sundays, though he knew that if the coaches saw him, they'd squeal. Even when had a hard time getting out of bed because of the pounding he'd taken the day before, his therapy was putting on the canvas Chuck Taylor All-Stars Converse hightops, going to the P.E. gym and getting in the pickup games with David Armstrong and the other members of the CU basketball team. The basketball players started practicing several weeks earlier, but they just screwed around on Sundays.

Timmy rationalized it two ways: One, he worked out some of the soreness. Two, the combination of the squeaking sneakers and his shot snapping the net was exhilarating. Timmy also was damn good and was even thinking of asking Coach Benson if he could go out for the basketball varsity this season. Timmy wouldn't be a big scorer for the varsity, but he knew he was as good as the backup guards already. Which was why he took this pass from David, pump-faked the varsity backup guard's sorry ass out of his jock, took two dribbles, went up in the air for the winning shot – and then popped down the perfect jump pass to David, breaking in alone. Layup.

"Game!"

The skins beat the shirts.

On the way home, he was getting stiff again, and he knew he should take a quick shower at home and head to the training room for a whirlpool, or ice, or both.

Bill Charles was sitting on the hood of Timmy's Pontiac. The head of the Black Student Organization was Timmy's friend, but he could be too much to take when you couldn't get him to talk about anything besides politics.

"We gotta talk," Bill said.

No, thought Timmy, I gotta listen.

৩

When Jake walked into his apartment, Kit already was there, so he chalked one up to progress in the relationship: She now had her own key.

"How many votes did you earn tonight?" he asked.

Kit had gone door-to-door, passing out pamphlets for Humphrey and Wayne Morse, and this remained a sore subject. Jake still was gaining respect for Humphrey, but not to the point of open advocacy.

"Humphrey's a hell of a lot better than either Nixon or, God forbid, Wallace," Kit said, pointing at leftover pamphlets.

"Does it really make any difference?"

Their debate was cut off when LBJ showed up on the 11 o'clock news, on the little TV with the picture that had more snow than Mt. Hood, and both Kit and Jake watched LBJ speaking at a podium in New York.

"One of my daughters asked me coming up here today," LBJ said, "'Tell me, Daddy, how it was that after losing a national election in 1960 to President Kennedy and then losing a state election as governor in California in 1962 to Pat Brown, how does it happen that Richard Nixon has been able to win his party's nomination for the presidency in 1968?'"

The president looked puzzled. "I told her that if she could give me a week or two, I would try to think of some reason."

Jake laughed, too.

As the station showed a still photo of Nixon, they heard snippets of the Republican candidate's radio speech. A coalition government in South Vietnam, he declared, would be "thinly disguised surrender." He said "far from ending the war," a coalition government "would only ensure its resumption under conditions that would guarantee communist victory."

Wait a minute, Jake thought. When had either LBJ or Humphrey said anything about agreeing to a coalition government? If they had, what was wrong with that? Nixon just kept making shit up.

# SIXTEEN:
## "IN-A-GADDA-DA-VIDA"

*(Thursday, October 31, 1968)*

Awakening, Kit Dunleavy lazily rolled over and opened her eyes. Even in the first-glance fog, she recognized Nixon next to her. Her shriek wasn't loud enough to wake up the neighborhood, but maybe those on the floor below.

"Happy Halloween," Jake Powell said from behind the Nixon mask. His voice was muffled and the plastic vibrated, humming, with each word. "Want some candy, little girl?"

"You..."

"I need your vote."

"You jerk."

"I've been called worse."

"You deserved it."

"*Who* deserves it?" Jake asked as he climbed out of bed and stood, throwing out both arms in a pose of presentation. "Your next president," he said, then pointed to the mask with one hand and after an instant, pulled it off with the other. "Or me," he said, pointing to his own face, "your next Halloween date."

"Both of you." She smiled. "But I've always been a soft touch for a guy with a pumpkin."

He grinned with widened, suggesting eyes. "How 'bout if I promise to buy you one later?"

"Okay."

Jake dived back into bed.

ᴄ∽৩

Neal Hassler was going over preliminary 1969-70 budget figures – already – when Jim Bellamy, the dean of the business department, stepped in.

"I just attended my first faculty senate breakfast meeting ever," Bellamy said.

"And to what did the faculty senate owe that honor?" Hassler asked.

"This," Bellamy said, sliding two stapled pages across the desk. "We passed it unanimously."

Hassler skimmed the Faculty Senate resolution, a statement of confidence in the Hassler administration and satisfaction with the university leadership "in challenging times."

"In other words," Bellamy said, "we all agreed the *Portland Herald* piece was a cheap shot. And we also are going to send a letter to the editor there, pointing out the exaggerations and inaccuracies."

"Thanks," Hassler said, "but that would take weeks."

"And a lot of paper," Bellamy agreed.

While Hassler was grateful, he was even more shaken that they thought he needed a vote of confidence. "How many had to walk out before it was unanimous?" he asked.

"Only three," Bellamy said, grinning. "Warner" – physical education – "said you should have called in the Marines. Mason" – philosophy – "said this was moot because a student-faculty-proletariat coalition should be running the school. And Gillespie" – history, prematurely senile – "left because he figured out he locked his keys in his car."

Turning serious, Bellamy leaned forward. "What's the doctor been saying?"

"Take the damn pills."

Bellamy fixed his gaze on Hassler's eyes. "Take the damn pills."

༄

Doubleheader Wyden hadn't become less of a problem, merely a different sort of problem. Now that they had won four in a row and were rated sixteenth in the country, the athletic director was at practice, strutting along the sidelines, acting like an architect watching his plans taking shape in construction.

At one point during kicking game work, Wyden cornered fullback Stevie Toland on the sideline for small talk. The problem was that Toland was on the first punting team, and when that unit was called onto the field, Toland missed his cue.

Howie Hallstrom strode over to the sideline. "Stevie," he told Toland with exaggerated politeness, "I know you're having a nice talk here, but your presence is required to avoid having our poor punter harassed by the opposition, who would like nothing better than to" – and now his exasperation was showing – "KNOCK THE BALL ABOUT FORTY YARDS BACKWARDS AND RECOVER IT FOR THE GAME-WINNING TOUCHDOWN!"

Toland took off.

Larry Benson, standing well down the field behind the receiving team, blew his whistle and hollered, "Let's go!"

Just when things are going well, Benson thought, along comes Doubleheader. Geez, he hoped Howie hadn't said anything too rash, but he guessed that must have been the case when Wyden stuck his head in Benson's office fifteen minutes after practice, said he wanted to see him and then left. Benson didn't move and went back to looking at the Washington game plan. In a minute, Wyden was back and sat down in Benson's office. A minor victory, Benson thought, but satisfying.

"Larry, we've made a little progress–"

"That's all?"

"Yes, at this point. But I've got to tell you I'm not happy with being shown up on the field like that."

"We were just trying to keep practice moving."

"Bullshit. You and your staff think you can avoid being accountable to me."

"I don't know why you'd get that idea. Bill, we all want the same thing."

"Just remember, your contract's up before next season."

"We're 5-2 and you're telling me not to feel secure."

"That's not what I said. Some boosters have been grousing. About you or your staff. Or both."

Benson leaned forward for emphasis. "You know the way it works," he said sharply. "A lot of those guys aren't happy unless they have something, or someone, to complain about so they can feel important. If I think somebody isn't doing the job, I'll take care of it."

༄

Todd Hendricks insisted on organizing the Halloween party and hosting it at the 22nd Avenue Boys Club. He promised he would have everyone out of the house by 11, even if he had to chase them out with his devil's pitchfork. He passed the hat – a helmet, actually – in the locker room after practice and, as a peace offering, trusted Jake to buy a couple of extra cases of beer to add to the stock. Because it seemed to be a way to ease some locker-room tension, Jake jumped at the chance. Jake only laughed when Todd said that Jake needed to buy the beer because none of Todd's other roommates were twenty-one. In Cascade that didn't matter when it came to buying beer, as long as you knew the right place. The Zippymart near campus – and Jake's apartment – would sell to fourteen-year-olds, theorizing that if you were old enough to try, you were old enough to get away with it.

The players also had agreed they would cut themselves off after one bottle. Okay, maybe two. They couldn't be sure how many outsiders would show up, so Jake had the extra cases and the money on the Zippymart counter when he heard the voice behind him.

"That's not for you, is it?"

Jake turned around.

"Oh, hi, Mr. Wyden. I'm just the errand boy," he said to the athletic director, who was carrying a carton of milk and four bags of candy.

As Jake took his change and lifted the case, Kit pointed at the beers and smiled at Wyden. "Want one?" she asked.

Wyden stared, and Jake chortled as he and Kit walked out of the store.

"You know," Jake said, "I'm thinking that might cost me more than the beer did."

"Sorry," Kit said, shrugging.

"Don't worry, it was worth it."

ভ

Vivian Amacher's two grandsons carried in the last boxes, straining under the weight. They plopped them on top of others in the corner of Annie Laughlin's living room, and for such a hurried and strained delivery, the result was surprisingly ordered and successful.

"That's it," said one of the grandsons, a thirty-five-year-old stockbroker. "All sixteen."

Vivian's daughter, Joan, was sitting with Annie on the couch.

"You sure this is okay with you?" Annie asked again.

Sipping her iced tea, Joan laughed. "If it wasn't," she said, "it would be a little late now." She noticed Annie recoil and grabbed her hand. "No, really," she assured her. "It's what Mom wanted."

The boxes were stuffed with Vivian Amacher's valuable biography collection, with works about virtually every American president – "everybody except Chester Arthur," she once bragged to Annie – and a wide variety of world figures, from Charlemagne to Churchill. When the receptionist from the Skyline Nursing Home called Annie to break the news of Vivian's death, Annie had wept. It wasn't a shock, but it still was wrenching. When Vivian's daughter called and invited her to the reception at her house – Vivian had requested cremation and no service – Annie went and was stunned to hear that the old woman had left a note intended to be an informal supplement to her will when she died. She wanted her biography collection, in specially marked boxes in storage in her daughter's attic, to go to Annie.

After Joni left, Annie opened one of the top boxes.

The first book she saw was Mohandas K. Gandhi's *The Story of My Experiments with Truth*. Two hours later, she still was reading, as she periodically took a bite from her dinner – a grilled cheese sandwich. The bag of Halloween candy was untouched on the coffee table near the front door. Trick-or-treating children were a rarity in her apartment building, but it didn't hurt to play it safe.

৩৩

As Jake and Kit approached the 22nd Avenue Boys Club, Jake put on his Nixon mask. Rick Winslow was in the front yard, picking up hamburger wrappers and soft drink cups, which probably had been tossed over the fence by passing students. Rick never been introduced to Powell's girlfriend, but he'd seen her with Powell outside the locker room after the Stanford game and had heard about how the narcs were going after her. At least he assumed that was Powell behind the Nixon mask. Then the significance of Kit's costume registered. She was a striped jailbird, dragging along a plastic ball and chain and carrying a tiny plastic pumpkin.

"You on the lam?" Rick asked.

They could joke about it, for now. The D.A.'s office apparently was going to leave Kit alone, at least until after the election.

"I just promised to be back at the jail by midnight," Kit said, immediately comfortable with the quarterback. "But, Rick, let me ask you something." She held up the plastic pumpkin, about the size of a baseball. "What would you think of a guy who got me into bed by promising to buy me a pumpkin and then gave me *this*?"

"Pretty weak," Rick said. "Sounds like something Powell would do. Wherever he is." He gestured at "Nixon" and said, "This guy is much better looking, by the way."

Two hours later, Rick walked into the crowded living room with a half-eaten wedge of brownie. Jake immediately hoped that someone they knew and trusted had made them, because brownies on campus were a risky proposition if you cared about keeping your sophomore quarterback from getting wasted with the biggest game of the season so far only two days away. Jake guessed some of the non-football-playing guests might be getting stoned in the basement, but the unwritten law – unwritten, but loudly trumpeted by Todd – was no drugs in this house. Rick seemed fine, except for sugar overload.

Marlo Thomas was arguing with Ted Bessell on *That Girl*, but because the sound was off, nobody was quite sure if it was about how *That Girl* could afford this New York apartment since she hadn't landed an acting job in six months. Rick balanced himself on the couch's armrest, sitting next to quarterback Tom Davis, who still was in a cast after his latest knee operation.

Jake had shed the Nixon mask. It was too hot, and he and Kit were among the few who had come in costume. Iron Butterfly's "In-a-Gadda-Da-Vida" would go on for, what, maybe forty-five minutes longer?

Suddenly, Todd quickly flicked the reject switch next to the turntable, silencing the music. Todd ducked most, but not all, of the tossed beer cans. Klaus Rockwell, the graduate assistant coach who had played with so many of the current Fishermen, was behind him.

# SIXTEEN: "IN-A-GADDA-DA-VIDA"

"Coach Benson sent me over," Klaus said. "I didn't tell him I was coming over, anyway, after we were done looking at film."

He had everyone's attention.

"Wyden called him," Klaus said. "He saw Powell buying beer, and he told Coach Benson he investigated and found out you were about to host a blowout for the entire student body at the house tonight, and that was a disgrace, especially because we were playing a very, very, very important game on Saturday. I told coach I would personally see to it everybody would be out of here by eleven. He said if any of you look hung over tomorrow morning on the bus, he'd lock up the bathrooms and tell the bus driver we're not stopping between here and Seattle."

Klaus looked at his watch. "One hour and fourteen minutes to closing time," he said. "We all straight on that?"

Heads nodded.

"Good," Klaus said, "now give me a damn beer."

Todd put Iron Butterfly back on the stereo.

Timmy Hilton and his basketball-playing roommate, David Armstrong, and their dates – all five of their dates – showed up a few minutes later. Soon, Timmy and David were talking with a red-haired Fisherman track runner whose fascination with shoes was well known in the football locker room.

"We wear flimsy goddamn sneakers," Armstrong said. "If some company ever makes real basketball shoes, they'd make a killing."

When the runner asked Armstrong what he wanted from basketball shoes, Timmy listened for a minute and then laughed. "Aw, stop talkin' about it," Timmy told the runner. "Just do it."

The runner pondered. "Just do it. Just do it!" he said, as if he was trying out a line in a play.

Timmy spotted Jake, kneeling cross-legged on the floor, in front of Kit's recliner. Jake was reading album liner notes as conversation swirled around him and Kit was nodding off. Timmy excused himself from his group, sat on the chair's armrest and asked Jake loudly, the only way he could be heard, "What'd you think of the bombing halt?"

"What?"

"The bombing halt!"

"What bombing halt?"

"Johnson called it off. No more bombing of North Vietnam."

Within five minutes, Jake and Kit were on the back porch, listening to a transistor radio. Timmy joined them for the 10 o'clock network news. Hanoi also had agreed to more extensive peace talks in Paris, beginning in a week. In return for the bombing halt, Hanoi promised not to attack cities in the south.

"He might get Humphrey elected, after all," Jake said.

"After this, are you still going ahead with the shit at the Air Force game?" Timmy asked, startling Jake. Timmy shrugged and said, "It's no secret. You have your meetings at Terwilliger's! Besides, Bill Charles came over the other night and said I had to get involved somehow. I said I'd think about it. But I'm leaning against it. Football is football. This isn't the Olympics, one or two men standing there with the whole world looking. I think you should leave this shit out of the locker room."

Jake nodded. "Promise," he said. "Not in the locker room."

Kit went into the house, the screen door snapping shut on the spring behind her. It was raining, but still warm enough for Timmy and Jake to feel comfortable on the covered porch. They got started again, as if they still were on that bus in Nebraska. Timmy talked about looking forward to playing in Seattle, where his dad could watch him, brag about him, maybe even hug him – then ask him if he was able to get through the door with that hair and tell him that Jesus still loved him.

Jake talked about the latest letter from Pittsburgh, and how his mother had stopped being chatty long enough to say she finally had heard about his nasty retort to the kid in Portland and how disappointed she and his stepfather were in him.

"She said, 'Your stepfather,'" Jake said. "It always used to be 'your dad.' I guess he's written me off. Well, that's fine with me."

By then, Kit was holding her fresh beer and listening at the screen door behind them. She suddenly figured out why he had dragged her to the pay phone the other night to call her dad. She was even happier that he had.

# SEVENTEEN:
## "PIECE OF MY HEART"

*(Sunday, November 3, 1968)*

The Fishermen wouldn't gather to watch the game film until later in the morning, but Jake Powell didn't need to wait. He had gone over the play from the end of Saturday's game over and over in his mind.

With Cascade leading 23-22 and a little over a minute left in Husky Stadium, Washington had a fourth-and-seven from the CU 40. Jake covered a Washington halfback coming out of the backfield, staying with him stride for stride. When the halfback curled in, Jake was behind him. When the pass came, Jake hit the halfback just as the Husky touched the ball. Perfect timing, perfect play. The ball hit the grass, the pass was incomplete and as he and the halfback rolled on the ground, Jake felt Alex Tolliver slapping him on the shoulder pads.

But then he heard the cheer, and his teammates already arguing. He bounced up to get in on the debate. One of the officials was pointing at the red flag on the ground and shaking his head as the Fishermen protested.

The call was pass interference, giving the Huskies an automatic first down at the 30.

Washington completed one more pass along the sideline, and then the Huskies' kicker drilled a tough 40-yard field goal with five seconds left.

Jake didn't say a word on the bus ride back south until about Portland. Timmy pulled Jake's bag off the seat and into the aisle, and sat down. "Look, it was a shitty call," he said. "Everyone knows it."

The coaches were split between the two buses, but Carl Steele and Rex Gamberg, seated in consecutive rows, were close enough to hear the exchange. Jake could see them talking in the next few seconds, but he couldn't pick it up – and hadn't really tried.

Gamberg leaned forward and whispered to Steele, "Don't you think the refs know who Powell is, too?"

Steele turned. "He played great," he said, softly. "We got screwed at the end on the road. That's football, not politics."

On Sunday morning, Jake was operating on about three hours' sleep, and fitful sleep at that. But the morning gathering at the Student Union cafeteria at least would distract him, and he wryly congratulated himself on the timing as he tried to get everyone's attention.

Finally, he did.

At least they didn't want to talk about the Washington loss.

The Air Force game was six days away. To make it more interesting, Air Force was undefeated and would be ranked in the top ten when the polls came out Monday. Sellout crowd, big non-conference game...and what?

The poet wanted to shut down the game. "We all gather together and run onto the field as one and chain and lock ourselves to the goalposts!"

The consensus response to that was that the police would have the protestors unlocked in two minutes, if they even got to the goalposts in the first place. "Besides," said the gay leader, "then we'd have to go into the football game and act for a little bit like that mercenary bullshit mattered." He nodded at Jake. "No offense, Powell. But I think you had a good idea all along. We sneak into the stadium on Friday night and paint the peace sign on the Astroturf."

"I was being a smart-ass!"

"I know, but it's a good idea!"

"How the hell are you going to get in and do that?"

"A few of us go to the Friday night high school games, hide until everyone's left, then paint away."

"They could get the paint off in time."

"Not *this* kind of paint."

Danny Gleason, the student body president, said they should pass out pictures of flag-draped caskets and lists of Oregonians killed in action. "Simple, but gets the point across."

A guy from the *Cascadian* yearbook argued for aggressive picketing at every gate and passing out brochures. "If all you do is hold up the game or talk about the war in general, you haven't made the point that you're doing this because the Air Force is dropping bombs on innocent people."

"*Was* dropping," Jake said.

## SEVENTEEN: "PIECE OF MY HEART"

"They stop bombing three days ago to get Humphrey elected, and we're supposed to forgive them?"

Kit Dunleavy, the newest member of a coalition with no membership list, who still felt awkward speaking up because she also would be covering the protest, was adamant, calling for peaceful picketing only. "Do we want to try to convince people or not? How would people react if we confront them in the parking lot or disrupt the game? It would defeat the purpose."

Actually, she was thinking about her father, who had decided not to make the long drive up for the game, as long as she promised to bring "her football player" home for Thanksgiving. But she was using her father as an example, and she was torn. Sometimes, she thought the only way to get men and women like her father – decent, but patriotic to the point of wearing blinkers – to come around on the war was to shock them. She wanted to win over people like her father, not drive them too far the other way.

As Kit talked, Jake realized that neither Annie Laughlin nor Bill Charles had said a word the whole meeting. Annie hadn't even gotten in her usual barbs at him. They must be plotting. When Kit finished, Jake called them on it.

"The picketing would be a good start," Annie said.

"Absolutely," Bill said.

"But it shouldn't be just at the game," Annie said.

"It should start at the airport," Bill said. "It should be at their hotel. Then it should be at the stadium. We need to get attention, and that's one way to do it."

"What else?" Jake asked.

Annie didn't try very hard to sound innocent. "What do you mean?"

"You know what I mean. You said 'a good start.' What else do you have in mind?"

"As a coalition, picketing might be enough," Annie said. "Individually, we can think about if there's anything else we want to do."

"I repeat, what do you mean?"

"I repeat," she said testily, "we can think about it. You, for example, can wear that armband. I think we should be shooting for something very symbolic and effective."

The guy from the *Cascadian* ended up moving to have a signup for picket duty, at the airport, at the hotel, at the game.

Hey, Jake thought, it was something out of *Roberts Rules*, at last. Hands made it unanimous, and they planned to set up a table in the Union this week with no secrets and no apologies.

"Hold it," Jake said, as a couple of them started to leave. "Don't do anything stupid. Don't get anybody hurt. Don't screw up the game."

Surprisingly, the *Cascadian* guy and the student body president made impassioned speeches, backing up Jake and Kit. They should make their point, they agreed, but not turn people off.

At Terwilliger's a little later, as Jake bit into his cheeseburger, Annie raised her right hand.

"I solemnly swear," she said, "we will not bomb the bus, bomb the locker room, poison the water bucket, bomb the stadium, or bomb or poison anything."

"Thanks," Jake said. "That clears a whole lot up."

                ∽

After the Fishermen looked at the films of the Washington game – and Jake received repeated reassurances, even from Todd Hendricks, that the pass interference call was bogus – Jake nervously approached Benson as they were leaving.

"Coach, can I talk to you for a few minutes?"

"Football or politics?" Benson said with a tight smile.

"Well, both, but mostly politics."

"Come by my house tonight. Nine o'clock."

Jake started the disclosure tour at seven. He borrowed Kit's car keys and made a call from the corner. A few minutes later, he was in Neal Hassler's living room.

The president listened as Jake outlined the picketing plans. Hassler didn't let on, but his reaction was relief, especially because the more militant Annie wasn't with Jake. Hassler told Jake peaceful picketing would be tolerated.

"Anything beyond that," Hassler said, "there will be problems. I will not have the people attending the game harassed. I will not have anyone from the Air Force, either the academy or the service, treated as anything but guests." He got up and walked around, looking outside from a room with no windows. "Disrupt the football game, and the student disciplinary actions, not to mention the legal ones, will be serious."

"I understand that," Jake said. "I can live with that."

"Good," said Hassler. "By the way, what's Coach Benson think about you being involved in this?"

Jake laughed. "I'm about to find out."

❦

Benson lived on a cul-de-sac on the south end of town, part of the way up Gilman Butte, the landmark everyone could spot for about the last thirty miles of the drive either way on Interstate 5. One of the Cascade rites of passage was the grade school hike up to the top of the butte. The view could be stunning, one of two ways. Either the kids could stand at the top and look down on the breathtaking Willamette Valley, stretching to the north, or have what usually was the first-time experience of actually being above the clouds.

When Jake pulled Kit's car into the driveway, two deer were in Benson's front yard. They bolted. Jake decided he was having that effect on everyone lately.

Patricia Benson, the quiet woman who always was waiting outside the locker room when Jake left after games, was in the living room, reading with the television on. She smiled and greeted Jake warmly as Coach Benson directed him toward his den, at the corner of the house on the ground floor. The kids, Jake guessed, must be upstairs.

Benson's den was a gallery of pictures, and he didn't say a word as Jake found himself drawn to look them over. Jake saw a young Benson with his dog and his parents on a farm; shots of his wedding with the men in military uniforms; and a photo of him with his wife and five children that ran with a *Times-Register* story after he was elevated to head coach. The football section featured a team picture of the 1942 Minnesota Gophers, and Jake quickly spotted his coach in the fourth row. Tightly aligned pictures showed the Cascade teams from the five years of Benson's head-coaching tenure, including this season.

Jake had spotted the military pictures first, but had saved them for last. He was thinking of his own father as he peered at the picture of a young – *very* young – Benson in flight helmet and uniform, sitting in an open cockpit. Benson said softly, "Army Air Forces, Pacific, 1944."

Jake had read quite a few stories about his coach and the press guide biographies, but he didn't remember anything other than the most vague of references to Benson's combat experiences. Benson had referred to them only briefly to Jake ("I flew during World War II") during the recruiting process, because Jake's high school coach had told Benson that Jake's father had been killed in Korea. But Jake never had heard any of his teammates talk about the coach's World War II experience, and he assumed few, if any, were aware of it.

"How come you never talk to us about this stuff?" he asked Benson.

"It's not something that comes up in casual conversation, is it? It was just something we did. We did what we had to do. Sometimes I just wonder what your generation is going to be saying to your kids if they're challenging you. *When* they're challenging you."

"We'll just ground 'em," Jake said.

As Jake went from picture to picture, of Benson standing next to a plane, of the pilot with his buddies outside the barracks, of a training class at graduation, he quietly asked the questions.

"What kind of plane is that?

"P-38 fighter, twin-engine."

"How old were you?"

Benson paused and put both hands on his knees as he leaned against the edge of the desk. "I was nineteen when I got my wings," he said. "Sixty-seven combat missions later, I was twenty-one and I felt thirty. I also felt lucky."

"Wow."

"When I went in, I was hearing guys tell me the definition of discipline was saluting everyone during leave and a making the bed the right way, and I learned that discipline is what you can call on when you need it."

He sighed.

After a few moments, he said, "I respect your passion on this. But I still have to say I don't want you or Keith Oldham, or any other players, picketing on gameday. On gameday, until the game's over, it's football. No armband, no picketing."

"Now you sound like Doubleheader and Gamberg! You say you want us to have lives away from football…"

"That's still true! This isn't too much to expect in return. How would that look to your teammates? You're about to play the number nine team in the country, you're carrying around a sign at the main gate and have to run in to get your uniform on for warmup!"

"But–"

"I'm not going to have somebody following you guys to see what you do before you have to be in the locker room. I want you to give me your word."

"All right," Jake said, reluctantly.

"Good," said Benson. "You came close on the recruiters. This time, if you – that means your people – do something to those players or any of the Air Force people, you are going to have a lot more important people to answer to than me."

Benson tapped an unsharpened pencil in the palm of one hand.

"I will consider it a personal betrayal if something happens to embarrass this program or this university on Saturday. Think about Neal Hassler and the others whose butts are on the line because they won't be coming after your people with fire hoses. Get that across to your friends. Nothing ugly."

Jake raised a hand and opened his mouth, but couldn't get it out.

Benson said, "You think you're not necessarily involved if someone goes overboard. But, damn it, you're going to have to accept some of the responsibility. And the armband? It should be a team thing or not at all. You *will* skip that. Who doesn't know where you stand, anyway?"

Most coaches, Jake knew, by now would have told him to clean out his locker and move to Russia. "Okay," he said.

Mrs. Benson was standing in the doorway. "Phone, Larry," she said. Benson walked down the hall to the bedroom. Jake went back downstairs with Mrs. Benson.

Humphrey was on the news, speaking in a packed Astrodome. "No one man can alone lead this country out of crisis and into a certain, happier future," Humphrey said. "But if you will trust me, I tell you that I shall call forth from America the best that lies within us."

The reporter said Humphrey had issued a statement, saying if President Thieu of South Vietnam refused to have his government participate in the Paris talks, the U.S. should go ahead without him.

The newscast switched to Nixon and a clip from *Meet The Press*. He was denying that he believed the bombing halt had been timed to help Humphrey in the election. "I must say that many of my aides and many of the people supporting my candidacy around the country seem to share that view," Nixon said. "They share it, I suppose, because the pause came at that time so late in the campaign. But President Johnson has been very candid with me throughout these discussions, and I do not make such a charge."

Talk about trying to have it all ways, Jake thought.

# EIGHTEEN:
## "CROSSTOWN TRAFFIC"

*(Tuesday, November 5, 1968)*

Nervously, Jake Powell voted in a general election for the first time. His hand quivered as he yanked down the handle inside the booth, snapping the curtain closed behind him. He was certain he wasn't going to remember how to work this damn machine and everyone in the grade-school gym near campus would be laughing at him when he crawled out from under the curtain. Or worse, that he would inadvertently vote for Nixon and Senator Wayne Morse's opponent and tip the balance, changing the course of history.

He scanned the tiny levers and flipped Humphrey for president, gently, and Morse for senator, with feeling. Thinking of Kit, he registered a vote for the D.A.'s opponent. As he slid the handle back to the right and the curtain popped open, he briefly felt exhilarated. Only briefly.

∽

Neal Hassler was convinced that as long as the picketers at the game were peaceful, it would be counterproductive for the university to drive them away or arrest them. Some of them would love it. They'd play dead or they would flop and scream, and the film would make the TV news.

The usual Potestio Stadium ushers, the volunteers from the Boy Scouts and the men's Active Club, obviously wouldn't be enough, so Hassler asked the campus police chief to line up added security at the stadium. He phoned the superintendent of the academy and warned him, but the superintendent didn't seem alarmed.

"We're used to this bullshit by now," he said.

∽

Annie Laughlin knew many Cascade cops liked to eat at Original Ollie's, one of those rare restaurants that could be all things to all people – coffee shop in the morning, conducive for a serious business lunch at noon, solid steakhouse and bar for dinner. She stood at the entrance to the lot for a minute and pretended to be counting her change. Convinced that nobody was watching, or in any of the other cars, she approached the empty police car parked closest to the back of the lot and slipped an envelope under the driver's side windshield wiper.

❧

The presidential race still is too close to call, Walter Cronkite said on the TV in Terwilliger's. Humphrey was slightly ahead in the popular vote, but Nixon seemed in better shape with electoral votes. It even could go to the House of Representatives.

"Wallace!" Jake Powell snapped, looking down from the screen. "Wallace is going to win this for Nixon."

"It doesn't make any difference," Annie said. "You still talk like the Democrats had nothing to do with this war! It's their war!"

"It isn't over," Kit said. "Besides, even if Nixon wins, maybe he'll surprise us."

Annie was disgusted. "Yeah, sure. He pulls us out on January twenty-first."

Jake ran through it again. Nixon would be president. Morse's Senate race still was too close to call, too, but if it came out the wrong way, Oregon would reject a senator who had the guts and the foresight to realize Vietnam would be a quagmire – and the wisdom to argue against getting deeply involved in the first place.

Kit's D.A. was going to win.

Jesus, what next?

❧

Kit was on the payphone at Terwilliger's, trying to be heard over the din, but not talk loud enough to share her conversation with everyone passing by on the way to the bathroom.

"Chris," she said, "you seem to be forgetting this was all your idea!" As she dropped another quarter in the payphone slot, she continued. "You're the one who left! You're the one who said we'd just see how things..."

She listened for a few moments.

## EIGHTEEN: "CROSSTOWN TRAFFIC"

"NO!"

Pause.

"*Stop it!*" she said. The girl coming out of the bathroom gave Kit a look, but such lovers' quarrels were common on this payphone, and one of the reasons there was a sign suggesting a five-minute limit on calls. "Stop it," Kit said softer, lowering her head even further.

A guy was standing behind her, hands in his pockets, searching for change.

"Goodbye," she said sharply, then slammed the phone on the hook and ran into the bathroom. Annie came in a minute later, when Kit was washing her face. Annie stood at the next sink and waited, finally handing Kit a paper towel.

"You okay?" Annie asked as Kit dried.

"I'm fine," she said, hoping the smoke in the place would be a sufficient explanation for her reddened eyes.

"If you ever need someone else to talk to..." Annie said, awkwardly.

"Thanks," Kit said. "I'm fine. Really."

"You can fool Mr. Oblivious out there," Annie said. "But you can't fool me."

"Annie..."

"Just let me know," Annie said over her shoulder as she pushed open the bathroom door.

# NINETEEN:
## "CROWN OF CREATION"

*(Wednesday, November 6, 1968)*

Kit had told Jake she couldn't go out to eat because she needed to study, and when he grimaced, she added that he should stop pouting about Nixon's victory and Morse's loss at the polls and hit the books, too.

At her tiny bedroom desk, Kit read twenty pages in her Western Civilization textbook, but didn't absorb a word. She gave up and went for a walk. The rain was falling softly, and Kit felt better after she flipped the hood of the windbreaker off her head and felt the raindrops on her hair and dripping down her face. She walked past the deserted tennis courts and down the hill, away from the campus, past the cookie-cutter apartment houses with bicycles and plants on the balconies, past the old rental homes with cars lined up three deep in the driveways, and then finally past the nicer homes, many owned by faculty members.

She came to Melville's Whale, the huge old house a retired professor had converted into a used bookstore and coffeehouse. In Cascade, it was renowned as a musty haven for readers and book collectors.

After the professor poured Kit's coffee in one of the communal mugs, she wandered into the children's section. Within a minute, she pulled out one of the familiar books with the plain blue cover – a Nancy Drew mystery in good condition, albeit minus the yellow dust jacket – and sat in the student's chair in the corner.

Before Nancy had done much sleuthing, Kit was turning a page when she noticed Annie across the room, in the fiction section. She was sitting and talking with Father Basinger, from the Newman Center. Before Kit made it through another page, though, Basinger left, and Annie turned and looked at the novels.

Kit was immersed in Nancy's adventure when Annie approached her.

"Flashing back?"

Embarrassed, Kit closed the book, but Annie waved off her sheepishness. "I used to buy every new one the week it came out,"

Annie said. "I've still got 'em lined up, in order, in my room at home, and I could give you a summary of every plot, in order."

Kit held up her book. "All right," she challenged. "*The Mystery of the Ivory Charm.*"

Annie squinted. "Number 13 in the series," she said. "They're rewriting those early ones, one by one now, and reissuing them, and that really stinks. Does the print look like a really old typewriter?"

Kit nodded. "Yeah, and with a really dirty ribbon." She looked in the front. "Copyright, 1936."

"Nancy's on vacation when a circus elephant trainer gives her an ivory elephant charm, and a little boy from India who lives with the circus hides on the train and rides back to River Heights with Nancy. Wel-l-l, it turns out that this little boy—"

Smiling, Kit held up the book, opened to about page twenty. "Enough! Don't ruin it for me!"

Annie looked around. There were perhaps ten other customers in the store, browsing. "You alone?" Annie asked.

"I told Jake I needed to study. And I did."

"But?"

"I just couldn't get into it. I went for a walk and ended up here."

"I've known the feeling. Too often lately."

Annie showed Kit the book she was carrying, a paperback copy of MacKinlay Kantor's *Andersonville*. "Actually, I needed this for American Lit. How about I buy this and we go play some pool or something? Maybe talk. Might do us good."

"Sure, why not," Kit said, thinking of plenty of reasons why not, but overruling them. "But where?"

"My car's around the corner," Annie said. "The tavern's not too far. Maybe fifteen minutes."

Annie had a three-year-old, two-door Plymouth. It was nothing flashy, nothing that stood out as a high school graduation present for a spoiled kid heading off to college, but still probably was in the upper echelon of student transportation.

Annie tossed a small stack of old issues of *The New York Times* into the back seat, making way for Kit.

They ended up a couple of miles beyond the city limits to the west, on the state highway that eventually led to the Oregon coast, and pulled into a gravel parking lot next to a place with a sign that billed it as the "My Way or the Highway Tavern." Kit had never heard of it. In the lot were a couple of motorcycles, three beat-up pickup trucks, a Volkswagen van and five nondescript cars. Inside, at first glance it could have been any tavern near campus, with the Hamm's and Bohemian lighted signs, a young and bearded bartender who might have been a graduate student or high school teacher moonlighting, a burger-dominated menu on the wall, barrels of peanuts in the corners, and a beat-up, cue-scarred pool table at one end.

Of the dozen or so customers in the place, four were at the bar and the rest were divided into two groups at the long tables closest to the bar.

Annie immediately walked up to one of the tables. Four dark men, all in cowboy hats, two of them with moustaches, were sharing two pitchers.

"*Anita!*"

To Kit's astonishment, they began talking rapidly with Annie – in Spanish. Annie was talking back to them – in Spanish. Kit had taken two years in high school, and she was able to follow the gist. They were doing well, they were happy to see her, and they had bought a million new shirts that week. Or something like that.

Annie eventually pointed at Kit and – or at least Kit thought – told the men that Kit was her good friend. Pointing at each in turn, Annie introduced Geraldo, Benito, Ruben and Juan. Annie hugged them all, and then gestured at the table nearest the pool table. Kit went over and sat down. Annie went to the bar and was back in a minute with a pitcher of beer.

"We don't have to play, if you don't want," Annie said, gesturing at the cue rack on the wall. Three cues were in the rack. A half-dozen were haphazardly stacked against the walls.

"Maybe later," Kit said. "How do you know them?"

"If I tell you the story, the *whole* story," Annie said, "will you tell me what's bothering you?"

Kit was pondering that when Annie looked her in the eyes, pointedly. "You won't surprise me, because I think I know," Annie said.

"All right," Kit said softly. "We trade stories."

Annie started slowly, with little emotion. "When I went to the migrant camp last summer, I thought they'd all love me for fighting for them. I stayed late one night, told the others to go ahead. I wanted to see what it was like at night. I was walking around like I owned the place, and maybe I thought I did because I speak Spanish. One guy said I needed to see the hut where the truck loaders lived. He said I wouldn't be able to believe what I saw, believe how they lived. So I went there. By myself. There were only a few of them there."

A few minutes later, the pitcher was empty.

Annie was leaning forward, her elbows on the table and her arms folded. She was looking down and her voice was flat.

She said, "Then it was the last guy's turn."

Kit had her cheek resting on one palm, one elbow on the table, and she had been shaking her head through the story. "Jesus," Kit said.

"That's when they came in," Annie said.

"They?"

Annie nodded at the table across the room. "Geraldo and Benito at first, then Juan and Ruben."

"Jesus, they didn't—"

"NO! Geraldo and Benito just stood there for a second. I was crying, I was numb, I didn't know, I was thinking maybe it couldn't get any worse, just so I don't get killed. Geraldo started yelling at them, calling them *pendejos* – assholes – and he came over and tried to help me. They started trying to beat the shit out him and Benito jumped in, too, and I was covering up and crying, and next thing I knew, Juan and Ruben were in there, too, and I could see knives and hear all hell breaking loose. I told myself to get up. Told myself to run. I couldn't. But before I knew it, Benito and Juan were handing me my clothes. There was blood all over. I didn't know whose. The other bastards were gone." Annie still wasn't close to crying. She was beyond that now; not desensitized, but beyond letting it show. "They helped me out of the hut, got me back to the camp entrance and I got out of there."

She hadn't reported it to police. The migrant workers' camp was an isolated world, apart from the gringo authority, the layers of mistrust probably impossible to penetrate. The rapists were a small group of men, men who were exceptions, and Annie had just gone to the wrong place at the wrong time. The grower wouldn't have cooperated, probably, not for this woman who was trying to stir it up, spouting the Cesar Chavez lines about decent treatment for the workers, almost all of whom were U.S. citizens or in the country legally. There probably would be some authorities, she thought, who believed she had gotten what she had deserved for trying to advance the cause of these people.

"At one point, for about two seconds, I thought, you know, how could I blame them. They're treated like animals, so they act like animals."

Kit jumped on that. "But–"

"No," Annie said, her voice getting sharper, "I didn't think that very long. They were pigs. Pigs! Even in those camps, you have to have more dignity than that, you can't let it do that to you, and Geraldo and the others weren't like that. Most of them weren't like that. I'm fighting for them. Not the assholes."

"So how did they end up here?"

"Father Basinger – you know him, don't you? – took care of it," Annie said. "He knows the whole story. He got them all jobs."

"I saw you talking with Father Basinger in the bookstore," Kit said. "Now I guess I know what about."

"I don't think you do, but that's another story."

Kit wondered if she should keep pushing. She decided to plow on. "I know you don't get over something like that, but ..."

"I'm still not." Annie paused and took a huge swig of the beer. "The abortion wasn't fun."

"Oh, God."

"Thought it would be so easy. I hated them. Didn't tell my parents, lined it up, no problem. Had it done. But it turned out to be so hard, Kit. So hard! It was one of theirs, but this was a baby! I couldn't even tell that part to Father Basinger." She was on the verge of sobbing. "Now you think I'm really nuts."

"Not at all. I'm glad you told me."

"Jake doesn't know any of that. I don't want him to know, okay?"

"Okay."

They sat silent for about a minute. Kit noticed that the four workers had been casting glances over occasionally, and she guessed they must have caught on that the story was being told. Finally, Annie sat upright. "Let's go talk with them for a bit," she said, "then we can go."

ᩇ

They were in the Plymouth in the parking lot next to the tennis courts, passing the joint back and forth. Kit had just finished telling Annie about Chris' visit. Everything about Chris' visit. "He's sending cards and flowers, and it's almost funny," Kit said. "That's really not his style. He says he's coming home at Christmas and wants to see me and get this straightened out."

"Straightened out? I guess I don't understand. He still wants to stay in New York and act?"

"Oh, yes," Kit said.

"I'm sure he's not screwing any of the actresses, right?"

"He doesn't even pretend that he isn't."

"But he wants some kind of commitment from you?"

"Just that I'll be there for him when he's home for a month and that I'll keep an open mind about us for the future."

"In other words, you screw him when he's home."

"Well, he did say he'd like me to think about coming to New York with him after I graduate. He says I could try to get a job at the papers and magazines back there."

"How's his acting going?"

"He finally admitted that as an actor, he's been a good waiter so far and he's getting a lot of help from his parents. He's carrying just enough hours at Fordham to not get drafted."

"Do it that way, screw up one class and you're in trouble," Annie said.

Kit took another hit. "I know," she said. "I don't graduate for at least a year, anyway," she said. "And maybe none of this matters now."

"Because of Jake?" Annie asked.

"Because of Jake."

Annie put both her hands on the steering wheel. "Good," she said. "There's nothing you can do about it now. It's not a big deal as long as you don't hurt Jake, okay? It's not like you screwed three of his friends or something."

"But I'm starting to think I might be pregnant," Kit said softly.

"Now *that's* a problem," Annie said. She snatched back the joint. "Probably ought to lay off this until you know."

"I know. I mean I know I should."

"Well," said Annie, "I'm here if you need help. Let me know."

"You mean an abortion?"

"I can't tell you what to do."

They sat in silence for a full minute. Annie took another hit, but didn't pass the joint. Finally, Annie started the car. "Tonight's our secrets," Annie said. "And if something happens sometime soon, keep an open mind, okay? And just tell yourself it could have been worse."

"You going to tell me what you mean by 'something' and 'could have been worse'?"

"Nope."

# TWENTY:
## "LIGHT MY FIRE"

*(Friday, November 8, 1968)*

For several days, Jake Powell had known his coaches were right about his divided attentions. He had a hard time concentrating on football, long before he was standing at the Cascade Airport railing, waiting for the Air Force football team to leave the plane.

His week had been a mess of depressing news, classes, practice and scrambling. Nixon's The One. Barring a recount reversal, Morse is out of the Senate. The Air Force offense looks unstoppable on film. The term paper on Thomas Jefferson was going to have to be written overnight next week; hope the bookstore doesn't run out of erasable typing paper. Though Kit had picked him up and driven him to the airport, she had seemed a bit distant, and he was wondering if the "let's-be-friends" speech was coming this weekend, or maybe next week.

Now, as he and the fifty other student protesters waited, Jake's biggest worry was that Annie wasn't around. At this point, he would prefer having his eye – both eyes – on her. His other worry was to make sure he was out of here on time to make the team's light "walk-through" practice in shorts and T-shirts.

As the roaring whine of the jet engines quieted and workers slid the laddered ramp to the door, Jake pivoted his homemade sign and looked at the message he had printed: "NO MORE BOMB-ING...PERIOD" Not bad, he thought, for a quick construction job that afternoon.

Kit watched from behind the mob. The plane was parked to the side of the commercial flights' usual two parking places at the small airport.

The first Air Force men off the plane looked to be officers, perhaps honchos at the academy. The students thrust their signs aloft and most started yelling, the messages diluted in the angry overlapping. Jake remained mute.

As the Air Force players started down the ramp, all of them lugging garment bags with spare cadet uniforms, Jake was reminded that these guys could have been sitting next to him in class. He was not looking at older, hard-edged, sneering mercenaries. They had distinguishing military haircuts, crisp blues and shiny shoes, yet had zits and shaving cuts. They carried thick physics textbooks and theme notebooks as well as their tote bags. They were going to call their parents and girlfriends collect that night. Jake recognized some of them from having played against the Falcons on the road the season before.

As the first of the Air Force group finished the hike from the plane to the storm fence that divided the outside waiting area and the tarmac, members of the baggage crew – which worked for all the airlines at this small airport – jumped into the cargo hold and started unloading the equipment bags first, so the Air Force staff could load them onto a rental truck. A group of about a dozen National Guardsmen circled the plane, standing watch. The Falcons were going straight to Potestio Stadium to wedge in their light no-pads workout before the Friday night high school doubleheader.

The students behind Jake cranked up the volume. They were behind sawhorses the police had set up at one corner of the waiting area.

"End the bombing forever!"

"Drop out of the war academy!"

"Stop the war!"

"Baby killers!"

Kit tried to take notes without taking her eyes off the scene in front of her.

As the Air Force men passed, skirting the small terminal building and heading to the bus at the curb, some players glared at the protesters. Most stared straight ahead. Yes, Jake thought, the players had been briefed: Ignore that shit, men.

One player, though, slowed his stride and finally stopped as his teammates continued. Tall and barrel-chested, this player seemed benignly curious rather than confrontational as he stopped and surveyed the group and the signs. Jake realized he was looking at Andre Orderia, the All-America center.

The voices exploded behind Jake – "Uncle Tom!" was the kindest – at the cadet. Without turning around, Jake tried to quiet them with an upraised hand, and one or two heeded him. Orderia looked at Jake and grinned, then leaned forward and spoke loudly, to nobody in particular. "You know, don't you, that without guys like us, you wouldn't have the right to carry those signs."

Jake offered a half-hearted salute, with the hint of a smile making it more friendly than sarcastic.

Kit noticed it, too, but she wasn't close enough to hear.

Orderia caught a policeman's attention and pointed at Jake. "Let him walk with me, will you, please? This is my pal."

The policeman looked puzzled, but nodded.

Jake squeezed between sawhorses and walked a few feet away from the crowd, just far enough to have some privacy. He reached out and shook Orderia's hand warmly. The handshake confused some of the demonstrators, but the shouts of protest continued.

"When I watched you on film this week, I didn't think you'd be nice enough to meet me at the airport," Orderia said.

"My girlfriend has a car," Jake said, laughing. "Wanna go get a beer?"

Orderia ignored that. "I'm still going to kick your ass tomorrow. Just like last year."

"You have to catch me first."

A *Times-Register* photographer took a couple of shots of this "confrontation." Noticing that, Kit started to fight her way through the other students, toward the sawhorses.

"Hate to tell you this," Orderia said. "But this stuff is getting old to us. And we're just a bunch of guys trying to pass calculus. You think we're all just itching to get to Vietnam?"

"Don't know. Does it matter?"

"Sure. It pisses me off when people assume I go to bed dreaming about blowing up an orphanage or some such stupid shit. And it really gets to me when some of you act like the North Vietnamese and the Viet Cong are sainted freedom fighters. They're fanatics who think nothing of massacring people – even civilians."

"I won't argue about that," Jake said slowly. "We don't have any business being there. Do you really think we should be?"

"Sometimes, I'd say, yeah, sure, they need us. Sometimes I think, 'What the hell are we doing?' Their leaders are crooks, their army's a joke, and their people aren't sure what they want. Other times, I want to say, 'Give me one of those damn signs, too.' I don't have some pat answer, like you people."

Out of breath, and with ink on her shirt because her pen got shoved against her in her fight to get through the pack, Kit reached the front of the mob on the other side of the sawhorses. But just as she did, an Air Force assistant coach who had jumped back off the team bus approached Orderia. "Knock it off!" he hollered at Orderia. "Let's go!"

Orderia took a step toward the bus, but stopped, leaned back and offered Jake his hand again. As they shook, Orderia said, "See you tomorrow."

That's all Kit heard.

On the way to the bus, the assistant coach was like a drill instructor with a first-day recruit.

"Jesus Christ, Orderia! That's all we need! You debating with the freaks! And then you even shake the guy's hand!"

Orderia didn't attempt to explain.

Jake went back behind the sawhorses, holding Kit's hand and leading her. Kit had stopped taking notes completely. The hothead guy who had been hollering about infant genocide challenged Jake. "What was that all about? Shaking his hand?"

"That's the best center in the country. He's going to *try* to kick my ass tomorrow."

"How do you know him?"

"We played them last season and I talked to him quite a bit at the Academic All-American dinner in Chicago."

The hothead glared at Jake, then squinted at the retreating Orderia, who was climbing on the bus.

"It's *him* blocking *you?*"

"A lot of the time," Jake said.

"Is it too late to get a bet down on them?"

⟪⟫

An hour later, as the West Coast Airlines flight from San Francisco pulled up to the terminal area, three men – in wool shirts, looking like either graduate students or dropouts – stood at the terminal's huge picture window.

They waited as the flight unloaded.

# TWENTY: "LIGHT MY FIRE"

They also kept looking at the Air Force plane, parked in the same spot as earlier in the day, now with six National Guardsmen standing watch around it.

Moments after the final passengers came into the terminal, two Cascade policemen approached the three men.

"Hey, guys, anything I can help you with?" one policeman asked.

"Our buddy must have missed the flight," one of the three men said.

The men looked at one another and as the officer stepped away, they wordlessly agreed it was time to leave. They felt the policemen's eyes on them as they went out the double doors at the front of the terminal, and as the conversation bounced around among the three.

"Those cops didn't show up just by accident."

"Oh, they might have. But put it all together and they're either being more careful than we thought or somebody talked."

"Our guy isn't going to be able to pull this off."

"Shapiro's gonna be pissed."

In the telephone conversation with one of them an hour later, Peter Shapiro of the Magicians was angry at first, then calmed down. He made a call to another Cascade number.

"Okay," he told Annie Laughlin. "You win. It's Plan 'B.' Just Plan 'B.' It's going to have to be good enough."

⌒

From across the room, the *Campus Daily's* rock music critic bellowed: "Kit, line seven!"

Kit was on her second page.

She picked up the receiver and punched the correct blinking button for once.

"How'd it go?" Annie asked.

"The story or the protest at the airport?"

"Both."

"Pretty uneventful and pretty undistinguished," Kit said. "I'm not sending this one to the Pulitzer committee."

"Maybe we'll have to give you something better to write about."

Kit laughed, and then realized Annie wasn't completely joking.

The sound of the clattering keys made the pause less jarring.

Annie asked, "And how are you doing? You okay?"

"I'm getting there."

# TWENTY-ONE:
## "FIRE"

*(Saturday, November 9, 1968)*

Three hours before the game, Jake and Kit crossed the Astor River footbridge, heading to Potestio Stadium. Jake held both Kit's hand and a protest sign. Kit had agreed to picket for a few minutes to allow Jake to feel as if he had participated in spirit, or to give it to a protester who hadn't brought a sign. Otherwise, Kit was going to concentrate on being a reporter.

Their hands were cold, but not frigid. It was going to be chilly that afternoon, but no rain was expected, so it would be suitable for both passing and more picketing.

Kit and Jake left the bridge and walked through the stadium's gravel parking lot, winding their way past the puddles and the muddy spots where the rocks had worn away. The concrete bowl stadium was a bargain, but there wasn't enough money left over at CU to pave the parking lot.

The players' gate was on the west side, and about ten demonstrators waited, with signs, for the Air Force team buses. Jake resisted the urge to skirt the outside of the stadium and go with Kit to check on how the picketing was going. He gave Kit a kiss and then a hug that turned into a deep embrace. Keith Oldham, the student senator-split end, got out of his car in the nearby players' lot. Spotting Kit and Jake, he yelled, "Hey, Powell, get your mind on the game!"

⁓

In the cramped locker room, Jake pulled out the stool from his stall. He put his coat and shirt on hooks and sat. Staring at the floor, he began his psych job. *Get ready to play. Forget all the other shit.*

The Fishermen dressed in virtual silence, if you didn't count Alex Tolliver's weekly throwing-up session in the back. For three years, Jake had been waiting for his fellow linebacker to lose it in a pile or in the huddle, too. When the kickers and return specialists went out for early work, Jake walked out of the locker room with them, but stayed in the end-zone courtyard. He was wearing his uniform pants and a T-shirt, and this was part of his ritual. He liked standing there, when the tape on his ankles still felt like casts. He enjoyed looking around, watching the ushers get in position, the equipment crews lining everything up, and even the coaches talking at the middle of the field.

"Hey, Powell!"

Andre Orderia, holding an opened game program, was sitting on the end-zone restraining wall. Jake walked over and sat down next to Andre. The Air Force center's program was opened to the "Meet the Fishermen" page.

Andre pointed at Jake's picture. "Got your hair cut since they took this?"

"I cut it myself," Jake said. "Twice a year."

They didn't say a word for a minute. Andre read and Jake scanned the stadium. Then Andre closed his program. "You weren't one of the guys screaming at the hotel at midnight, were you?"

"Nah. Had curfew."

"We did, too. Lights out at 11:30, lights on at midnight to see if somebody would get the assholes in the parking lot to shut up."

"Sorry."

"That's OK," Andre said. "Gave us a chance to sneak your pom-pom girls out of our rooms."

Andre flipped a page. "Just out of curiosity, do your coaches give you shit about your politics?"

Suddenly, it was the same coach and same tone of voice as at the airport, this time from the locker room doorway. "Orderia, get your ass in here!"

Orderia didn't stick around to get an answer.

❦

At halftime, Cascade was up 22-19 and both quarterbacks – Rick Winslow and Terry Brown of Air Force – had thrown for over 200 yards. The Fishermen flanked out Timmy Hilton often, rather than leaving him in the backfield, and he caught five passes in the first half. The Fishermen or Falcons would have the coverage perfect and the ball would be right there, the only place it could be to be completed, or the receivers would make great catches.

# TWENTY-ONE: "FIRE"

In the locker room, the Fishermen rested and waited for the coaches to go over adjustments, and then try to push some emotional buttons to send them out fighting mad.

In the student section, Kit sat with her roommate, Lisa, and as they talked, they were only nominally paying attention to the Air Force falconry team putting on an exhibition, with Commander II – the majestic falcon – flying loops over the stadium and striking at the lure swung by his handlers.

The falcon soared back above the stadium, circling, gliding, and looking.

Suddenly, Commander II was plummeting, in free-fall, not graceful flight, and when the falcon slammed into the carpet, the handlers sprinted to the carcass.

*Oh my God*, Kit thought, quickly understanding. Somebody shot the falcon!

❧

When the Fishermen came out of the locker room for the second half, the quiet was eerie. They charged out, sprinting to the bench holding a three-point lead over an undefeated opponent and maybe nine people cheered.

Jake was the last one out of the dressing room.

Kit was standing by the bench with the rally squad, waiting. How she'd gotten past the guards at the bottom of the stairs, Jake couldn't guess. She waved him over. Jesus, he thought, this isn't the time to talk. But he went.

"They got the falcon," she said, shaking her head.

"What do you man, 'got'?"

"Shot it. That's what they're cleaning up out there."

"You sure somebody shot it?"

"Well, nobody stood up or anything. It just came down. But you could tell. A few people are saying they could hear it, but I didn't. Had to be from outside the stadium."

Annie. It must have been Annie. Annie had to set this up. How could she do this?

Around him, his teammates were trying to figure out what was going on. The coaches were trying to get all of their minds off whatever the hell happened and back onto the game. Jake resisted the urge to head straight back to the dressing room, change and hunt down Annie.

⌒

Although the crowd had cheered every Fishermen completion, and went appropriately nuts when they scored one of their six touchdowns in the 49-36 win, the end of the game didn't trigger a raucous celebration. After watching the clock hit all zeroes, the Fishermen hooted and hollered and patted, bracing for the onslaught of fans, friends, and family pouring out of the stands.

It didn't come.

In the seats, some of the students and fans were clapping rhythmically to the fight song and celebrating, but not even the startling number of security guards around the field could explain this lack of rowdiness. A few of the players ran over to the railing and talked with friends or parents who had come down to the first row, and some were quickly – and haphazardly – briefed about the falcon.

In the locker room, Benson stood on a taping table and waved for their attention.

"Big win, men!" he said, hoarsely. "We've answered the challenges, and we're going to keep on answering them!"

The players yelled their approval, but still without the sort of usual post-victory enthusiasm that carried through the walls and into the visiting locker room above them.

Benson waited for quiet.

"Some of you might have heard that something happened out there at halftime. I don't know much about it, but it looks like somebody shot down their mascot falcon."

He gazed straight at Jake Powell.

"Nobody in this room better have had anything to do with it," he said.

Looking around the room, Benson added, "But I'm not going to let that ruin this: You just beat the number nine team in the country, and there wasn't one thing fluky about it. Good job, so enjoy this and then start thinking about Colorado."

# TWENTY-ONE: "FIRE"

Rick Winslow noticed that Jake quickly peeled off his uniform, put on his clothes and hustled out the door – without showering – moments before the reporters poured in.

Half the questions to Rick were about football: About how he was able to throw for 400 yards; how he was able to lead his team past the ninth-rated team in the country; and how he was going to be able to tell his grandchildren about the day he couldn't miss.

The other half were about the falcon.

∽

Jake and Kit found Annie at Terwilliger's, sitting at the bar among some friends. Jake didn't notice that Father Basinger was four stools down the bar. Kit did, but didn't say anything.

"Was it you?" Jake asked Annie.

"I didn't shoot it."

"I know that. But you planned it."

"It's a bird," Annie said. "Half the people who were so horrified go hunting every year and try to shoot something."

"That's different," Jake said.

"I know it is," Annie said, so earnestly that Jake decided she was hoping he could be won over. "This at least made a point. It was symbolism."

"What?"

"If they were so offended by this, why aren't they screaming about what the planes – the planes that the falcon stood for – have been doing in the bombing in Vietnam? It was only one bird. I don't like anything dying, Jake. You know me and animals. But it was a huge point."

She snatched a drumstick and pointed it at Jake. "Now sit down and have some chicken. Or do you feel bad about the way we kill seven million chickens every day, too?"

"Jesus, Annie!"

Everyone in Terwilliger's was watching and listening. It was impossible to cause a scene in this noisy place. They had managed it.

"I don't know how you did it," Jake said. "I don't know who you put up to it. I don't know how nobody saw it and nobody got caught.

At this point, I don't give a shit. I don't want anything else to do with you, period. You've ruined the Coalition, too."

"The Coalition isn't the cause, Jake. The cause is much bigger than that. But we'll make sure everyone knows that this wasn't the Coalition, if that makes you feel any better."

Still sitting on her pivoting stool, Annie reached out and put both hands on Jake's shoulders.

"We're beyond the point of just standing there and whining! They won't listen to reason. We've held signs, we've reasoned, we've campaigned for candidates, we've screamed – and the war goes on! And it won't matter who wins the election, either."

Jake pulled away.

"Aren't you supposed to call a radio station and brag and take credit for this?" he asked. "How's everybody going to understand your point if you don't explain it?"

"You'll think about this, too. Tomorrow, you'll be glad this happened. This and nothing more."

Jake grabbed Kit's hand. "Let's go."

As Jake and Kit took their first steps toward the door, Jake didn't even turn around when Annie called out. "Jake, really, it could have been worse!"

He thought she was being a smart-ass, but if he had turned around, Annie's imploring look would have convinced him otherwise.

Jake didn't notice Kit's long look back at Annie as, hand in hand, Jake and Kit walked to the door.

❦

Jake and Kit went to the *Times-Register* first. Next, they stopped at the Cascade television station, where Jake read his statement and answered questions for a reporter, all with a cameraman filming. Then Jake called the *Portland Herald*. Finally, he headed to Coach Benson's house.

Benson was hosting a party. Jake guessed the guests were boosters, sports writers, friends and coaches. The door was open, but Kit and Jake rang the doorbell anyway. Benson was civil to Kit when Jake introduced her. Jake, he just looked at. Shit, Jake thought, he's not just mad; he's hurt. When Jake handed Benson a sheet of paper from the small stack, the coach didn't even look at the mimeographed statement.

"Jake, one question for now. Promise me you didn't know."

It wasn't a question, but Jake wasn't going to point that out.

"No," he said, flustered. He didn't mean no, he couldn't promise, so he plowed on. "No, coach, I didn't know." He pointed to his extra sheets. "I hope this explains a little."

Benson wasn't going to read the sheet. Not yet. "You know who did it?"

"I have a pretty good idea."

"Who?"

Jake didn't say anything.

"We'll talk about this more tomorrow," Benson said.

"Thanks, coach."

"Don't thank me yet."

"So you know, we're going to President Hassler's now."

"Jake, he's here. He's had to be on the phone most of the time. I'll give this to him." Benson waved the sheet. "Trust me. If you think I'm angry, you should see him. No, I take that back. You shouldn't see him. I'll tell him you were here to see us both."

He shut the door. Jake didn't move, and Kit put her hand on his shoulder. Suddenly, he turned and drove his fist into the porch pillar, then strode off to Kit's car.

On the other side of the door, Benson didn't move. Suddenly, he turned and drove his fist into the alcove wall so hard, he had an ice bag on top of his hand 15 minutes later as he sat in his den with Hassler. Benson watched as the president silently read.

A STATEMENT FROM JAKE POWELL, CHAIRMAN OF THE CAMPUS COALITION AGAINST THE WAR

For immediate release

We organized a peaceful protest at the Air Force Academy-Cascade football game. We were protesting United States military and political policies as they pertain to Vietnam. In particular, we wanted to emphasize that the bombing halt does not excuse Air Force practices of the recent past, as so directed by the United States government and military leaders.

We deeply regret the halftime incident. As a coalition, we had no advance knowledge of anyone's plans in this regard. We understand we share the blame. We are not certain who fired the shot or shots, but will at least for the moment accept responsibility and express our deepest apology to anyone who was offended, including the representatives of the United States Air Force Academy and the fans in attendance. I believe the vast majority of those involved in this coalition and the antiwar movement in general share my disdain for this kind of conduct.

Nevertheless, we will continue to forcefully state our beliefs about the American military involvement in Vietnam.

Peace.

❦

"Think the papers will run it?" Jake asked Kit, reading it again as he sat on the end of the bed.

"Maybe part of it," Kit said. "They have to get all that stuff in about the game. You guys did beat mighty Air Force, after all."

"I almost forgot," Jake said, and then held up the paper again. "I still don't understand why you wouldn't let me say we were disowning whoever did this."

"Because we don't know the whole story."

"Come on, we do, too. As much as we need to know."

"I don't know that," Kit said.

# TWENTY-TWO:
## "THINK"

*(Sunday, November 10, 1968)*

When Jake Powell appeared in Larry Benson's office door, the coach was wearing gym shorts and a T-shirt and had the *Times-Register* sports section spread out in front of him.

"We have our Sunday morning basketball game in a little bit," Benson explained. "It's our therapy before all the films."

Benson quickly said that while he believed Jake didn't have anything to do with the shooting, he was holding Jake responsible as the leader.

"But coach…" Jake began. He knew it sounded like whining, so he stopped. He tried again. "How do we know somebody wouldn't have gone too far even if we hadn't organized the picketing?"

"That's what I told President Hassler last night. I promised him you didn't know and that you would have tried to stop it if you had." Benson locked eyes with Jake. "That's all true, right?"

"All true. I wondered if something else might be up. But I let everybody else know I thought anything else would be bullshit."

"So was it Annie Laughlin?"

"As far as I know, she's never shot a gun in her life."

"I'd assumed that. But she recruited somebody."

"I don't know."

"Jake, we're suspending you for one game."

Jake's initial reaction was relief: At least he was keeping his scholarship.

Then the relief changed to anger. He hadn't *done* anything.

"This is something we have to do," Benson added. "Your group made your point. I'm making mine. I'm using you to make the point to others, too. You've got a lot of rope, but you're accountable, too. And sometimes accountability isn't fair."

Jake sighed. "Want me at practice?"

"Of course," Benson said, a wry smile forming. "I know how much you *hate* practice."

In the locker room later, Jake was still trying to decide how mad he was when Carl Steele walked up. "This is supposed to be top secret," Steele said, "but the athletic director – your buddy – told us to throw you off the team. Larry told him no. He went right over his head to President Hassler, and Hassler said it was up to us."

Steele was walking away before Jake could react. But he turned back, suddenly, and added, "And I think I've figured out who did the shooting."

Jake said, "That's more than I know."

Steele gave him a long look of assessment. He decided Jake was telling him the truth.

❦

Father Basinger gave lip service to the church rule that only Catholics – confirmed or converted – could take communion. Yet he knew that non-Catholics often took the host and wine in the Newman Center, and he never quibbled with it. Still, he was surprised to see Annie Laughlin, kneeling, waiting for the host.

"*Corpus Christi,*" he said, and placed the host on her tongue.

"Thank you," she said, garbling it because the host was in the way.

The guy next to her at the rail grunted, letting Annie she hadn't gotten the protocol right.

She didn't care.

# TWENTY-THREE:
## "REVOLUTION"

*(Friday, November 15, 1968)*

Larry Benson could hear the buses idling outside his office window and smell the diesel fumes. The Fishermen were leaving for the airport and the trip to Colorado in a few minutes. As students hurried past the Hobson Court complex on their way to classes, the players milled around on the sidewalks, saying goodbye to girlfriends as if this were going to be a two-year tour of duty in Vietnam rather than a forty-hour excursion to the game in Boulder.

Loading his briefcase, Benson tried to convince himself he was overreacting, worrying so much about this game. The Fishermen were back in the top twenty, at number nineteen, and if they beat Colorado and Tillamook State, they would finish 8-3. Yet there were so many sideshows, it would be a miracle if they were cranked up for this game in Colorado.

The coaches yelled about the sloppy practices. They harped on the goals: Finish strong, move up in the polls, and end the season with the Fishermen's best record in years. They warned the players that the state of Colorado was primed to shower abuse on them because of what happened to the Air Force Academy Falcons – and to the falcon.

Benson didn't consider Jake Powell indispensable, but it wouldn't help that the Fishermen would be playing without one of their starting linebackers. Jake practiced with the team, but he wouldn't be going to Boulder. He worked so hard, Benson had a few regrets about suspending him, but he stuck by his decision.

Colorado was in fourth place in the Big Eight, yet the Buffaloes might go to a bowl game because their league was more flexible.

Benson snapped the briefcase shut and started down the hall to the bus. The receptionist was reading the *Campus Daily*. Even upside down, the headline got his attention: **SDS LEADER TAKES CREDIT FOR FALCON**

He went over and started reading over her shoulder, not noticing the byline.

⚭

The morning before the story ran, Annie showed up at Jake's place with two coffees and a bag of donuts. A red-eyed Kit instantly realized Annie had timed her arrival to miss Jake, who had left for his first class. "I'm going to give you the *real* story now," Annie said.

"What story?" Kit asked.

"The story for the *Campus Daily*. The falcon."

"You really want to do this?"

"Yes. It's not much of a statement if I'm not willing to stand behind it."

Kit had to prod Annie a couple of times, and accept that Annie still dodged a few questions.

"I think that's it," Annie finally said. "Except now you get to answer one."

"What?"

"Why were you crying when I showed up? Did you find out for sure?"

An hour later, Kit left Jake a note, saying she was skipping Fiction Writing – and all her other classes – to go to the *Campus Daily* office and write. On her way, she realized she probably needed a comment from Jake, too, so when he came out of Fiction Writing, she was waiting.

Now, on Friday morning, the *Daily* story was the talk of the campus – and of the town.

In the story, Annie said that she could promise that the Campus Coalition Against The War leadership had nothing to do with it. While she said she hadn't pulled the trigger, she refused to say who it was – or even if she knew who it was. She was vague enough to avoid being in handcuffs, but overt enough to be claiming credit. She also pointed out that nobody had attacked or harassed any human members of the Air Force contingent. How would everyone have felt if they had run out of the stands and, say, thrown blood on the Air Force quarterback in the middle of the third quarter? Or done something even worse?

# TWENTY-THREE: "REVOLUTION"

In the practice locker room, a few of the players still were loading their equipment bags, trying to be ready before the call to head to the buses. Others were finished and were sitting, reading the *Daily*.

Rick Winslow called over to the suspended Jake Powell, who had shown up to be with his teammates before they left him behind. Rick pointed at the story. "Jake," he said, "you really call Annie Laughlin that?"

"What'd he call her?" Todd Hendricks asked.

Rick read aloud. "'Arrogant, selfish, and short-sighted.'"

Jake nodded. He wondered how long it would be before he would forgive Annie. He was torn between now and never.

಄

When teacher Mike Schwartz walked through the door of the vacant South Cascade High classroom, Annie was seated at a desk in front, scribbling in a lesson-plan book.

"Hi," Annie said.

"Annie," he said, "I don't think this is a good idea."

"Why not?"

"We were just reading the *Campus Daily* in the faculty room. I think you better take the day off and see if the dust settles."

"Are you asking me?"

"I'm telling you."

Annie picked up her books and left. She wouldn't let herself cry.

಄

There was only so much they could take, Neal Hassler told himself angrily. There was a difference between rebelliousness and destruction. Though police already had questioned a stonewalling Annie, neither they nor the D.A. would be able to make a much of a case only with Annie's vague admission. They would work at trying to charge her with at least destruction of government property and malicious mischief, but tongues would have to loosen.

Hassler called the dean of women.

"I'm expelling Annie Laughlin," Hassler said.

Pause.

"I know that," Hassler said. "But I think I know how to take care of that. Find her. Tell her to be in my office at four this afternoon, and that if she truly is going to stand behind this, she'll be there."

She showed up.

"Your half-assed confession was pretty gutless," Hassler said. "You must not be very proud of what you did."

Annie smiled. "The cops tried that, too," she said.

"You think you could get away with laughing in our faces about this?"

"I'm not laughing," she said. And she wasn't.

"You're protecting someone," Hassler said.

"What do you mean?"

"The shooter."

She said nothing.

Hassler said, "I hope it's worth you getting expelled."

"You can't do that."

"The hell I can't."

"I'll appeal to the student conduct board. I'll demand it to be open. You'll have television cameras in there. You'll have twenty-seven reporters in there. It'll be 'The Falcon Murder Case.' You don't want that spectacle here, do you?"

"You won't appeal this. The *only* reason I'll regret doing this is you might be made a martyr. Maybe you'll learn that the First Amendment isn't a license to do whatever you want. Another school will admit you after a respectable delay, and I'll even recommend that somebody give you a second chance. But it can't be here. Of course, it also means the university is pulling you out of your student-teaching assignment."

Annie got up and started toward the door. "Nice try," she said.

"You know Kit Dunleavy, don't you?" Hassler asked.

Annie stopped.

"Of course, you know her," Hassler said, on the verge of mocking her. "She's your friend Jake Powell's girlfriend. She wrote that story this morning."

"What about her?"

# TWENTY-THREE: "REVOLUTION"

"I've been talking to the D.A. about that drug probe and Kit's story. We've decided that it's up to me. To get re-elected, the D.A. grandstanded about calling Kit before the grand jury. I'm guessing – okay, it's a little more than a guess – that the D.A. can back down if he can put it off on me. I'll be the, quote, university president who says the university would prefer not to see one of its students harassed in a clear violation of freedom of the press, unquote. And without the university going along, the D.A. reluctantly concludes it would be a waste of the public's time and tax dollars to pursue this case and this young woman. If you don't appeal, you ride off into the sunset for a year. Kit doesn't have to worry about it. You appeal? You make a stink? I tell the D.A. he's on his own limb. He's got to call Kit before the grand jury. It's my guess Kit says she won't reveal her sources. She's in contempt of court. She goes to jail for a few days, maybe longer. She gets a lot of sympathy and notoriety, but she's also got a record and a lot of other problems down the road you don't even think about."

"You're bluffing!"

"I'm not."

"I'll call a press conference right now and tell them you're blackmailing me."

"Think anyone would believe you? Or care? You're an extremist who would make anything up. You – or somebody – shot a bird in the middle of a stadium, remember?" Annie glared as Hassler said, "You brought me down to your level. We'll announce this Monday."

Hassler had counted on Annie having enough principle to worry about a friend, and enough humanity to care. He had counted on a limit to Annie's ruthlessness, and he had guessed that there might even be more to it than friendship with the Dunleavy girl. He was right – to what extent he didn't know, but he had been right enough to win. Yes, he congratulated himself.

Then he rushed into the bathroom and threw up.

&

Damn, Howie Hallstrom thought as he entered the bar next door to the hotel and joined the other assistant coaches. College women are getting younger every year. He was thirty-five. These women looked half his age to him. Shouldn't they be out babysitting or something?

Finally, Hallstrom got the bartender's attention. Carl Steele joined him and helped carry the glasses and beer over to the corner, where the assistants were standing and shouting. Some high school player – Hallstrom couldn't remember which one – once told him how the Colorado recruiter bragged that the legal drinking age was eighteen for the weaker 3.2-percent beer. In bars like this one, adjacent to the Boulder campus, customers could get tame beer and no hard liquor.

They gave up trying to carry on a conversation halfway through the house band's lame attempt to cover "Ruby Tuesday." They just stood and watched, signaling and screaming the order ("PITCHER OF COORS") from the waitress who finally discovered them, noticed the Fisherman caricature on Hallstrom's green sweater and asked in his ear if they were from Cascade. He nodded.

The band had just gone on break when Benson walked in, looking unhappy after going to dinner with Doubleheader and a couple of former Fishermen players who lived in the Denver area. The assistants got to stay at the hotel and watch the movie – *Bullitt* – with the players.

"It really wasn't that bad for a while," Benson said. "He was so excited about all the money that's going to be donated when we finish 8-3, he was almost tolerable. Then he started talking about this being the second season of the Wyden era, another forward step in his administration. Even when he's trying to compliment us, he can tick me off."

If they finished 8-3, they were Wyden's coaches. If they didn't, they were a bunch of bozos he had inherited.

❧

For weeks, Jake had been complaining that he was going to be in Colorado on the Friday night when shaggy-haired Welsh songsmith Donovan P. Leitch appeared in concert at Hobson Court.

After Jake told her of his suspension, Kit went to the information and ticket counter in the Student Union and paid ten dollars for two tickets. It was going to be one of her ways to bring him out of his funk.

When she handed him the envelope in his apartment and he pulled out the tickets, he exclaimed, "Wow! I'd forgotten all about this."

Kit smiled. "You could have just faked a sprained knee."

"What?"

"It would have been easier just to fake you're hurt than to find a way to get yourself suspended."

At least he laughed.

Donovan worked without an opening act. Twenty-five minutes after the scheduled 8 p.m. start, the head of the student body's entertainment and arts committee welcomed everyone – and then added a warning. Hobson Court's lower bowl seating area was all constructed of wood, and the fire marshals always were scared to death that the building was a potential inferno. "They mean business this time," the student said. "No smoking – of anything!" He waited for the laughter and hoots to die down. "Look," he said, "I'm not just saying it this time. They're telling us no more concerts after tonight if you don't pay attention!"

That triggered shrill whistles and boos.

"There," the student finally said, shrugging, "I've said my peace. And now," he said, pausing for effect and to let the lights go out, except for the spotlight at the one portal at floor level, "Donovan P. Leitch."

As Donovan walked through the portal and up the stairway to the stage, carrying his acoustic guitar as the spotlight followed, the small bright flames appeared at half the seats. Kit was one of the thousands holding a lit match aloft. After that went out, as Donovan was into his first song, many of the students around them lit joints. Jake was surprised that Kit didn't, but he also was distracted by Donovan's song selection.

Jake ended up singing along.

*"Oh, no, must be the season of the witch..."*

༺༻

After the concert, Annie was sitting at the top of the stairway outside Jake's door.

Kit saw her first, and her eyes widened. Jake noticed Kit's reaction first and then spotted Annie.

Jake stopped halfway up the last flight. Kit kept going.

"Hi," Kit said.

"Hi," Annie said.

Jake said nothing.

"Hassler threw me out of school," Annie said flatly. If Jake had been more prone to be sympathetic, Annie's lack of anger would have worried him. Annie without emotion wasn't Annie.

"You should be able to appeal, shouldn't you?" Kit asked.

Jake started up the final few stairs and was passing Annie when she said, "I'm not fighting it."

Jake got the door open. He turned. "Kit, you coming?"

Kit scrambled to join him in the doorway. "Jesus, Jake, did you hear what she just said?"

"I heard," he said.

Jake strode into his apartment, leaving the door open. Kit remained in the doorway and turned back. "Come on," she told Annie, nodding her toward the door. "He'll get over this. Let's talk about it."

Suddenly, Jake was back in the doorway.

"I said how I'd react if she crossed me on this," he said to Kit. "I'm only keeping my promise. Now, are you coming in or not?"

Annie stood up slowly.

"Kit, don't get caught in the middle on this," she said. "Call me tomorrow."

# TWENTY-FOUR:
## "IN SEARCH OF THE LOST CHORD"

*(Thursday, November 21, 1968)*

The Colorado collapse was an aberration. Larry Benson knew that. In Boulder, the Fishermen's coaches adjusted the gameplans, hollered, told the players that they had the character to come back, and stacked up the defense against the run even more than planned. Nothing worked in a 31-7 loss that ended under such foggy conditions along the Rocky Mountains, the film taken from the press box level in the fourth quarter was useless. To make matters worse, Timmy Hilton suffered a concussion in the third quarter and had to leave the game.

They had to rebound in the final game, the intrastate rivalry against Tillamook State. If they did, this still could be a pretty good season. The Fishermen were 6-4 and had a chance at finishing second in the league. Benson's teams were 0-4 against TSU. To some of the boosters, he knew, the problems against Tillamook State were the most important element of his coaching record. They didn't care as much about the Fishermen's recent dominance of the California schools, their return to the upper echelon of the league, and their entertaining style of play. Nope, they would find ways to grouse every season if the Fishermen didn't have at least nine wins, though a victory over TSU could lessen some of the sting.

Cascade and Tillamook, on the Pacific Coast Highway, were eighty miles apart. The teams could go into that last game without a win between them, and it would be a bitter sixty minutes. A writer started calling it "The Battle of Oregon" many years ago, and it stuck.

The joint meeting of the CU and TSU booster clubs in Portland was another game-week tradition, and so were the friendly wagers and taunts tossed back and forth among friends who had attended opposite schools.

Danny Dixon, the TSU coach, was a roly-poly Marine veteran of the island fighting in World War II, a drawling Texan who considered the toughest challenge of play-calling to be whether to run the fullback to the left or the right. At this luncheon, Dixon had the first turn at the microphone.

"I always get fired up during the Battle of Oregon week, and this is no different," Dixon thundered. "I thought about the Fishermen Sunday morning and threw up."

There was laughter all around. *Oh, that Danny.*

Benson liked Dixon, which was convenient because they attended the same events about twenty times a year. Dixon was a good man and a superb motivator. They also had figured out over beers that they were in the Pacific theater of combat at the same time – Dixon fighting on the ground, Benson flying overhead. After that, they were going to hate each other over a football game? Benson knew their disparate approaches were good for football in Oregon. Both programs were competitive in the Pac 8, even nationally. Oregonians didn't have a clue about how tough that was in a state of this size. Yet Benson was getting sick of listening to some of the parroted rhetoric about the images. Dixon's program had "discipline" because his players had short hair, no facial hair at all, and ran a no-nonsense, ground-oriented offense. TSU had some great players, some great young men, but that wasn't any monastery, either.

Dixon was done, and it was Benson's turn. "We're not proud of the way we played at Colorado, but we'll bounce back," he said. He fully understood that to the Fishermen fans in this room, there was only one way to walk off that field in Tillamook on Saturday and be proud – after a win. "I don't need to be reminded of our record in this game the last few years," he said, "and I'll certainly remind our players of that."

A lot of the Cascade boosters nodded at that one. *Yes, Larry, remind the boys, will you?*

"I know a lot of you also want to know if Timmy Hilton is going to play," Benson continued. "At this point, we don't know."

☙

The Newman Center's meeting room was jammed with reporters, including Kit Dunleavy. Father Robert Basinger was confessing.

"I was surprised I was able to do it with one shot," he said, "but I practiced a lot to get my eye back. I will continue to maintain it was the most effective symbolic protest we could come up with. It was not my idea alone, but I will accept full responsibility and whatever punishment comes from both civil and church authorities – for everything involved."

Even before he asked for questions, ten hands were up. He pointed at a woman from a Cascade television station.

"Why didn't you come forward when Annie Laughlin did?"

"I wish I would have," Basinger said. "We had talked about it. I thought we were going to do it together, but she jumped the gun." Basinger smiled sardonically. "No pun intended. She said she wanted to keep me out of trouble, but I decided I had to admit my role in this."

༄

As the semester wore on, Rick Winslow more frequently felt noticed on campus. There was the glance of recognition from other students as he passed them along the 23rd Avenue commons, the smile from the girl at the cash register in the bookstore, one student nudging another at the adjacent table in the Student Union. *Hey, that's Rick Winslow. You know, the quarterback.* It had taken a while, especially because he was not physically imposing. Timmy teased him that as skinny as he was, he looked more like a violin player than a quarterback.

Only two months ago, Rick had been perfectly willing – and expecting – to spend the season standing on the sideline, charting the plays on a clipboard while Tom Davis rang up big numbers as a senior and then came over and told Rick how he did it. Now the *Portland Herald* had run a big blowout on Rick this week, charting how his sophomore stats compared to the other top-drawer quarterbacks of recent years. His one-game performance against Air Force was not only a school record for passing yards, but also the best the *Herald* could dig up by a college sophomore ever. "He's one of those late bloomers who's going to be even better in college than he was in high school," Howie Hallstrom was quoted as saying in the *Herald*.

This was the first week he was feeling big-time pressure. Now that he was the proven quarterback of record, now that they already were talking about career school records and maybe future

All-America status, he would either produce against TSU...or maybe watch those looks from women take an ugly turn for a week or so. Now he was both embarrassed and surprised by the review on numbers here in Spanish.

Maya Leon, the teacher, was a gorgeous, dark-skinned graduate student from Peru earning her tuition by teaching this beginning section. She'd written numbers on the board and asked someone to say them in Spanish. When they were done, she said they represented her prediction of Rick's statistics – 25-for-31 passing, for 312 yards – and the final score in next Saturday's game: 34-10, Cascade. Until today, he had no indication that she had even understood who he was...or knew anything at all about the game that the silly Americans called football.

As he was walking out of Spanish, Maya Leon smiled at Rick and said, "My boyfriend says you will kick the Trappers' asses."

"Muchas gracias," he said.

He'd see what he could do.

As they walked out the door after class, one of Rick's dialogue buddies caught up with him and said, "Too bad about the boyfriend."

ॐ

Maybe he was out of touch, Neal Hassler decided, because only now he was beginning to realize that the football game against Tillamook State was the most important university event of the year. He had heard that the *Times-Register* was putting out a special supplemental section tomorrow on the game. They hadn't done anything that thorough about the financial crisis in higher education. Dollars were drying up, tuition was skyrocketing, and some of the best professors were bailing out because they could make much more money in other states. Yet football was all anyone wanted to talk about this week. Well, that and the fire department's insistence that no more concerts could be held in Hobson Court because of the students' contempt for the no-smoking pleas before some singer's concert last Friday. Amazingly, the priest's admission that he had done the shooting already seemed to have taken more steam out of the Falcon shooting controversy, a trend that had started when Hassler announced Annie Laughlin's expulsion. Hassler was surprised that everyone seemed to realize that just because the Newman Center was in the campus area and catered to the university constituency, the university president couldn't control the priest – apparently no more than could the pope.

Hassler was offended when the vice president for finance off-handedly added in a budget meeting this week that a football win against Tillamook State might help general contributions.

"Let me get this straight," Hassler said, sharply enough to cause four departments chairmen to look up in surprise. "If the football team beats TSU, we can break ground on the new married housing on Monday?"

The old married-student housing complex was a string of huts across the street from the track and field stadium, Burleson Field, on campus. The huts were erected during World War II, and the plan then was that they would be only stopgap housing and come down after the war. Nearly a quarter of a century later, they still were in use and were a campus eyesore.

Hassler took a call from Paul Weaver, one of the university's most prominent alums, a contributor in the capital campaigns. Foundations were far bigger contributors, but as an individual, Weaver ranked at the top of the list. When Weaver started out by saying he didn't want to make too big a deal out of football, Hassler knew Weaver was going to do just that. With all this talent, Weaver said, this team should have done better. He said that if the Fishermen lost Saturday, "it might be time to make changes." He made no financial threats. He didn't mention what changes.

Why could football turn otherwise intelligent people – lawyers, educators, whomever – into babbling idiots? Hassler had been at presidents' conferences when his counterparts from other schools, including one of the most brilliant historians in academia, salivated and ran off at the mouth about the football team making the university proud – or bemoaned the lack of success as a "disgrace." Don't need that garbage, Hassler thought. Sure would make it a lot easier for everyone, though, if they beat TSU.

൭

Annie met Kit at The People's Bakery.

In mid-afternoon, the place was nearly deserted, so they had a corner of the bakery to themselves as they sipped their coffees.

They talked for twenty minutes, and very little of it was about the falcon.

∽

The seniors asked if they could delay the start of practice a few minutes so they could preside over a team meeting after everyone was dressed. No offense, they said, but without the coaches.

"No problem," Hallstrom told captain Alex Tolliver. "We'll just go have a pitcher or two at Terwilliger's."

"Fifteen minutes," Benson said.

As the coaches waited on the practice field, Benson sat on the edge of the trainers' table along the sideline, talking with reporters. What else could these guys want to know? Already this week, he had spoken at one breakfast, two booster luncheons and one media luncheon, and also after three practices. During the rivalry week, the writers bothered to show up regularly. Yes, he said, they'd be able to adjust if they didn't have Timmy Hilton. No, he said, he didn't know if there was a bigger rivalry anywhere.

This would be his seventeenth Battle of Oregon as an assistant or head coach. The players were in the programs for only four or five years, and some of them weren't as fanatical as the fans. That was the part that sometimes got to him. The fans always want to talk history, but all the seniors know, Benson thought, is that they are 0-2 against the Trappers – and they don't want to go out 0-3.

Back in the locker room, Tolliver said, "I don't want to leave here saying I've never beaten the goddamn Trappers." Alex cussed only about one thing: The Goddamn Trappers.

When it was his turn, Jake Powell said he was tired of visiting Roseburg every summer and having to listen to the shit from rednecks who went to Tillamook State – either now or in the past.

"I guess it's a miracle I'm standing up here," he said. "A lot of other coaches around would have tossed my ass out off the team a long time ago."

"And with good reason," Timmy Hilton said, smiling.

That did get a laugh.

"I'd do anything to win this game," Jake declared.

Todd Hendricks smiled wickedly. "Anything?" he asked.

"Anything," Jake said.

Todd sprang up from his locker and scurried into the training room. Jake was afraid he knew why. He was right. Seconds later, a grinning Todd was back, holding scissors and the clippers they used to shave hair off their ankles before getting taped.

"We're about to have a team bonding experience," Todd said.

He turned on the clippers.

Other players yelled and laughed. "Yeah!" "Take it all off!"

Jake sighed.

"Let's go," Todd said. "I saw how they did this in the Army."

Jake walked with Todd to the sink, looked in the mirror for a second and said, "So long."

෴

About halfway through practice, Steele noticed that Powell kept playing with his helmet, as if it didn't fit. There wasn't the usual mane between his helmet and the neck ring he wore above his shoulder pads. And about four times now, somebody had called Powell "Butch."

Walking back up the hill after practice, Jake finally took off his helmet. They hadn't done a bad job of it, but a crewcut on Jake was a shock – at least to the coaches. He could have been a trainee in Camp Pendleton, rather than a picketer outside its gates.

෴

Timmy heard pads pop as he jogged around the perimeter of the practice field in the rain. He felt left out – and very wet. When you were a part of the practice, running through the drills and the plays or talking with teammates during the lulls, the rain wasn't bothersome. When you were off running by yourself, in helmet and shorts, the drops got between the facemask; the T-shirt underneath the practice jersey seemed as if you'd just taken it out of the washer, during the wash cycle; and the mud clamped onto your calves.

He still felt a little sluggish, although five days had passed since he suffered the concussion when he slid into a retaining wall at Colorado. He knew the trainers were watching every sluggish step. The doctors had declared that without a miracle recovery, he shouldn't play Saturday against Tillamook State. You don't screw around with concussions, they said.

"I just got my bell rung," he insisted.

He knew it was more than that, because even that night, the headache wouldn't go away and he felt dizzy each time he got up and tried to move around the apartment.

"How ya' feelin'?" David Armstrong called out from the couch.

"I have an idea," Timmy said dryly. "Let's see if you can go a whole hour without asking me that again."

"Come on, how ya' feelin'?"

"I feel okay."

"And?"

"I don't know. Doc's taking another look tomorrow."

Timmy wasn't sure who wanted him to play more: himself or David. The Cascade and TSU basketball teams played four times a year, and they hated each other even more than the football teams did.

❦

Back in Jake's apartment after eating and arguing at Carlo's Pizza, Kit was exasperated.

"At this rate, the church is going to forgive Father Basinger before you forgive Annie," she said sharply.

"No doubt about it," Jake said. "I'm not very good at turning the other cheek, either."

Jake insisted that Father Basinger's statement didn't change anything.

Kit headed toward the door. "I'm going to let you get your rest," she said. "And let you think some more."

Jake caught up and hugged her. "Don't be silly," he said. "Stay."

"It's not silly," she said, accepting the hug, but not returning it. "I'm not staying."

## TWENTY-FOUR: "IN SEARCH OF THE LOST CHORD"

"Okay, I'll walk you back," he said.

Until they were halfway to the sorority, he was convinced she was going to change her mind and go back with him.

# TWENTY-FIVE:
## "WAITING FOR THE SUN"

*(Saturday, November 23, 1968)*

Gazing blankly ahead, Larry Benson sat on a bench in the corner of the tiny coaches' locker room, waiting for the writers to scramble into position around him. They knew enough to be solemn.

Flatly and wearily, he gave Tillamook State credit "for a fine game."

Dusty Harris sounded almost apologetic to be asking anything. "Would you have won with Timmy Hilton?"

"I don't know. We're not going to make any excuses."

A writer Benson didn't recognize coughed as if it set up his question. "Does this make the season a total disappointment?

"No. Not after all we've been through, as a team, as young men, as coaches."

He knew what they wanted to ask: Oh and five against the Trappers, Larry, what about it?

Nobody brought that up.

There was silence, except for the scratching of pens. They were all caught up with him, and now a few of them were underlining his last sentence, doodling, evaluating their handwriting, doing anything to avoid looking him in the eye.

Benson's teenage son, Charlie, came in and sat in a corner.

"It's just that I wanted to win," Benson said. Well, no kidding, he thought, so he tried again. "This game is blown into strange shapes and proportions. But the game is still for the young people, and I wanted our people to have the experience of winning this game. It's not to settle a bet, or what the coach wants, or what the alumni want. It's still for the younger people."

The writer Benson didn't recognize had gotten up his nerve.

"Do you think your job is in danger?"

༄

It was only a stupid game, and yet Jake Powell couldn't stop sniffling, reaching for his eyes and coming away with damp knuckles. He didn't really care that this had been his last football game, unless you counted future touch games in the Sunday recreation leagues. He had accepted that, even looked forward to moving on, not because he hated the game, but because he was ready to escape its hold. But it had ended 33-32, 33-to-goddamn-32, because they couldn't stop 'em when it counted. He'd missed about three tackles himself, tackles that could have left the Trappers short on the third-down plays, including one in TSU's game-winning drive in the final minutes.

But they lost, trudged up the ramp, out of TSU's stadium and into the basketball arena, where Benson walked around the basement dressing room and thanked each of the seniors. Until then, Jake had managed to be stoic. He even ignored the shit from the idiotic fringe of the TSU fans, who told them to go back to their LSD. But now, as he had been for five minutes, he was on the verge of tears. Over a stupid football game. And this on top of everything else.

❧

Timmy wondered if he should have told them to stop shining those lights in his eyes because he was going to play whether they cleared him or not. If he had played, the Fishermen would have been so far ahead, TSU's grind-it-out offense would have done nothing but kill the clock and keep the point margin under 35. He was certain he would have been great, and he didn't feel at all arrogant for thinking that. It only made him sadder. And then mad.

❧

Rick Winslow was ten minutes into his shower, staring into the water as it ran down his face. He laughed bitterly. Maya Leon had been about *sesenta* – or sixty – yards off. The reporters had told him he had thrown for 250 and change against the Trappers. Big deal. The Fishermen lost...to the Trappers. He supposed he would remember his two touchdown passes in the wild fourth quarter, the second one to Keith Oldham when they were trailing 27-24. He really thought it was going to be their day when they botched the snap on the extra-point attempt, but Rick, the holder, managed to heave a pass for the two-point conversion that made it 32-27. Even after TSU took a 33-32 lead, he thought that had just set the stage. This was why they'd been practicing that two-minute drill forever, and they would pull it off, just as they pulled it off against UCLA. This time, though, they got only as far as midfield before they ran out of downs.

Rick would remember that final fourth-down play, when they had caught the Trappers in the exact line stunt they expected, had the trap block all set up and had the hole open from here to Pendleton. But Rick got caught thinking too much, looking ahead, and turned the wrong way, and when he figured it out, it was too late. He was buried, short of the first down. He walked over to the sideline, in tears. Larry Benson met him.

"I lost the game!" Rick managed to blurt out.

"Stop that!" Benson said sharply. "You keep your head up! You did *not* lose this game!"

But Rick couldn't forget. If they'd gotten that first down, they would have needed only one more first down to be in field-goal range and...

If...if...if. This goddamn season was turning into too many "ifs." Now, he thought, they'd have to wait another year before they kicked the Trappers' asses.

∾

Neal Hassler never before had visited the Fishermen's locker room after a game. Today, he felt the urge. He wanted to see what he could do to dilute the gloom.

Benson accepted his handshake with a tight smile. The only sounds in the players' locker room were the showers running in the distance and pads being dropped on the floor.

∾

Bill Wyden took it surprisingly well until Jim Jerold, the Tillamook State athletic director, searched him out after the game. Anyone could see Jerold coming about three blocks away because of his orange sport coat. Jerold said it had been a hell of a game and a credit to state of Oregon college football and all that shit, but Wyden was certain that the son of a bitch was just trying to rub it in with phony kindness. Cascade was 0-2 against the Trappers in the Wyden era. What else mattered?

◠ꙩ

Kit and Lisa decided to wait out outside the basketball arena, near the team bus, and see if Jake wanted to ride back to Cascade with them.

Naomi Reynolds, the professor's wife and Chris' mother, headed for the parking lot beyond the arena with a group of friends from her Cascade repertory company. They had come in four cars, met near one of them and drank beer and vodka for two hours, then went into the game.

Naomi noticed Kit near the bus and peeled off from her group. "Be right there!" she hollered at the twenty-something English teacher, her latest leading man, and waved at her friends to keep going.

"I've been reading your articles," Naomi said. "You're getting very good, young lady."

"Thanks."

"And they're sure giving you a lot to write about."

She looked at Lisa. Kit took that as a signal to introduce Lisa. "This is Chris' mom."

Chris' mom plowed ahead. "He's going to be here for Christmas," she said.

"I know. He's even writing me letters this time."

"He wants to see you."

"I know."

"He gets sappy about you."

"I know."

"He's a good kid."

"I know that, too."

"Okay," she said, laughing. "Just so you know."

A few strides away, she turned around and said on the move, "And wait 'til next year!"

Jake had emerged from the dressing room and was just close enough to hear that.

"That's the problem," he said when he reached Kit and Lisa. "I don't have a next year."

## TWENTY-FIVE: "WAITING FOR THE SUN"

He rode back to Cascade with Kit and Lisa, but didn't say a word for the first thirty miles.

&#8766;

Howie Hallstrom and Carl Steele were the first two on the bus. Neither of the coaches felt like standing outside the arena, making small talk while they waited for the players.

Hallstrom lifted his briefcase with both hands, and then threw it down against the seat. He looked at Steele and shook his head.

"You know," he said, "someday we'll look back on this and... and..."

"And still cry," Steele said.

&#8766;

Alone in her apartment, Annie listened to the entire game on the radio. She never had done that before. She listened for Jake's name, and didn't hear it often.

# TWENTY-SIX:
## "WHITE ROOM"

*(Wednesday, November 26, 1968)*

Bill Wyden spelled it out for Neal Hassler, who had returned to Cascade after a two-day trip to a seminar in Los Angeles. Larry Benson's five-year contract ran through June, or the rest of the university's fiscal year. That had been the arrangement at Cascade for as long as anyone could remember. When Hank Gardenia moved up to briefly become the athletic director and appointed Benson as his successor, the former coach resisted some mild pressure to "modernize" the arrangement for Benson and have its expiration date shortly after a football season. The way Gardenia looked at it, it would give Benson about six months of severance pay if the shit hit the fan, and that seemed fair to him. None of the assistants had contracts at all.

Wyden argued they couldn't stand pat. It wasn't only the "it's-time-for-a-change" post-season letters to the editor and the athletic director. Some of the big-money boosters were steamed about the collapse in the final two games. "Paul Weaver said he talked to you last week," Wyden told Hassler.

Hassler nodded. "What are you getting at?"

"We at least have to take a look at this. Larry's still popular with a lot of people, I know. I like him myself. But if we decide he stays, I think we have to tell him to start clamping down on his program and make some staff changes."

"Staff changes? Which coaches are we talking about here?"

"Can I be blunt?"

"Please."

"A lot of the boosters want Larry out. The only way Larry can stay and we can have any credibility with the boosters is to show them that we did something, that things are going to change – even if Larry's still the coach. I think that means three, maybe four new coaches."

"Who gets let go?"

Wyden shrugged. "Doesn't matter," he said. "We just have to show them we're doing something."

Hassler stood and walked over to the corner of his office.

"Bill," he began, "a lot of people are saying the same things about me that you've just said about Larry." Wyden said nothing, so Hassler continued. "He's running a competitive program. Right? He's not cheating. Right?"

"Well..."

"Two weeks ago, we were rated...what?"

"Nineteenth."

"Out of how many teams in the country?"

"Hundred and something. But that was two weeks ago – the rated part."

"I know. But tell me, are the people who are telling you how unhappy they are, are they all just going to stop going to the game and stop donating money and buying tickets if we don't fire Larry or make him sign some sort of blood oath? Or tell him he's got to give the boosters the scalps of some of his assistants? I wanted to win that game Saturday, too, but aren't these people just blowing hot air? Paul Weaver will get over it. So will the others."

"Dr. Hassler, I don't think it's that simple. Larry's not so much the issue as the direction of the program. There's a general feeling, especially in Portland, that this program is out of control."

"Would it have been, quote, in control, unquote, if we'd scored two more points on Saturday and beat the Trappers?"

"Dr. Hassler–"

"You talk with Larry. You say what you think. If you want to tell Larry to evaluate his staff, fair enough. But I'm not going to overreact to a few blowhards out there. Larry's the coach here next season, as far as I'm concerned. I want him to have a new contract soon. Okay?"

❧

Even after that post-practice session with Wyden four weeks ago, Benson hadn't taken seriously the possibility of not being back next season. While he'd heard the grumbling about that loss to Tillamook State, he was convinced he had built up enough goodwill during his seventeen seasons in Cascade, both as an assistant and head coach, to overcome this disappointment. Yet when the reporters were skittish about asking about his future in the interviews for the postseason wrap-up sessions, he wondered what they had heard. Wyden seemed to be avoiding him. The staff already had met and charted out the recruiting plans for the next few weeks, shooting to land a couple of junior-college defensive backs or maybe a good defensive lineman, because that's where they needed immediate help. They would hit the road next week. Or would they?

Benson found Wyden. "What's the story, Bill? I've got a staff with plane tickets in their pockets for recruiting. I've got the all-star game coming up." He was one of the coaches for the North in the Hula Bowl in Honolulu. "Is there going to be a problem here?"

"You're the coach, Larry," Wyden said.

"Am I getting a new contract or not?"

"We need to talk about changes. I told you that a few weeks ago. And that was before that finish."

Benson was seething. He wished he had gone straight to Hassler.

"I told you, Bill," he said. "I told you that if you want me, you live with my decisions on this staff. This is a good staff and I want to keep it together. You know, everybody told me after last season that I should ask for an extension then, but I was too stupid to do it."

Wyden reminded himself that Dr. Hassler had mandated a new contract. His options were to stall and see if Hassler was forced out soon, or go over the president's head. He hadn't ruled either out.

"Larry, I've decided to recommend that you get a new contract," he said. "But there's no rush. Your old one has months left. I need you to be more open-minded about this. Think about whether the staff needs new blood – maybe all new blood."

"Bill, I wanted to win more games. Maybe we should have. But was this a bad staff when we beat Stanford and UCLA?"

Wyden raised his hand. "Larry, give me some credit. I haven't ordered you to do anything, have I? I want to put this on hold until you think this through."

❧

The day before, Bill Wyden had told Dusty Harris to call this afternoon because Wyden might have something to say then. Harris almost had written a speculation story on the spot for today's paper. He could have batted it out in five minutes, saying Bill Wyden wouldn't comment on the future of Larry Benson, and something might happen on Wednesday. No matter how many times Harris tried to get Wyden to hint that he was on the right track, Wyden had refused to help. Just call back in twenty-four hours, he said.

When Harris called, Wyden said he didn't know what all the fuss was about. Harris believed Wyden just enough to write the story as if he believed him completely.

> By DUSTY HARRIS, Herald Staff
>
> Bill Wyden, the Cascade University athletic director, Wednesday lined up in solid support of Larry Benson, the Fishermen's head football coach.
>
> Wyden declared that Benson "can be the coach for the next 20 years, if he wants, and if I have anything to do with it."
>
> Wyden's stance should quiet talk that criticism from a few vocal critics could force Benson out of his job.
>
> Benson's contract is due to expire at the end of June, but renewal now is expected to be a formality.

&#x221e;

Annie Laughlin and Peter Shapiro were on a bench in Memorial State Park, twenty-five miles outside of Cascade. Annie had just told him the whole story.

"I should never talk to you again," Shapiro said. "But I'll give you credit for coming up with something almost as good."

"Better."

"That's debatable."

"But you can't question the price I'm paying. It'll end up taking me longer to graduate than you did. And that's *if* I can get back into school somewhere."

&#x221e;

"It'd keep me out of trouble," Timmy Hilton said with a smile.

Even after all he'd gone through already today, Benson managed to laugh. At least Timmy hadn't come in and announced he was taking a year off for a visit to Tibet. Timmy was asking for permission to go out for the basketball team, as soon as the doctors gave him the go-ahead.

"Timmy, they've been practicing for weeks. They've got their first game next week! Even if Coach Vickers let you come out, you'd be that far behind."

"Coach, I know I can play with those guys. I did all right on the freshman team. I want to try."

"How about school?"

"I'm all caught up."

"How about getting hurt? You blow out a knee, you could cost yourself a ton of pro football money."

"I could get hit by a bus, too. Besides, if I don't go out, I'd be playing in the pickup afternoon games in the P.E. gym."

"Let me think about this, okay? When are you seeing the doctors again?"

"Monday."

"Let's see what they say, and we'll go from there."

"All right," Timmy said. He waited a moment. "Coach, I don't know if this will just make you feel worse, but I wish I would have worked harder at talking them into letting me play on Saturday. I'll always feel bad about that."

"We'll get 'em next year."

◦◦

Half an hour south of Cascade, Jake Powell decided that Kit drove like his grandmother. The drive to Medford, which should take two and a half hours, was going to take forever. Maybe she was too caught up in briefing him about her family.

At least she was talking to him. Preoccupation was a big thing with her lately, and he wasn't sure whether it was all because of his refusal to forgive Annie, or something else.

Kit said he'd like the sofa bed in the family room, that Uncle Cal would bend his ear about his old football days at Medford High, and that if Tillamook State came up, he should avoid calling them the "Fucking Trappers." Her dad would grouse about lumber not selling as well as it should, but when he said something about how things would pick up now that the Republicans were getting back into power, Jake should bite his lip.

Kit said her dad knew all about Jake's politics. After the Air Force week, who didn't? Her dad wouldn't agree with him on much, but he wouldn't automatically hate Jake. Because Jake put on those football pads, he had a touch of immunity in her dad's eyes. Her younger sister, the high school senior, would find a reason to walk into the family room at five in the morning to see what Jake looked like asleep, to see if he snored or if Kit had sneaked down in the middle of the night.

"Despite everything," Kit said, "if you don't eat the stuffing with your hands, they'll like you." She laughed. "After Chris, they'll be happy you're not an actor." She took her eyes off the road just long enough to take one more look at his hair. After a week of coaxing, Jake was able to get a little on top to respond to the direction of his new comb. "They'll like you more the second they see your hair."

When they had reached Roseburg, Kit announced, "Last chance." For days, she had been lobbying for Jake to stop to see Annie's parents, who had been so good to him after his mother and stepfather moved to Pittsburgh. Jake knew they would have gotten around to asking him to try to forgive Annie.

Jake was weakening. He thought President Hassler's expulsion of Annie was too harsh. Even if she were charged with anything, Annie probably would get probation at worst. He also was impressed with Annie's most recent actions. Some of the information came via Kit, and the rest via the campus grapevine.

Annie stepped in and told the rest of the SDS and Bill Charles, among others, that she had decided to accept the unjust expulsion because it would advance their cause. It was so obviously excessive, she said, the fence sitters might see the need to get involved. Annie asked them to forget those plans to demonstrate at Hassler's office.

In Kit's story, Annie outlined her plans to first spend a year traveling and advancing the SDS cause, especially if Nixon didn't pull the troops out of Vietnam in his first week in office.

"Jake, I think that's the only thing Annie regrets," Kit said now. "The way it's affected you two."

"She should have thought of that before."

# TWENTY-SEVEN:
## "HAIR!"

*(Thursday, December 12, 1968)*

When Larry Benson and Howie Hallstrom checked in at the main office of Wheat Ridge High School in Beaverton, where they were about to pay another visit to a potentially difference-making tackle, the school's football coach was waiting. After the handshakes, the coach told them he had just gotten a call from President Hassler's office, handed Benson a message slip and said that the woman had asked Benson to call ASAP. The Wheat Ridge coach pointed to an unoccupied counselor's office and said, "Dial 9 to get out."

"Oh, shit," said Hallstrom, thinking the worst. A pink slip by phone.

After placing the collect call and being patched through to Hassler, Benson listened for a minute. To Hallstrom, standing by the desk, it seemed like five. Benson finally shook his head. "Anybody talked to Timmy?"

Benson looked at his watch.

"That's cutting it tight," he said. "We'll be spending at least a half-hour with the player here, then heading back."

Pause.

"All right, I'll be there," Benson said.

Disgusted, Benson turned to Hallstrom. "Hair again."

"Just hair?" Hallstrom asked.

Benson filled him in.

༄

Jonathan Vickers, the stern young X's and O's basketball coach who became the Cascade program's first full-time assistant in 1967, took over the reins when head coach Don Barnes suffered a severe heart attack two weeks before the first game. Vickers' stint as head coach might be for just one season or it might be permanent, depending on how both Barnes and Vickers did. Despite their worries about their ill coach and their misgivings about his replacement, the Fishermen adapted. They beat Seattle Pacific, George Fox College, and Eastern Washington in their first three games.

Backup guard Timmy Hilton jokingly asked why they couldn't schedule the football season this way. "We'd *own* George Fox!" he said.

After practice on Wednesday, with the opening road trip to Spokane for a game against Gonzaga coming up, Vickers asked Timmy to stay. In a matter-of-fact tone, the coach told Timmy he needed to get a haircut by the next afternoon. It wasn't a bitter ultimatum or anything close, and he might as well have been reminding Timmy to pack his basketball shoes.

"Why?" asked Timmy.

"Because you need one."

"Coach, I don't think I do."

"Well, I do. When you're representing this university, you should meet some standards of appearance."

"Whose?"

"Mine. At least to start with. To win, this program needs discipline. Besides, you're not even on one of our scholarships, so we did you a favor by even taking you on the team."

A favor? He already was the third-best guard and threatening to break into the starting lineup – if Vickers was open-minded!

"If Lou Alcindor was on our team, would you tell him the same thing?" Timmy asked, referring to the UCLA star center whose hair was every bit as long.

"Sure would."

Timmy loved his hair, loved toying with it and getting it just right. He loved his father, the barber and Pentecostal minister, but he didn't drastically cut his hair for his father; and he was going to do it for Vickers? When he did go home, he didn't pick out his hair as he usually did, and it could look much shorter than it had on campus the day before. Timmy surmised he could pass Vickers' inspection by snipping here and there himself, then scrunching his hair instead of lifting it with a pick. Yet Vickers' attitude ticked him off, and he wasn't going to back down.

Timmy pivoted and went down the stairway to the locker room, where he filled in David Armstrong, whose blond curly hair wasn't much shorter than Timmy's. "Guess I'm not playing basketball any more," he told David. "It was fun while it lasted."

# TWENTY-SEVEN: "HAIR!"

The next morning, a phone call from Bill Charles, the head of the Black Student Organization, awakened Timmy.

"We're not taking this lying down," Bill said.

"I *am* lying down," Tommy said.

"Well, get your ass out of bed and we're going to get something done."

"How'd you find out about this?" Timmy asked.

"I've got my sources," Charles said.

෨

The rattle in the lock awakened Jake, and he turned to the door in time to see Kit walk in. Almost like old times, Jake thought.

They were due to turn in their Fiction Writing projects this morning. Jake had one more final exam today, but he had gone to *Barbarella* the night before with a couple of teammates and had gotten a full night's sleep. Without Kit, he had to settle for Jane Fonda in his dreams.

This exam would be a cakewalk. Professor Athearn served up broad essay questions in every History of Oregon test, and Powell knew he could bluff his way through it.

"Where's your story?" she asked.

Jake tossed her a theme folder with his short story, about a magic soccer ball.

Kit sat down on the floor, opened the cover and started reading.

As Jake turned on the water in the tub, climbed in and started trying to get clean without a showerhead, he wondered again what had gone wrong. Kit hadn't stayed over since they returned from the Medford Thanksgiving trip, which had gone well – at least as far as he could tell. He hadn't said "Fucking Trappers" or responded to her sister's teasing flirting. He had helped Kit's mother clean off the table and hadn't blown up when her uncle asked how he could stand playing with all those "nee-gras." He had civil conversations with her father, even about politics, and he discovered Kit's father wasn't so much for the war as he was against the "disrespectful" dissension. By the time they left for Cascade, he seemed convinced that Kit and

Jake didn't throw shit – real shit – at the police and that they weren't the only anti-war protesters in the country who were that civilized.

After returning to Cascade, Kit said the final weeks of the semester were so frantic, they both would be better off if she slept at the sorority.

When Kit was done reading, Jake was dressed.

"B-plus," Kit said, closing the folder and smiling.

"Good enough," he said.

"Good morning," Annie said, strolling through the unlocked door.

To Jake, this seemed a setup. Kit looked at him, shrugged and said, "Time for you two to talk." Jake walked over and picked up his coat and acted as if he had a class that started in two minutes.

"NO!" Kit said. "You're staying here and you're talking. Or I swear to God, *I'm* never talking to *you* again."

Jake froze. Instead, Kit gathered up her coat and books and left.

Annie stood in front of the Bobby Kennedy poster, staring and saying nothing.

Jake went over to the sink and poured a glass of water. Annie turned to watch. "Jesus," she said after a second, "there are sea animals growing in that glass!"

Jake smiled darkly and held it up, squinting at the filthy glass. "Well, what have they ever done to me?" He held the glass out, making a silent toast, then downed the water in one long drink.

He hadn't turned around when he started, and was looking at Annie in the mirror.

"I don't know if I can ever completely forgive you," he said tentatively.

"Ninety percent would be good enough," Annie said.

"I know you believed in what you did. But do you really think you accomplished anything?"

"I don't know," Annie said, softer now. "But if we just stood by and–"

"Stop it!"

As he shouted, Jake grabbed the glass, lifted it and cocked it, as if he were about to throw it against the wall.

Catching himself, he turned and faced her, pleading with both hands, the glass in one of them. "You don't need to make a speech with me, okay? I know why you did it!"

"Then why–"

"Because I damn near begged you not to do anything like that! I said you'd be risking our friendship, and you went ahead and did it anyway!"

Jake slammed the glass back down, but it didn't break.

Annie sat on the bed, running her hands through her hair and looking down. "There's more to this than you and me," she said.

"I guess that's where we're different, Annie. I think about that. You don't."

"I thought about it. A lot. If I hadn't, I would have gone along with what–"

She stopped.

"What?" Jake asked.

Annie put her head back in her hands. "Some of them wanted to blow up the plane, too," she said.

"What?"

"The Air Force team plane. Some of the Magicians wanted to blow it up."

"Jesus..."

"Not with anyone on it, at least. It was parked off to the side at the airport."

"When?"

"Saturday. It was going to go off about when they thought it'd be halftime."

Jake strode over to the corner, angrily, and then turned around.

"That could've killed somebody," he said.

"They swore way they had it planned, nobody would be hurt."

Jake sat on the bed, next to her. "So why didn't it happen?" he asked.

"The police and feds were guarding the plane," Annie said.

"Guess they weren't as stupid as you thought."

"I made sure they weren't."

"And how did you do that?"

"I told the police."

For an instant, Jake thought she was going to cry. Instead, she looked straight at him, her eyes reddened and wetter than usual, but still defiant.

"Just the Cascade police," she said. "Wrote a note, went downtown, and left it on a cop car outside Original Ollie's."

"When was that?"

"That week."

"And what did the note say?"

"You can't tell another soul this." Jake noticed she didn't even pause to make him promise. "The note said they needed to guard the plane close because the Magicians – I didn't name them – were planning to do something."

"They had somebody on the inside? Like on the airport crew?"

"I'm pretty sure they did. That's the only way they could have been that confident."

Jake exhaled loudly and shook his head. "They're going to get you in over your head sometime."

"I can handle it."

"Can you?" He got up from the bed and started pacing. He grabbed a sweatshirt off the floor, just to have something in his hands. "You say that, but if they're fanatics, you know that sometime you won't be able to talk them out of something – and you might get caught up in it!"

Springing up from the edge of the bed, she grabbed the sweatshirt from him, dropped it and took his hands. "Don't you see? That's why the falcon thing was so important! It got the message across, and it was a lot better than the alternative!"

Jake looked at her for a few seconds. "I won't ever agree about that," he said, flatly.

"But don't you understand a little more now?"

Reaching slowly, he hugged her. It was not a passionate embrace of lovers, but a reaffirmation of friendship. As he held her, he asked, "Did you tell Kit this when she wrote the *Daily* story?"

"No. Not everything. Don't you, either. At least not now."

Jake pulled away and looked at her, excitedly. "I *am* going to tell President Hassler!"

"No!"

"Why not? I never understood why you didn't fight it more, anyway! And it might help keep Father Basinger out of hot water."

"No! It just opens a bigger can of worms. If Hassler changed anything now, he'd have to explain why, the FBI would come back at me and want to know the whole story, and I'd have to dodge all that, too."

"You could–"

"I'll get back in school somewhere – maybe even here. I want to travel around the country. I want to see some people."

They hugged again. Jake rocked her from side to side. "When are you leaving?"

"Next week. I'll go by and see my parents and keep going."

"I'll miss you."

She laughed. "I know." A second later, she added, "We'll – I'll miss you, too."

✺

The latest run of letters accused Neal Hassler of turning the campus into an open-air latrine. The papers had a field day with an epithet-spiced SDS brochure distributed on campus, declaring that Annie Laughlin, the courageous SDS spokesman and leader, had been railroaded.

So, what the hell, he thought, this couldn't be any worse.

The meeting was with the five men: Timmy Hilton, Bill Charles, Larry Benson, Bill Wyden and Jonathan Vickers. Hassler had invited the football coach to round out the group, and Benson was the last to arrive. He had let Hallstrom drive back from Beaverton, and it was a miracle they had avoided a speeding ticket. Hassler noted how Benson carefully surveyed the conference room arrangement, and then chose to sit at the opposite end of the table from the president. Hilton and Charles were on one side, Wyden and Vickers on the other. Benson was in the second position of neutrality – or authority.

Hassler tried to lighten the mood. "I probably should have worn a referee's shirt, or at least brought a whistle," he said.

Only Timmy smiled.

On one side, the arguments – both from Timmy Hilton and Bill Charles – were that the "Afro" hairstyle was an expression of black pride and, regardless, judging the merits of appearance as a condition of being allowed to participate in any university program was a bad precedent.

On the other, Vickers argued that his authority would be undercut unless he was allowed to set the standards during his assignment as head coach. While saying that, he glanced at Benson. Wyden said he agreed, but tried to soften it. "The last thing we want is to risk losing our star football player over this," he said.

Hassler asked Benson what he thought.

"I'm here because you asked me to come, President Hassler," Benson said. "I'd rather stay neutral here."

"No," Hassler said, "I want to know what you think. Timmy's on a football scholarship. It's your issue, too."

Benson pondered for a moment. "My personal feelings are obvious about this," he said. "Personally, I support Timmy's – or anyone's – right to wear his hair how he wants to."

Amid the reactions on either side of him, he held up his right hand.

"It isn't simple, though," Benson continued. "Look, I believe that we make way too big of a deal of this now. And when we – the older generation – react the way we do to it, we make it more of a badge of rebellion than it should be. I tell my kids I don't like what their bands are doing to set the hairstyles – right before I tell them to turn the music down. But I think there are a lot more important things to measure discipline by. We have a dress code on the road, for example. That's common sense. That's class. And we have any number of other standards for players, involving things a lot more important than how they wear their hair. I don't think that should be the defining issue, the one where we draw the lines in the sand."

Vickers snorted. "That's why..." he said, and then stopped.

"That's why what," Benson said.

"That's why you can't beat TSU."

As Benson made a move to get out of his chair, Hassler yelled, "Enough!"

Benson sat down. He continued, "Despite that cheap shot, I will say there's a professional side to this, too. There's a part of me that says coaches should be allowed to set their own rules."

Hassler jumped in, "I don't agree with that. We can't have different standards across the board at a public institution. Whatever I decide here, it's going to be a policy." He fixed his gaze on Wyden. "And it's going to be a policy for stars and benchwarmers alike."

He let that sink in.

The fact that this had been in the afternoon newspaper, Hassler said, forced his hand. He would have preferred to ask everyone to put this on hold and talk it out, but that would be difficult to do now.

Vickers wouldn't back down.

Neither would Timmy, who said he wanted to play on the basketball team, but because his scholarship was in football, he could live without it.

Bill Charles roared, "It's the principle!"

Later, as they filed out, Wyden glared at Benson. "You already were on thin ice," he told the coach. "This won't help matters."

$\infty$

The *Herald* wasn't sending anyone to Spokane with the Fishermen basketball team. That was a sore spot with Dusty Harris. How the hell can you cover your beat if you're not with the team? And this release, telecopied to him by the Cascade publicity office during the dinner hour, raised as many questions as it answered.

After getting the release, Harris tried to reach Vickers at the hotel in Spokane. The hotel operator said she had been ordered not to put calls through to the players' rooms, so he couldn't get to Timmy Hilton. Harris tried to reach Bill Wyden at home. He was out of town, Wyden's wife said. Harris tried the university president, Hassler, at home. No answer. He didn't know he could have walked four blocks and found Hassler at the theater in downtown Portland, seeing *Star-Spangled Girl*. So Harris finally started typing.

By DUSTY HARRIS, Herald Staff

Cascade University president Neal Hassler Thursday declared that that "hairstyle will not be an issue" in deciding who could and who couldn't play on athletic teams at the school.

# THE WITCH'S SEASON

A Negro member of the basketball team, Timmy Hilton, protested acting coach Jonathan Vickers' order to cut his hair or skip the team's Friday night game against the Gonzaga Bulldogs, the Fishermen's first road game of the season.

Hilton is a junior reserve guard on the basketball team, but is better known as an All-America tailback on the football squad. There was no indication how the decision would affect the coaching status of Vickers, who was elevated following head coach Don Barnes's recent heart attack.

# TWENTY-EIGHT:
## "TUESDAY AFTERNOON"

*(Tuesday, December 17, 1968)*

The alumni association director called Neal Hassler to report that the mail there was similar to the president's. Both offices received irate letters from writers who declared they wouldn't donate any more money, and Hassler guessed that some even came from legitimate donors.

That morning, the *Portland Herald* editorial page piped in again, saying he had undercut his basketball coach and displayed the administration's trademark permissiveness. The editorial sarcastically congratulated him for consistency, also in keeping with his "decision to allow militant Black Student Organization leader Bill Charles to be the commencement speaker at the upcoming mid-year graduation ceremony."

Angered by the editorial, Hassler called Clifford Carlson at the public affairs office and asked him to call the *Herald* editor and point out that Bill Charles was a member of the mid-year graduating class and that his fellow graduates had *picked* him to be their peer speaker. The relatively low-key mid-year graduation ceremony, with far fewer students participating than in the spring ceremony, didn't even have an official commencement speaker. Hassler told Carlson to emphasize that even the student body leaders who supervised the vote had impressed upon Charles that a commencement wasn't a political rally and that if he got out of line, the university might rescind the students' right to pick a member of their classes to speak in the future, either along with a commencement speaker in the spring or alone at the small mid-year ceremony. Besides, Hassler said, the ceremony was four days before Christmas and the numbers of students going through it and families attending were going to be even lower than usual.

Carlson said he would do all that. Hassler could tell he wanted to say something else, so he asked Carlson, "Is there something else going on?"

"It's out," Carlson said.

The grape and strawberry issue was back in the forefront as well. So much had happened since his latest food ruling, Hassler had almost forgotten about it. Hassler had told the food service director that orders would be drastically curtailed for the second semester, living up to the sentiment of the students' fall vote. When the director cringed, Hassler insisted there would be no going over his head on this one.

Carlson's sources told him that the director of the Oregon Farm Union tipped the *Herald* about the decision. The director cried to the paper that this was another case of the students – not the administrators or the taxpayers – running the university. Driscoll, the *Herald* reporter, called, read Hassler the quotes from the head of the Farm Union and asked for a response. Hassler spoke slowly. "This is not a boycott," he said. "This is an adjustment of the academic year's order, in accordance with the wishes of the consumers – in this case, the students."

If the governor hadn't jerked him around earlier in the year, Hassler wouldn't have tried this.

☙

Jake had gone to *Rosemary's Baby* with Kit over the weekend, but it was damn near platonic – even during the scary parts. Afterward, she kissed him as if she meant it, but said she had to return to the sorority that night. With final exam week coming up, she said, she thought it would be better for both of them.

"What's going on here?" he asked that night.

"What do you mean?"

"Come on, you know exactly what I mean."

"I need some time," she said. "Please, leave me alone for a few days. Wait. Please." She hugged him, and he thought he felt moistness – maybe remnants of a tear or two? – on her cheek. Then she broke away and ran up the stairs.

After he waited too many days, he found her note inside the door. "Terwilliger's. Tuesday 6."

Jake was waiting for her, sitting at one of the four-chair tables on what occasionally was the dance floor.

Kit walked in at 6:10, ignored his attempt to kiss her, sat down and started talking.

"Annie's going to travel and do SDS work."

"I knew that. So?"

"I'm going with her."

"*What?*"

"I'm going to skip the next semester, go with her for a while, and write something about it. Maybe for the *Daily*. Maybe for a magazine. Maybe even a book. We're going to leave right after I'm done with finals."

"You're not even going home for Christmas?"

"We're going to stop through Roseburg and Medford, but not for long and we'll be on the road before Christmas. We're going to the Christmas protest vigil in San Francisco, then heading east."

"And neither of you thought to even run this by me?"

"I only decided for sure today."

"But you've been thinking about it?"

"Jake, I decided to go for it! I don't want to say later I should have done it!"

Jake felt the knives. Two at once. From Kit and Annie. One in the heart. One in the back.

He slammed the mug on the table. Kit suddenly couldn't say anything. Maybe she had a tough time talking, Jake thought, when she was pretending to cry.

❧

In the restaurant at the Portland Athletic Club, seven boosters surrounded Bill Wyden.

"Now, Bill, I'm not a racist," one said. "I bought a table to the NAACP dinner this year. I thought it was a tragedy when Martin Luther King was shot. But I think that if Benson is going to continue to bring in this many Negroes, they have to learn how to handle them."

Another booster said, "If you want my opinion..." – he always gave it, wanted or not – "...Larry has lost control. You need to make a change at the top. Clean house."

Paul Weaver, the biggest contributor at the table, finally spoke up, and he gave the impression he believed everyone else was part of an opening act and he was the star. "We were telling you all this even back during the season," Weaver said. "Everyone at this table is going to take a long look at cutting contributions – or cutting them off – if you don't do anything. If Larry stays, he's got to change his whole staff, except Gamberg. We have to know that something's being done. Now damn it, are you going to keep jerking us around, or are you going to do something?"

"Whoa," a fourth booster said. "I think that's a little severe. And for chrissakes, why don't we talk a little louder? Maybe the whole room can get in on this."

Booster No. 1 softened the tone. "You just can't win with the militants. You give in to them once, they expect it all the time, everywhere, in all the sports. If they want to be one of the militants or do whatever the militants tell them, they don't belong in uniform!"

Wyden knew a couple of these men regularly called Portland newspapermen and made it sound as if Wyden asked for their counsel daily. Wyden himself wasn't above planting material with the press, especially with Dusty Harris and the columnist at the *Herald,* Leonard Beechman, and he knew the boosters had those financial figures, too.

"We're planning on keeping Larry on for next season with a new, shorter-term contract," he said, thinking of the president's stand. Hassler wasn't locked into his job, either, but he was the boss for now, and Larry was just popular enough, especially in Cascade. "I can tell you that much," Wyden continued. "We can't just clean house now in the middle of the recruiting rush–"

"That's your fault for putting this off!" Booster No. 1 argued.

"There's a lot involved here," Wyden said. "I've told Larry I'll get into the specifics on his contract and everything else after he comes back from coaching in the Hawaii all-star game."

❦

Hassler was sitting in his den, trying to finish a crossword puzzle between his convulsions of sobs. They weren't loud, weren't even audible. But he could feel them, gripping him, shaking him, more within his spirit than in the open for anyone else to notice – if anyone walked in. Knock that off, he told himself.

He couldn't understand why these fits struck him. The pills didn't hold them off. He wasn't grief-stricken, he wasn't angry, he just felt at these moments as everything was coming at him. But he also didn't tell anyone, not even Eleanor. What was next?

# TWENTY-NINE:
## "GOIN' UP THE COUNTRY"

*(Saturday, December 21, 1968)*

The envelope, postmarked Medford, had no return address, but Jake recognized Kit's handwriting. Still standing at the mailboxes at the entrance to the stairway, Jake ran his fingers over the outside of the envelope, tracing the outline of the layers of cardboard enclosed. He tore open the envelope and then unfolded the note wrapped around the cardboard.

> *Forgot to give you this.*
> *Love, Kit.*

He separated the two pieces of cardboard. The spare apartment key fell onto the floor.

The second letter was from Tony Brantley, the defensive end who took off in the spring to campaign for McCarthy in New Hampshire, eventually switched to George McGovern and worked for him through the Democratic convention. Tony was in his hometown of Butte, Montana, working part-time tending bar in the raucous M&M Cafe, the miners' favorite, as he took classes at Montana Tech to keep the draft board off his back. The tips were great at the M&M, Tony bragged. "Only problem is if they don't like what you say, they threaten to throw you down the mine shaft," he wrote.

Tony announced he was coming back next semester, whether his credits from Montana Tech were accepted or otherwise, and hoped to show up in early January, a week before classes.

Could he crash on Jake's floor until he found a place to live? (Sure, Jake thought, if you're not claustrophobic. Besides, you don't have to worry about Kit being here.)

How come they didn't beat the Fucking Trappers? (Well, maybe if their best defensive end hadn't run out on them, they wouldn't have given up 33 points.)

Coach Benson's safe, isn't he? (Must be, it's a month after the season, and they're out recruiting.)

How'd Jake do on his finals? (Okay, and he was still on track to graduate in the spring.)

Was Jake going anywhere for Christmas? (Well, he had been planning to go to Medford with his girlfriend, but now he was going to stick around Cascade.)

Was Jake brokenhearted that Julie Nixon really was marrying David Eisenhower? (That's today, isn't it?)

Jake sat down to write him with the answers.

❧

Hassler was on automatic pilot in the Student Union ballroom for most of his speech to the CU Alumni Association's Parents Council breakfast, a function held as a prelude to the mid-year commencement ceremony in Hobson Court.

He again emphasized that the university still is a great place of learning, the turmoil is overblown, semesters continued unimpeded. He targeted those who were smiling. "Maybe everything hasn't been smooth, but what generation has done everything its parents wanted? I know mine didn't."

Hassler thought the applause was more than polite, more than the usual expression of ceremonial gratitude that the speech was over. After the breakfast ended, several parents introduced themselves and variously congratulated him for keeping the university from imploding, expressed sympathy for him because he was caught between the crossfire, or challenged him, especially about allowing Bill Charles to be selected as that day's commencement speaker.

"Again," Hassler said, "he is *not* the commencement speaker. He's a graduating senior addressing his peers, and they selected him. He's got ten minutes, no more. When the graduating seniors pick him to speak, believe me, it would have caused more problems to veto him than it will to let him talk. He'll be fine."

He hoped he was right.

❧

# TWENTY-NINE: "GOIN' UP THE COUNTRY"

In Medford, Kit's parents hadn't been thrilled about her trip from the start, including because they questioned the wisdom of driving around the country in the first month of winter.

They were even less thrilled after they helped reload Annie's car with Kit's things following the girls' brief visit. The trunk, back seat, and even the floor all were jammed with the girls' luggage, loose clothes, books and other gear. Kit's early Christmas presents – a huge, embossed blank journal and an Olivetti portable typewriter – were buried amid the rubble.

"You better hope you're not stopped," Kit's dad said. "They'll get you for having an obstructed view."

Kit's sister, the high school senior, laughed, thinking that if there was some pot in there somewhere – and she assumed there was – the cops would have to search for an hour to find it.

Kit's mom got her to promise to call at least every other day.

Then Annie put the car in reverse. Kit's parents and sister waved until the car was around the corner. As the car disappeared from view, Kit's mom said, "I still don't trust that girl."

"Which one?" Kit's sister asked.

∾

At the podium that afternoon, in his cap and gown, Bill Charles opened by thanking his fellow graduates for selecting him and the administration for not attempting to veto the choice.

Then he angrily said the American system and the educational world still treated blacks abominably, and that the system – and the American way of thinking – needed massive retooling. He alluded to the murder of Martin Luther King and to the riots that followed, and spoke of the anger so many blacks felt because a man who advocated civil disobedience, not violence, had been cut down. "Is it little wonder that young people are turning to leaders who advocate more decisive and open rebellion?" he asked.

*Oh, shit*, thought Hassler.

But then Charles softened. He said he still had hope, that progress was being made – far too slowly for his liking, but it was being made. He said, "As I look out at you, my fellow graduates, and, yes, even your families and our faculty and administration here, I see the potential for difference-making, for change, for progress."

When he finished, the reaction was mixed, but Hassler noted that he had taken only nine minutes and kept it clean.

# THIRTY:
## "JENNIFER JUNIPER"

*(Friday, December 27, 1968)*

As he entered the Berkeley coffeehouse, Rick Winslow spotted Jake Powell's girlfriend. She was at a corner table with two other women he didn't recognize, and she was leading back against the wall and writing in a hardback notebook in her lap. What was her name again? Kit? That's it. Kit Dunleavy.

"Hey, Kit," Rick called and walked over. "I didn't know you were from down here, too."

"I'm just visiting."

He introduced her to his buddy from high school, Trevor, the Cal-Berkeley student who had called Rick at his parents' house and invited him over for a night on Telegraph Hill. Plowing on, he asked when she was going back to Cascade for the next semester.

"I'm not going back," she said.

"How come?"

"Long story."

"Sorry."

"That's okay. You couldn't have known."

Five minutes after Rick left, Annie Laughlin and Peter Shapiro joined the small group. They had just been to the *Berkeley Barb* offices, where they talked with the editor about a planned Sunday night anti-war vigil on the California-Berkeley campus – one designed to follow up on the success of the gathering in Golden Gate Park on Christmas night.

"How's the book going?" Shapiro asked Kit, nodding at her notebook.

"I'm almost done with the part about the Golden Gate Park vigil," Kit said. "I can't let myself get too far behind."

"You ever going to type it?"

"Later. It's pretty much a journal, and it seems more natural to write it out longhand first."

"What you going to call this?"

"Not sure yet. Got any suggestions?"

Annie jumped in. "How about, *Guys Ask Too Many Questions?*"

"Not bad," said Kit.

In Annie's car a few minutes later, as they were heading back to the Victorian house in the hills, Annie asked Kit, "How you feeling? Still okay?"

"Still okay," Kit said.

"You sure you're fine with me leaving for the inauguration?"

Kit smiled. "There are ten people in that house, and you've got them all looking out for me," she said. "That should work, don't you think?"

"As long as you stay away from the brownies."

෴

The needle on Jake's Salvation Army stereo already was going bad, so his copy of Donovan's "The Hurdy Gurdy Man" album was scratchy. It didn't help when he kept lifting the arm and dropping it to hear "Jennifer Juniper" over and over.

The package from his mother and stepfather still was on the counter. The box didn't arrive until the day after Christmas, and waiting to open it was his subtle protest for its tardiness. Hell, even he had gotten his box off to Pittsburgh – sweater for his mother, a Pendleton shirt for his stepfather – well in advance of the holiday.

He decided he had made his point, even if he was the only one who knew he had made it, and opened the box. He opened the present from his stepfather first, and it was a new hardback copy of *Paper Lion*, the book about George Plimpton trying to play quarterback for the Detroit Lions. It had been out for three years, but the movie version – with a stage actor, Alan Alda, playing Plimpton – had only been in theaters a few weeks and Jake planned to see it soon.

"Not bad, stepdad," Jake said, clicking the beer bottle in his left hand against one of the empties on the counter.

The gift from his mother was in a wrapped box that had fit neatly along the bottom of the package. Inside, he found cushioning layers of newspapers surrounding a picture frame. He carefully lifted it out and held it up.

His father, in his military uniform, was smiling at the camera. Smiling at the son he didn't get to see grow. Or play football. Or get in trouble.

# THIRTY: "JENNIFER JUNIPER"

Jake borrowed a hammer and a nail from the guy on the first floor. When he had gotten the picture both up and finally straight, he nodded at the image.

"Merry Christmas, Dad," he said.

# THIRTY-ONE:
## "I HEARD IT THROUGH THE GRAPEVINE"

*(Tuesday, January 7, 1969)*

Larry Benson was exhausted and depressed, and tired of flying. He had been enjoying himself in Honolulu, coaching the North squad in practices – if that's what you could call those laughter-filled sessions in shorts and T-shirts – for the Hula Bowl all-star game. Mostly, it was rest and relaxation. The Pearl Harbor tour was far more meaningful for Benson, the World War II pilot, than most of the others. If they walked up the beach from their Waikiki hotel, they came to the R&R processing center for soldiers on leave from Vietnam.

Benson's sister called the hotel five minutes before the teams left for a luau. She was crying.

"Dad's gone," she said from Minnesota.

George Benson was dead, of a heart attack, at 71.

Larry suddenly remembered his father fighting to keep the livestock business afloat during the Depression, managing to keep his son and daughters from understanding the magnitude of the problem. They had moved into a smaller place that felt like a meat locker in the winter, but they didn't feel desperate. Then George Benson got himself back on his feet, and the family back into a home with heat and a room for each of the children.

Larry remembered his father never quite understanding why Larry and Patricia had left Minnesota after their college graduations, taking off for the frontier.

Larry remembered his father's wearing the Cascade Fishermen sweaters and sweatshirts in Litchfield and telling everyone about his son's team until damn near everyone in the little town knew.

Larry remembered a lot more, too.

His sister insisted he stay and coach in the Hula Bowl before coming to Litchfield. "You know he'd be telling you to stay," she said, sobbing.

He made it to Litchfield on Sunday, the day before the funeral, and then took off the day after to go to the national coaches' convention in New Orleans. The plan was to go from the convention back to Litchfield for a few more days, then land back in Cascade the next Monday night, the 23rd. By then, he would have been gone from Cascade for over two weeks.

Carl Steele met him at the gate in New Orleans and told him how sorry he was about Benson's father. Before long, Benson could tell that something else was bothering Steele, and he asked him point-blank what it was.

Steele came back with a question of his own. "Have you talked with Patricia or anyone in Cascade today?"

"No, why?"

"The *Herald* and *Times-Register* both ran stories today, saying you have to shake up the staff, among other things, if you want to stay."

"Well, it isn't true. Wyden's blown some smoke, but it isn't going to come to that."

"Any of those writers call you to ask you about it?"

"Nope, and I know where it came from."

Fifteen minutes after arriving at the hotel, Benson called Wyden.

"Larry, I want you to think about making some changes," Wyden said. "Let's put this on hold until we're both in Cascade."

"Are you trying to get me mad enough to quit? Just so you don't have to pay the six months on the contract?"

"Of course not."

"You doing this because of the meeting about Timmy's hair?"

"I was mad ... but no."

"Then let's knock off this leaking to the press."

"But—"

"I'm not saying it's you. But you must know who's doing it. You call those Portland jerks and tell them to knock this off."

"Have you thought about this? At least they're not telling me to fire you, or else."

"Have you thought about *this*, Bill? They could be going after me through the assistants. They might as well just order you to fire me. Is that what they're doing?"

"They don't tell me what to do."

# THIRTY-ONE: "I HEARD IT THROUGH THE GRAPEVINE"

"Bill, I'm not quitting. I'm not firing anybody. You asked me to think about it. I've thought about it, and I'm not going to make any changes."

"We have to at least talk about the possibilities."

"We just did."

∽

The *Herald*'s latest editorial about the "misadventures in Cascade" finally got around to asking why Neal Hassler had allowed Bill Charles to "transform a commencement into a political rally of objectionable tone." At least this time, it conceded that his fellow students had picked him to speak.

Governor McMichael was in town for some political schmoozing. He called Hassler in the morning and said he would stop by after lunch. Well, Hassler mused, it was better than busting into the office unannounced.

When the governor arrived, he demanded to know why he hadn't put more restrictions on Charles.

"That was two weeks ago!" Hassler said. "His speech is getting worse every day! He didn't say anything obscene–"

"There are different definitions of obscene."

"–and we didn't have any trouble."

"Neal, every time we turn around, it's something else. I'm going to call the members of the state board. When they meet at the end of the month, I hope and expect they'll ask for your resignation. From what I can tell, they might even do it without any input from me."

Hassler had taken his damn pill, as he'd told Eleanor when she called for the third time, and he wondered if it were time-released ambivalence. Under its spell, he seemed to have mixed feelings about everything. He didn't know whether to quit on the spot and jump with joy, or tell the governor that they'd have to drive him out of this office with a bulldozer and tear gas.

McMichael must have thought it was shock. "You're in a ball-buster of a job," the governor told Hassler. "But for your own good, you need to understand that you can't be effective now. There are just too many people who have written you off. You can make this easier for everybody, including yourself, by resigning and maybe going back to teaching."

Hassler said, "I want to go to that meeting. I want to talk to them. After that, if I think staying on the job will hurt this school, you won't have to fire me. I'll quit. But I want to be heard."

McMichael answered quickly. "That's fine," he said.

The governor knew how the board would react, Hassler realized with a sinking stomach.

The governor wasn't even down the stairs when Hassler's shivers returned, enveloping him in frustration and confusion. He thought: Look what it's doing to you!

He knew he would resign, but he wanted it to be on his terms. If the governor had been in this chair, and he tried using that charisma crap on the student militants, the rioters would have shut this place down. Damn right, governor, this isn't an easy job. Maybe when your term expires *you* could try this.

# THIRTY-TWO:
## "CRIMSON AND CLOVER"

*(Friday, January 10, 1969)*

Rick Winslow didn't want to be mistaken for a lineman, but he decided the hits might not be as painful the next season if he added a few pounds of muscle. So he spent an hour every other day lifting weights, and this time, he walked in just as Jake Powell was finishing his second of three sets at the bench press.

"Bulking up for the pros?" Rick asked.

Jake laughed. "I'm thinking of going into pro wrestling," he said. "I want to be Tough Tony Borne's tag-team partner."

Tony was an Oregon legend. He also was about 5-foot-5 tall and 5-foot-5 wide – and not fat. Tony looked like Paul Bunyan's caddy in the wilderness.

Rick told Jake he had seen his girlfriend – ex-girlfriend – in Berkeley and that Kit had said to say hello.

Jake said thanks and went back to the bench press.

᎐

"It's definite now. If Benson wants to stay, he has to fire four assistants," booster Paul Weaver said triumphantly. "I told Wyden we wouldn't give another dime. He said he'd take care of it. It'll break one way or another the middle of the week."

He and another man were standing in the floor-level hallway of Portland's Memorial Coliseum, an hour before the Seattle Super-Sonics-San Francisco Warriors game, one of the Sonics' four games in Portland each season.

The other man, *Portland Herald* columnist Leonard Beechman, thanked him for the tip.

᎐

"Holy shit," Jake said a second after answering the knock and opening the door, "when I said I had room for you in this place, I didn't know you hadn't stopped eating since you left."

Tony Brantley had gained forty pounds since last spring. The omelets at the M&M Cafe in Butte, Tony sheepishly explained, were made of four eggs for the customers and six for the bartenders. And nobody said you had to stop at one omelet.

"But at least I have hair," Tony said dryly.

"You should have seen it six weeks ago," Jake said, running his fingers through his brush cut.

Over the next few hours, Tony talked about New Hampshire and the ecstasy when McCarthy did so well in the primary and nudged LBJ toward quitting. He told about Chicago during the convention, about trying to hand out McGovern literature there, but getting caught in the crossfire and almost in the roundup. He talked of disappointment in settling for Humphrey and then retreating to Butte.

Tony knew the outline, but not the details, of what had happened in Cascade during his absence. Jake filled in some of the blanks.

"So I suppose the women love fat guys in Montana," Jake finally said, trying to lighten the mood again.

Tony shrugged, "I knew one of the waitresses from high school. There was a pool table in the back. What about you?"

"Don't ask."

"What about you?"

"Dumped."

"At least she came to her senses," Tony said. He instantly could tell he had gone too far. "Shit, sorry. You over it?"

"Not really."

"Tell me about it."

Jake showed him Kit's note and told him about Rick Winslow seeing her in Berkeley. Tony snorted. "The next note's going to say, 'Can't we be friends?' Hell with her. Let's go down to Terwilliger's and look for a couple of women we won't respect in the morning."

Jake laughed. "You just want to find the bookie for the Super Bowl."

"I just might," Tony said. "I'm taking the Jets and the points. You heard that Namath guaranteed it, didn't you?"

"Just give me the money. The Colts'll kill 'em."

# THIRTY-TWO: "CRIMSON AND CLOVER"

❦

When Rick Winslow and Todd Hendricks sat down in the living room and compared notes about their Christmas breaks, Rick mentioned seeing Powell's girlfriend – ex-girlfriend – in Berkeley.

"Shit, know what I heard about her today?" Todd asked, gesturing with his beer bottle for emphasis. "She's one of Professor Reynolds' harem!"

"Oh, come on..."

"No, she really was. One of the Hansen sisters told me. Said some guy in one of her classes is one of the guys screwing Reynolds' wife and he told her he was at the Reynolds' house and Kit was there."

"So?"

"It was eight in the morning or something. And Kit had just come downstairs. In her underwear. This guy told one of the Hansen sisters that he later figured out the girl was the *Campus Daily* reporter, the football player's girlfriend. Don't ask me which one, though."

"Which one what?"

"Which Hansen sister," Todd said. "I always get 'em mixed up. My only question is whether Powell knew about it. He's just weird enough to share her."

Rick got up and paced. Finally, he said, "I don't think he knew. And, Jesus, I don't think you know Jake very well if you think he wouldn't care."

"Maybe that's why she's his ex-girlfriend."

❦

At the SDS' house in the Berkeley hills, Kit finally had enough of Annie's grilling.

"I didn't get this many questions from my parents," Kit she said, laughing.

"I just want to make sure," Annie said.

Kit had enough names, addresses, and phone numbers of Annie's friends in the Bay area and on Annie's route to Washington, D.C., to keep her busy for a year if she tried to get in touch with everyone. Annie was planning to be back by February 1, after the inauguration.

"Last chance," Annie said. "We could go back to Cascade and then I could go east from there."

"No thanks," Kit said. "I'll stay here. Like we planned."

∾

During the pre-dinner cocktails at the Hasslers' house, Clifford Carlson – after getting some encouragement from Eleanor – gave it another shot.

Quit now, he told Neal.

"No," Hassler said, shaking his head vehemently. "I'm going to take it to the board meeting. Then I'll resign. Not before."

"Hell," Carlson said, "you don't even want to stay in the job. You can resign and still go to the state board anyway. You think they won't let you talk?"

"When I talk to them, I don't want to be a lame duck."

"Neal," Carlson said gently, "you already are a lame duck."

# THIRTY-THREE:
## "WHEELS OF FIRE"

*(Tuesday, January 14, 1969)*

Benson decided to take a walk on campus before confronting the mealy-mouthed pencil pusher. This crap isn't letting up; it's picking up steam.

The night before, when he finally returned home after the all-star game, convention and funeral travels, his wife showed him Leonard Beechman's column in the *Herald*. The column disclosed that "major contributors to the Oregon program" had gotten promises from the administration that Benson "definitely" would have to fire some assistant coaches to get a new contract.

Benson went from the offices to the Student Union, picked up coffee and a *Campus Daily* and sat in the cafeteria. He felt better. On the street and in the Union, quite a few of them nodded warmly. *Hey, coach. Hi, coach. How's it going, coach?* Long hair, short hair, women, men, professors, students. He even got a greeting from the guy in front of the Union wearing the sandwich board sign that proclaimed:

FUCK THE DRAFT RALLY

TUESDAY 3 P.M.

ON THE COMMONS

But this speculation bothered him. He had gotten wind about Wyden's gathering with the boosters at the Portland Athletic Club, and he knew that kind of maneuvering had been going on for months. This time, it had to be some Portland booster with a thick wallet and a thicker ego bragging to Beechman.

Wyden still was trying to play it both ways. In the *Times-Register*, which usually got its quotes correct, Wyden was saying: "Larry Benson is not resigning, and unfounded speculation is malicious and harmful." Then why'd he help start it? How effectively could they recruit in the state? The high school kids and their parents could be wondering if the assistant coach who had pitched Cascade to them might be gone.

Benson wondered if he weren't overreacting because of fatigue and sadness; but damn it, he wasn't changing his mind. If they wanted his ass, they could have it, and that's what he told Wyden.

"If you really want me here, put the contract on the desk, and let's get going," he said. "Four years, three years, two years, whatever."

Wyden didn't move.

"If you want to stay," he said, "you're going to have to let assistants go."

At least he seemed apologetic about it, but that didn't calm Benson. "You were going to do this all along! There's a newspaper on your desk there, where you say in black and white that it wasn't going to happen. Are you calling yourself a liar?"

"No! I promise you, that was not the plan. Now, though, I have to guarantee some credibility with the money in Portland. If you stay, we've got to get them off our back by doing something." Benson thought Wyden was about to cry. "Larry, I've defended you! If I hadn't stood up for you, you'd be going for sure, too, and I'd really be a hero with these people."

"You're asking me to make good coaches the scapegoats."

"Come out of the clouds, Larry. You think this is easy for me? Hell, I like these guys, too. I want you back. If that's all there was to it, it'd be automatic. You sit at this desk for a while. Look through these files and think about the budget and where the money's coming from. Go around the state and hear the way people talk about us—"

"I do."

"I mean when you're not around. They talk about us like they're ashamed to give us another dime because of all the shit that happens on this campus – and, yes, even on your team. You tell me how we can afford not to pay attention to these people."

They measured each other. "What's it going to be?" Wyden finally asked, softly.

"I don't know yet," Benson said. "This is the middle of January. Most of the other jobs have been filled. We put these guys on the street, what are they going to do?"

"What are they going to do if you quit? Then we're talking about a whole staff."

Benson got up, but stopped in the doorway. "I'll let you know tomorrow morning. But I want you to know right now, I'm going over your head on this."

Wyden shrugged. "Go ahead. It won't work this time."

When Benson called, Hassler said, sure, come over. His voice seemed flat, emotionless. Benson hoped it was just the flu, but when he saw Hassler a few minutes later, he knew it wasn't. May this not happen to me, Benson thought. No job is worth this.

When he broached the subject of his new contract, Benson felt even then as if he were encroaching in Hassler's isolation.

"Larry," the president said finally, "the system stinks. I'm not fighting it any more. My support won't mean much at this point."

Benson didn't even ask which system. Maybe it was all the same system. The truly important – Hassler's milieu. Or the relatively trivial – Benson's. All part of the same system, the system that had those idiotic letters sitting on Hassler's and Benson's desks. The system that had the boosters proud of themselves for being able to overwhelm a pencil pusher, then being able to brag about the power they wielded. The system that made this sensitive educator, who more than any other had prevented the campus from shutting down, into a villain – for both sides. The system that made them both feel helpless.

Benson told himself: Make calls to the editors, the other boosters, the parents, the faculty, and the friends. You could fight it, if it was worth fighting. You could call the columnist at the *Times-Register* and put it all on the table. Say you can be quoted on all of this. But then he asked himself: Even if you win, is it worth it? The system stinks.

∾

In an interim stop in Chicago on the way to Washington, Annie felt as if she had made it to the Democratic convention – a few months late. She walked around Grant Park, hearing the echoes of the protests and the squabbles with Mayor Daley's police. Then she got back in the car and drove to Addison Street, not to seek the landmark Wrigley Field, but to get a half-dozen of the little hamburgers at White Castle on the way to the house in Evanston, where one of Shapiro's Magician buddies was letting her crash for the night.

⟳

The coaches had promised Samuel Haliburton, the director of minority affairs, they would attend this meeting with the representatives of the Black Student Organization.

Benson had forgotten about it until his secretary reminded him. Five o'clock in the Lettermen's Lounge. This was all he needed now. He called Patricia and said he'd be home as soon as he could, but don't hold dinner.

In the meeting, after a general discussion of minorities' roles in the athletic department and programs, and of the need for more black coaches, Bill Charles' successor as the BSO president, Ron Miller, said the university hadn't done enough to promote the black players for honors. "You coaches don't do it, either," Miller said.

Benson, who had just spent a week in Honolulu with a black senior, linebacker Alex Tolliver, and was one of the first Pac 8 coaches to hire a black assistant, Stan Simmons, didn't say anything. At this point, he thought, what's the use?

Marv Cantrell, the baseball coach, waited for Benson to explode. When he didn't, Cantrell did. "I'm sorry, Ron, but that's idiotic. There aren't too many people at this university who have done as much for–"

"Thanks, Marv," Benson said, cutting him off. "But don't bother."

The meeting broke up, in part because Benson got up and left. Haliburton and Cantrell chased him, catching up with him at the arena doors. Benson didn't seem mad, and that alarmed Cantrell even more. But Benson was hurt. That much, Cantrell could tell.

# THIRTY-THREE: "WHEELS OF FIRE"

"Larry, ignore that," Haliburton said. "You know that's bullshit. I know that's bullshit. Everybody knows that's bullshit."

"Why didn't you tell them that?" Cantrell asked, pointedly.

"Oh, it doesn't really matter," Benson said.

Cantrell didn't like the sound of that. Benson was playing with his keys, and he abruptly left.

At home, he ate with his youngest daughter and wife. After the chicken, he talked with Patricia.

"If you're sure, I'm sure," she said. "Just make sure you're sure."

Benson went to his den and typed. He only had to rip, wad, replace and start over once. He showed the page to Patricia. He phoned his oldest son, Don, a CU junior, and his oldest daughter, Jane, a freshman. When son Charlie got home from basketball practice, Larry showed him the letter. When daughter Cindy got home from ballet class, he showed her. She was only twelve, but she got the drift. Patricia told Angie, the youngest. All five kids knew. Dad's planning to quit his job tomorrow. Dad's just had enough.

∽

Kit's typing, both off the top of her head and in transcription of her handwritten passages in her hardback journal, had become as much a part of the house's regular sounds as the Hendrix albums. She wondered how much better the material would have been if she had ridden with Annie to Chicago and Washington, D.C., but she was excited about the evolution of her project so far. The anti-war Christmas vigil in Golden Gate Park got her started, and she was turning it into an "outsider's" curious look at the movement and the leftist world in the Bay area, with Annie only one of the handful of men and women she had observed and interviewed so far.

It also kept her mind off other things.

"Thought of that title yet?" asked one girl, a folk singer who also was in the second tier of SDS leadership, as she sat down at the table in the living room and peeled a banana.

Kit laughed. "I still don't know if it's ever going to need one," she said, leaning forward, lifting the paper guide and squinting at the page. "But I'm open to suggestions."

She laughed and pointed at a copy of the *Berkeley Barb*. "How about *Barbed in Berkeley?*"

∽

Todd Hendricks started drinking beer at noon. Now, fourteen hours later, Rick Winslow wanted to put a muzzle on him. But that was one of the drawbacks of Hoot's, the 24-hour restaurant near the campus. By this time, after last call at Terwilliger's, everybody eating breakfast was talking a few decibels too loud − and laughing a little too much.

Jake Powell walked in with Tony Brantley, and Rick waved them over. Tony peeled off for the bathroom, but Jake came right over and slid into the booth next to Dan.

"Thanks for telling me about Kit," Jake said. "Sorry if I didn't say it then."

"You're better off without the bitch," Todd said matter-of-factly, reaching for his toast.

Rick kicked him under the table − an instant before Jake grabbed his shirt near the collar. "Take that back."

Todd seemed surprisingly unconcerned. "What is this, the god-damn third grade?" he asked, shrugging off Jake's grip. Jake stood up.

"Shut up, Todd," Rick said, trying to head off what he knew might be coming. "Jesus, Jake, he didn't really mean that. He's drunk."

"Come on," Todd said, "the way she was screwing Professor Reynolds, I thought you'd be saying the same thing."

Jake froze. "What?"

"She was walking around the professor's house in her underwear, big guy!"

To Rick, Jake seemed more stunned than mad. "Jake, it's just stupid gossip. Don't jump to conclusions."

Jake walked away with Tony.

## THIRTY-THREE: "WHEELS OF FIRE"

Five minutes later, when Todd was at the cash register paying the check, Rick said he was going to take a leak, which was true enough. On the way, he found Jake and Tony in a booth in the back.

"Jake, I apologize again for Todd," Rick said. "He can be such a jerk, I know. But he isn't one."

"That's okay," Jake said, waving a hand. "But so you know, she must have been with his son."

"What?" Rick asked.

"Reynolds' son. He used to be Kit's boyfriend. I guess he is now, too."

# THIRTY-FOUR:
## "THE HURDY GURDY MAN"

*(Wednesday, January 15, 1969)*

First, Larry Benson apologized.

"This is going to affect you all," he said.

He looked around at the other coaches, whose fates undoubtedly would be intertwined with his. Eight assistants – Howie Hallstrom, Carl Steele, Dennis Olesiak, Stan Simmons, Rex Gamberg, Pete Salisbury, Ted Wolf and Klaus Rockwell – waited.

"I'm resigning," Benson said.

They weren't shocked. They knew this had been a possibility. Yet the reality of it was stunning.

"Is this under pressure?" Benson continued. "I suppose so, depending on your definition. But at least resigning," he added, with a dry smile, "sounds better than 'quitting.' I just don't want to sift through all of this any more."

Pete Salisbury spoke up. "Larry, can't you sleep on it for a day? Or two? Geez, we all knew what you've been through the past few weeks. Don't do something you'll regret in a week."

Olesiak stood. "How many of us need to quit to get you – and the rest – through this? And which ones?"

"Cards on the table, right?"

"Absolutely, Larry," Olesiak said.

"Some of the biggest hitters in this are after me, not you. You guys know that. I throw 'em some heads, it's a compromise. It's got nothing to do with who can coach, who's doing a good job. It's politics. They want blood. Somebody's blood. So they can take some credit."

Olesiak tried again. "What if we quit? How many?"

"Look," Benson said, "it wouldn't put an end to it. It might buy me a two-year contract, but the people who don't like me won't let up unless we go 10-1 next year. I could be out after a year. If I thought it would save my job and a few of the others here for years, and I *wanted* to coach here the way things are, then maybe I could do it. But I'm just sick of this. And if I leave, some of you might even be able to stay."

He knew this was playing right into the hands of his biggest critics, those who would be ecstatic when they heard the news. They'd be picking up the phone to tell each other, "It worked."

It wasn't just the pressures of losing a couple of games they should have won. It wasn't just this garbage with the boosters over his job and all their jobs; the same garbage that goes on everywhere, he knew. As he stood talking to them with his resignation letter in his coat pocket, he simply didn't want to coach here any longer. Nothing against them, nothing against the university. It was the system. Right now, the system stinks.

"Can we go to the president on this?" Simmons asked.

"Already have. Won't work. Neal Hassler's got more important things to worry about now. I don't think he's going to be president much longer, either."

Finally, Benson said he was going to give Wyden the news. He hoped they could round up as many of the players as possible by early in the afternoon, and maybe they could announce it soon after that. In the office down the hall, he gave Wyden the letter.

"Sure this is what you want to do?" Wyden asked.

"It's the way I've got to do it," Benson said. "What I want to do is bring the whole staff back, go 12-0 next season and tell those men in Portland we don't need their money. But we don't have a chance to do that. I'll make this easy as long as you pay me through June, through the contract."

Wyden nodded. "Deal," he said somberly. He reached out. "No hard feelings."

Benson shook his hand. Later, it hit him that Wyden might have thought it was more than a business handshake.

༄

When Paul Weaver got wind in Portland of what was happening, the booster called one of his friends.

"It worked," Weaver chortled.

༄

# THIRTY-FOUR: "THE HURDY GURDY MAN"

At the locker-room meeting, Timmy Hilton almost made Benson want to run back up to Wyden's office and steal back the envelope.

"Aren't you quitting without a fight?" Timmy asked.

"I've fought," Benson said, "but I just don't have it in me right now to fight any more."

Nobody had been able to get in touch with Jake Powell.

◯

Jake was in the library, trying to study. The problem was that he kept pulling Kit's latest letter out of the envelope and re-reading it, so he wasn't making much progress on *A History of Britain*.

She was full of bright talk about her writing and her adventures with Annie, as if Jake had fully endorsed her exit and the project.

She didn't mention Professor Reynolds' son.

◯

Dusty Harris was grateful they hadn't called a press conference, because it was his guess he wouldn't have been able to get to Cascade in time, and then they'd be playing catch-up. He did what he could from Portland.

By DUSTY HARRIS, Herald Staff

In an unexpected decision, Larry Benson Wednesday resigned as head football coach at Cascade University.

Benson announced his shocking move after a meeting with the university's athletic leaders and, later, a grim gathering with the players.

A small alumni faction has been critical of Benson, and the coach obviously was disturbed by it.

Benson issued the following statement: "Last week from the American Football Coaches Association convention, I assured Bill Wyden that it was my intention to remain as head football coach at Cascade University.

"However, upon my return to Cascade, I reluctantly concluded that in the existing atmosphere of rumor and innuendoes, it would be impossible for me to carry on in the manner in which I felt necessary to make continuing progress with our program.

"Consequently, I felt the best course of action was for me to tender my resignation. This action certainly was difficult for me to initiate but was, in my opinion, necessary."

Benson's decision came out of the blue. Athletic Director Bill Wyden did say, however, "since recruiting is in full swing, we must name a successor as soon as possible."

༄

Jake was passing the second-floor landing, heading upstairs, when a guy came out of the non-orgy apartment on one side. Jake knew him just well enough to bum a beer occasionally, plus make small talk on the landing about the weather and sometimes football.

"You sorry about Benson?" the guy asked.

"What'ya mean?"

"Benson quit. You really hadn't heard?"

"No, they didn't announce it at the library."

༄

At 11, Dusty's phone rang at home. It was an officer from the Portland branch of the Fishermen's Booster Club, one of Benson's supporters, angrily telling him, "You guys were used."

Shit, Dusty thought, that's our job.

# THIRTY-FIVE:
## "MAGIC BUS"

*(Thursday, January 16, 1968)*

As Jake was about to tear up the Chicago-postmarked card without reading it, he gave in and looked at it as he walked toward Hobson Court.

> Dear Jake,
>
> On the way to Washington to watch the Inauguration. Hope to talk to you about it someday. Other things, too.
>
> Annie

She hadn't said "we." Hey, Jake wondered, maybe Annie and Kit had separated on their travels, arguing over whether they should murder the Naval Academy's goat mascot or West Point's mule. And Washington wasn't that far from New York, where Chris lived, was it?

He dodged six speeding bicycles on the sidewalk in the final block before reaching the arena. After a seventh almost hit him, he exploded, although he knew that the campus custom was to ignore the "NO BIKE RIDING ON SIDEWALK" signs. He grabbed the handlebars of a three-speed as it went past, ran a few steps with the bike as he tried to wrestle it to a stop and glared at the skinny biology major who looked back at Jake as if he were nuts, but managed to keep the bike upright and moving forward.

"Walk the damn bike!" Jake yelled, but the rider was able to pull away, still looking back over his shoulder.

Jake felt like a Chicago cop.

Inside the football office wing, Jake wondered if the next coach, as Larry Benson always had, was going to tell his players they could just storm down the hall, past all secretaries, and poke their heads in his office. Somehow, Jake doubted it.

Coach Benson was in, and he was talking on the phone. He looked up, smiled at Jake and gestured to a chair.

"Dusty, I'm sorry," Benson said, "I just wasn't in the mood to do much talking yesterday."

Must be the old guy from the *Herald*, Jake thought.

"Can't I just leave it at what I said yesterday in the statement? That much is true. I was tired of the brush fires."

Benson raised his eyebrows and smiled at Jake.

"Dusty, that's really all I want to say. The other stuff about coaches, well, that doesn't matter now. I'm not saying you have it right. I'm not saying you have it wrong, either. I'm just saying either way, it wouldn't matter. I think they were after me."

He gave a get-on-with-it gesture with his hands. Jake laughed.

"No," Benson said finally. "I've talked to a lot of my friends in the business, but I really don't know what I'm going to do."

He was doodling with a pencil now.

"Thanks, Dusty. You've always been fair with me."

He hung up.

Jake smiled. "Coach, you ever thought about going into politics? You've got that dodging down."

"Jake, that's all this job has been," Benson said. "Politics. And not just your politics."

"If I had anything to do with you quitting, I feel terrible." Jake pondered the sound of that. "I feel terrible, anyway, but..."

Benson held up a hand. "This involves so many things. Minor. Major. It's all in there. Yeah, you're in there, too, just part of all of it. It's this business and it's the times. Both. You heard me with Dusty. I'm just tired of all this."

Benson had another call, his secretary said, from Al Rodgers. After a second, Jake remembered why the name was familiar. Rodgers was the Wisconsin coach who had just taken the Chicago Zephyrs' NFL job. When Powell got up to leave, Benson smiled and asked, "So when do you plan to run for senator, anyway?"

Jake stuck out his hand. "Think 1986 would be rushing it?"

Fifteen minutes later, Benson had an offer on the table from Rodgers, a long-time acquaintance, but not a close friend. No hoops. No interview. Benson had twenty-four hours to decide whether he wanted to be an NFL offensive line coach, back in his native Midwest.

⁓

# THIRTY-FIVE: "MAGIC BUS"

With Kit questioning, taking notes, and taping the conversation on several different reels at the Berkeley community center, Peter Shapiro talked for over two hours about the Magicians' willingness to take drastic measures for their causes. Traditional dissent and discourse, he argued, weren't effective in a nation in which the establishment controlled the media, and the major political parties prevented any radical voices from being part of the process.

"Do you really believe you're going to change enough people's minds that way?"

"We're getting their attention."

"So?"

Shapiro snapped, "Are you being a smart-ass reporter or making a point?"

"Both," Kit said.

"What do you mean?"

"Pretty much everything you're against, I'm against. Everything you're for, I'm for. But when you go too far, I almost feel ashamed for agreeing with you. Getting their attention and getting things done are two different things, and I think a lot of the radical movement does far more harm than good."

"We're trying to cause change. We really are."

Kit's look gave her away.

"You don't believe that?" Shapiro challenged.

"I believe you believe it."

"But?"

"But you're discrediting your own cause."

"Now you sound like Annie."

"Words I thought I'd never hear," Kit said. "'Annie Laughlin, voice of reason.'"

❧

Another *Portland Herald* reporter, Cathy Davenport, interviewed Neal Hassler for a story about the upcoming board meeting. To break the ice, she asked Hassler what he thought about his football coach's resignation. "The system stinks," he said. She asked him if she could pass that along to the sports department. "Why not?" he said.

# THE WITCH'S SEASON

By DUSTY HARRIS, Herald Staff

Larry Benson, who quit as Cascade University's football coach 24 hours earlier, was at his office on Thursday, answering phone calls from friends.

Meanwhile, athletic director Bill Wyden was trying to line up Benson's successor.

The tremors caused by Benson's resignation had calmed slightly Thursday, but rumors continued to circulate that alumni pressure inspired Benson to step down.

Beleaguered university President Neal Hassler finally commented on Benson's departure. "The system stinks," Hassler said succinctly on Thursday.

Benson continued to maintain he simply wearied of attempting to run his program under a heavy burden of criticism, speculation and innuendo. A prominent booster – a Benson supporter – said Benson bowed out after refusing to fire members of his staff. Another called the anti-Benson campaign "a black eye to the reputation of the university."

Also, CU student body president Danny Gleason, known to support radical causes, told reporters: "Under very difficult circumstances, Coach Benson was running a clean and competitive football program in line with the academic mission of the university. As long as the system allows outsiders to dictate hiring and firing decisions, big-time intercollegiate athletics will continue to be a cesspool. In this case, the university should have been telling boosters it would not fire Coach Benson, and if they didn't like that, tell them they could put their money right back in the wallets."

After word of his resignation spread, Benson was linked with the vacant coaching jobs at Stanford and California. He said he had no plans for the future, however, and had spoken with representatives of no other programs.

# THIRTY-SIX:
## "WHILE MY GUITAR GENTLY WEEPS"

*(Friday, January 17, 1969)*

Neal Hassler lectured himself at the breakfast table. Try to take it easy today. Put together more notes for the State Board meeting next week. Read the mail, but don't bother with the ones minus return addresses. You know what kind those always are, and you don't need any more of those. Hope nothing else happens and hope the next call isn't something worse.

If it's like yesterday, try to ignore Clifford Carlson hanging around like some Yorkshire governess and acting as if there's nothing to do at public affairs. Why doesn't he just take out a thermometer and take your temperature and remind you to finish your broccoli at lunch, too?

If the governor checks in, say, "No, sir, I won't quit now." Tell the state board's secretary the agenda looks fine. Might as well get it over with, right at the start of the meeting, so putting ol' Neal first is fine.

What's that, Eleanor? Pretty good. Feel pretty good today. Better than the last couple of days, guarantee you that. Slept like a log last night, for a change. By the time I get to the board meeting, I'll be so fresh, they'll think they're hearing from William Jennings Bryan, brought back from the dead to the podium.

Hey, she even laughed at that one.

The office? Oh, no, dear, it's nothing more than busywork now.

That much is true.

Bye. Love you, too.

Thought for sure the car needed gas. It's half full. Or, as the state board would say, half-empty. Oh, that's a good one, Neal. Almost as good as the one Carlson told you yesterday. How'd that go?

How many reporters does it take to screw in a lightbulb? Give up? What difference does it make, because they're always in the dark, anyway.

What a nice day for January. Chilly, but nice. Wait, who's punching a time clock here, anyway? Just take a little drive, past the campus, over the bridge and keep going on the River Highway. See if you can avoid getting caught behind one of those crawling log trucks on the way back and soak up the atmosphere underneath the canopies of tree limbs. Look at guys pulling off the road to put their boats in the river and wonder what the hell they do for a living to be able to do this on a Friday, and then get close enough to see the white water breaking. Guess what they're talking about at the little cafes – Nixon's inauguration, changing the oil in the truck, whatever – or, better yet, go in one of those places and join in the talking.

⌒〇

For a couple of days, Carl Steele had been wondering whether he owed it to his family to learn to like the insurance business, or anything more stable than coaching. As he was deciding whether simply to mimeograph his resume or pay more to have it printed up, it struck him that he wasn't even sure he wanted to work at some of the places he was going to send it. He had a young daughter. Did he want to subject her to a vagabond coaching brat's existence?

"Why are we doing this?" Steele asked fellow assistant coach Pete Salisbury, who also was addressing envelopes as they shared a copy of the NCAA Register.

Pete also had a non-football option. The owner of The Landing Dock, Pete's former moonlight-hours employer during his graduate assistant days, was bugging Salisbury about becoming the manager and maybe eventually a minor partner.

"Isn't it obvious?" Salisbury asked. "Anywhere you go the boosters can be jerks, the athletic director a moron, some of the players unteachable, and the salary too damn low."

"Well," Steele said, "now that you put it that way..."

They both knew they were hooked.

⌒〇

Larry Benson finished telling Al Rodgers that the Zephyrs had an offensive line coach and promising to come to Chicago to sign the contract and tour the team offices late in the next week. His secretary said the next call was from Sam Reynolds. Professor Reynolds?

# THIRTY-SIX: "WHILE MY GUITAR GENTLY WEEPS"

*The* Professor Reynolds, the most popular showman-lecturer-educator on the campus? And who was rumored to run coeds through his bedroom as if he were holding office hours?

"Coach," Reynolds said, "I know this is short notice, but I was wondering if you could come by and talk to my 11 o'clock Political Science 202 section today? Hell, if anything around here has been a lesson in politics, it's been the athletic department since last fall."

"Oh, I don't know," Benson said, "I understand you're a tough act to follow. I also understand you're not big on football."

"No, I'm not," he said. "But I play devil's advocate sometimes, too. You don't have to give a speech. Just some opening remarks and then questions. Just like a press conference."

"I hope your students are smarter than that."

☙

Nice guys, these truck drivers, fishermen and country folk. The toast is a little light and soggy, now that you mention it, but the waitress keeps calling you honey, and when was the last time you heard it from someone besides your wife? Weird, isn't it, that you can drive just a few miles from town and be in another world altogether, where they probably don't have to worry about this side and that side coming at you. The bill's so small, you might as well leave a tip larger than the check, so at least in one place, you can be a hero for a few minutes before you go maybe a little farther east, then turn around.

☙

"Coach, what about Winslow?"

"One of the toughest quarterbacks I've ever seen," Benson told the students of Political Science 202, and not just the young horticulturist in the fourth row along the wall who had asked the question. "And already one of the best."

It still was early in the semester. This class was so huge, not everyone knew yet that Rick Winslow – an embarrassed Rick at this moment – was directly behind his smartass friend, the horticulturist.

They talked about hair, the suspensions, outside pressures, boosters, winning and losing and that damned draw play on third and eight against Stanford because what kind of call was that? ("Are you a journalism major?" Benson asked.) The positives, the negatives, the highs, the lows.

Benson was forty-four years old. It had been twenty-five years since he felt truly young, because he didn't feel truly young after the first time he went up in that P-38, not knowing he would return alive. Yet he knew once again that if all there was to this business was the young people, he would have remained young in some ways right along with them – and not walked away from this damn job. That's what Benson was thinking as he pointed at another longhaired guy in the front row.

"Why can't you change your mind?" the student asked.

For one thing, Benson thought, he'd shaken on a deal with Wyden. He told them the rest, about it not being just the young people. "It's so more than that now," he said. "It always has been, I guess. It's just too much more now."

At the bell, he got an ovation. Because they were getting up to leave, he was going to call it a standing O. Then he wondered why the man, another professor he guessed, was charging through the students at the door, going against the grain, rushing toward Reynolds.

❧

"The truck driver's all right, but he's pretty shook up," one state patrolman told the other, who had just pulled up.

"And the guy in the car?"

"No way. Truck driver said he got out and looked, saw there was nothing he could do, went over to the side and started to wait. And that's when it really got to him, he says."

"Any chance it was the truck driver's fault?"

"No, look at the truck's skidmarks, for Chrissakes. This guy drove right into the fucking truck."

They were a couple of miles outside Calistoga, just beyond the Johnson Bridge, where the road crosses the river and switches to the south side.

# THIRTY-SIX: "WHILE MY GUITAR GENTLY WEEPS"

A compact blue car, still smoking, was crushed against the front of the logging truck, as if it were a crushed beer can.

Nobody was going to be able to revive Neal Hassler, but they were going through the motions of trying.

○○

It took a few hours for the news to reach Cascade. Professors rushed into other classes. Janitors, without being told to do so, dropped the flags to half-staff. Students stared in shock. Bells rang.

Jake Powell was in the Student Union when he heard. A guy in a Dodgers sweatshirt walked up to the crowded table closest to Jake's and said something softly, then left, twisting a copy of the *Campus Daily* between his hands. As heads shook or dropped into hands, Jake got out of his chair and leaned over to the girl at the end of the table.

"What he say?"

"President Hassler was killed. Car wreck. Might have been suicide."

Jake left his books on the table and purposefully walked out onto the patio, which was deserted because of the cold. He took three quick steps, kicked one of the metal chairs away from a table and then, with his vision blurring, pounced on the chair. He threw it over the stone patio railing, into the shrubs below. He didn't feel any better when he plopped down into another chair, dropping his head into his hands.

Fifteen minutes later, he went outside, retrieved the chair from the bushes, carried it through the front door and the cafeteria, and back onto the patio. As a few curious students watched from the cafeteria windows, Jake quietly put everything back in order. He had decided it was the least he could do.

○○

In Washington, D.C., when she heard, Annie Laughlin cried for the first time since the gang rape. She couldn't even completely explain it to herself, but she left the apartment and went down to the Ellipse, eventually sitting on the stairs of the Lincoln Memorial.

She asked herself if she had helped turn that car into the truck. Of course she had. Is this guilt? No, she decided. It was regret. Not regret about advancing her causes, but regret about some of the fallout.

From a payphone, she called Berkeley and got Kit Dunleavy on the first try.

"I'm not going to take no for an answer again," Annie said. "Now it's really time to go back. If you don't, I'm going to get him on the phone and tell him everything myself. I'll break my word if I have to."

# THIRTY-SEVEN:
## "THE WEIGHT"

*(Monday, January 20, 1969)*

In his final act as team captain, Alex Tolliver spread the word about attending the memorial service as a team, with notes on the bulletin boards in the weightroom, in the locker room, in the Lettermen's Lounge, even in the Student Union. The football players were to meet in the south end zone of the arena – the same spot where they congregated for the basketball games. Bring girlfriends, buddies, parents, whomever with you, but meet there. The coaches and their wives joined them, too.

Tolliver brought his Bible. He was shocked that Timmy Hilton had, too.

About forty players – or half the roster – were in the seats behind the basket when several of them elbowed or tapped one another, even if they had to reach around their girlfriends.

Jake Powell and Kit Dunleavy had come through the portal and were walking toward them. Holding hands.

*∽*

The night before the memorial service, Jake spent three hours at his favorite little cubicle in the library stacks. This was his refuge. There must be five-hundred of these desks in the library, but Jake always was disappointed – and even mad – when he came to this one at the end of a biography row, nearest the Roosevelts, and found someone else encamped. This time, he was lucky. He intended to start Sir Philip Sidney's *The Defence of Poesy*, but he ended up leaving his stuff on his desk, going up a floor and picking out *Catch-22*. His folded-corner bookmark hadn't been flattened.

Back at his desk, Jake started with the chapter called, THE SOLDIER WHO SAW EVERYTHING TWICE, and made it to MILO THE MILITANT before he folded a page there, closed the book and packed up.

At his apartment door, he dropped his books as he fiddled with the damn lock, which still wouldn't surrender without a two-handed wrestling match. He finally won, shoved the door open and was bending down to pick up his books when he saw Kit. She was sitting on the bed and obviously had been asleep.

He stared.

"I hope you don't mind," she said tentatively, "your landlord let me in."

"No," he said. Slowly, he retrieved his books, walked in and closed the door. "So this was the plan all along?" he said quietly. "I'm the safety valve. Good 'ol Jake? You know, I missed you, but I don't think I can forgive you, either."

She wasn't moving.

"I was wrong," she said, measuring her words. She had been prepared to defuse anger, not to face quiet scorn. "I was wrong, but not the way you think. And you were wrong."

"I'm listening."

"I'm pregnant." She let that register. "Three months pregnant. I don't know how I fouled it up, but I did."

"Mine or Chris'." The non-question shocked her. He knew about that time with Chris!

"Probably yours," she said softly. "But I can't be sure."

"Just tell me the whole story," he said bitterly. "I want to know the whole story. The truth."

As she was about to answer, Kit suddenly wondered. "Did Annie tell you?

"*Annie?* She knew?"

"I guess Annie didn't tell you."

"No."

"Well, how do you know about this if Annie didn't tell you?"

"Does it matter?"

"Sure."

"A guy on the team heard about it from someone who was at Reynolds' house and saw you. He thought you were screwing the professor, but I put two and two together. I figured Chris paid a visit – in more ways than one."

Kit was shocked. The guy who was sleeping with Chris' mother. He had been introduced to her in the kitchen, the morning after she and Chris...

"Chris was just home for a few days," she said. "It was just once. He came home to see his grandfather."

"Why didn't you tell me?"

"I guess I was ashamed. And I knew that was it."

"And you told *Annie?*"

"I made her promise not to tell you. I'm glad she didn't."

"Terrific."

"They'd just told me I was pregnant. I was going to get an abortion."

"Jesus, did you?"

"The sorority had its connections. I didn't want to make you a martyr. I didn't want to have to tell you I didn't know if the baby was yours. I was going to disappear, have it done and make excuses."

"You were going to?"

"I couldn't. Annie and I talked it through. She told me to tell you about the baby. Then she said *she* would. But I told her she had given her word."

"Well, she kept it."

"She told me to at least tell my parents, and I said I might... eventually. I was going to try to decide between an abortion and just taking off after the semester ended, or having the baby somewhere and putting it up for adoption."

"Jesus, you're still pregnant, right?" He stared, trying to see if she were showing.

"Yup. The day after I talked with Annie, Hassler expelled her. Annie argued with me about it again. She finally told me that if that was the way I felt when the semester was over, and I hadn't done anything, I could go with her, probably to Berkeley, to buy time."

"So this stuff about researching and writing was bullshit?"

"Not at all. But I'd decided to go with Annie before I decided to do that, too. I have to tell you, though, I think what I'm writing is good. Better than I dreamed."

With Jake still numb, she told him everything about Chris, about not knowing which one of them was the father. "No excuses," she said. "I knew better, right from the start. You're goddamn right I was ashamed, really ashamed, but I really fell in love with you."

For the first time, she was crying.

"Now let me tell you something more about Annie," she said, sniffling. She spelled out Annie's deal with Hassler, to keep her from being the D.A.'s campaign sacrifice. "Even after that, Annie was worried the D.A. still might go after me and didn't feel guilty about getting me out of town for a while. I made another promise to Annie. If I didn't have the abortion pretty quick – and she was against it – I'd come back and tell you. When Annie heard about President Hassler dying, she called me and said this was the time. I decided she was right. So here I am."

He sat down with Kit.

"I'm glad," he said. "And I'm sorry."

"Same here."

"What about Chris?"

"He's a nice guy. I really loved him. But it's over. He just wants different things. I don't love him anymore."

She paused.

"What?" Jake asked.

"There's a bit of a double standard here, you know."

"Meaning?"

"Seems like we ran into about ten girls you'd screwed."

"Two."

"Yeah, right," she said sarcastically.

"And neither was after we got together. You and Chris, that happened after we got together."

"I'm sorry. But it's not like it was someone off the street – or I'd just met at Terwilliger's."

"What if it's his kid?"

"I don't know. I've thought about that about a million times. I don't think it is. I think it's yours. But, Jake, I can't be positive."

"So what are we going to do?" he asked as they hugged.

"Let's go to the memorial service tomorrow," she said.

৩৯

Classes were canceled. When the service ended, Benson whispered to Alex Tolliver, and they began passing the word to the players. Meet downstairs, in the football practice locker room for a final reunion. They had gotten the food service to roll in coffee and donuts, and if Bill Wyden wouldn't pay for it, the coaches – the ex-coaches – would.

## THIRTY-SEVEN: "THE WEIGHT"

Downstairs, Benson walked to the center of the room one more time. He told them about his final walk with Hassler.

"We're all going to remember these times," Benson said. "This was a good man, and the times ate him up. I hope we all learn from this."

A few minutes later, when the coffee drinkers were on their second cups and a few of them were beginning to leave, somebody turned on the television in the corner and tuned to the noon news. Jake didn't spot Annie in the clips of the protesters, and he scoffed at himself for trying.

"I ask you to share with me today the majesty of this moment," Richard Milhous Nixon, the thirty-seventh president of the United States, began. "In the orderly transfer of power, we celebrate the unity that keeps us free."

Jake didn't feel like celebrating. He took Kit's hand again, and they walked away.

# THIRTY-EIGHT:
## "NIGHTS IN WHITE SATIN"

*(February 2004)*

The house was in the same place, but little looked the same. As Jake Powell and his entourage climbed the front porch, he asked the television photographer to hold off on taping for a minute, and then knocked on the heavy front door. Ken Howe, the university history professor who owned the house and had supervised the gutting and rebuilding, cheerfully had given his permission for the visit on the telephone, but Powell didn't want to ambush him with lights in his face.

"Senator!" Howe said, smiling, yet surveying warily.

Powell shook his hand, and then introduced the group. His wife. His son, a Seattle advertising executive. Bill Flanagan, the *Prime Tuesday* reporter, and Kevin Naples, his photographer.

"Come in," said Howe, who looked as if he probably had put down his pipe to answer the door.

As they were approaching the third floor on the stairway, Howe turned as he climbed. "You aren't going to recognize much," he said to Jake, his closest pursuer.

"Believe me," interjected Kit Powell, one step behind her husband, "that's a good thing."

As they had agreed, Naples began taping as they stepped into what used to be the attic. The alcove was Howe's office, with a desk, a computer workstation and two file cabinets. The walls were plush paneling. The bathroom fixtures were gone, and the only remnant of the old plumbing was the sink that went with the wet bar.

Jake Powell nudged his son, Robert, and pointed.

"That's where I had my posters," he told Robert Powell, who was thirty-four years old. "Gandhi. Donovan. Hendrix. Bobby Kennedy."

"You forgot Dick Butkus," Kit said.

"Who?" asked Robert.

The exchange was a cute opening in the *Prime Tuesday* story that ran three days later.

By then, Bill Flanagan was back in the New York studio. The first five minutes of the piece was a recap of the "controversial friendship" between "maverick Oregon senator Jake Powell" and "radical fugitive Annie Laughlin" and now he was going to get into the material the network had been relentlessly – yet vaguely – promoting since the weekend.

Flanagan turned to another camera, heralding a change of pace.

"So that's a look at Jake Powell's Cascade of 1968 and the present, at the history of the friendship," he said. "Certainly, it was a tumultuous time, for Jake Powell, for his campus, and his country. Jake Powell is right: This all needs to be framed in that context."

Flanagan turned to another camera, heralding a change of pace.

"During Powell's run for the Senate, in the 1992 campaign against the four-term incumbent Republican, the consensus was that state Democratic leadership knew he couldn't win because of that past and advanced Powell as a sacrificial lamb. He was a successful lawyer and was happy in Medford, where his wife, Kit, the author of the '60s landmark look at the radical student movement, *Barbed in Berkeley,* was the editor of the *Medford Tribune-Post* newspaper. Even he didn't expect that to change. But disclosures about the incumbent's bizarre personal misconduct suddenly surfaced, and Republicans' renewed attempts to question Powell's past didn't deflect the spotlight. After one of the more shocking upsets in Oregon political history, Powell set about establishing a solid reputation as a hard-working, effective freshman senator. In 1998, Republicans hammered away at Powell's refusal to disown his friendship with Laughlin, who was on the run after she was implicated in the bombing of several military recruiting offices in 1969 and '70. But Powell was re-elected."

Flanagan now walked toward yet another camera.

"When we told Senator Powell we were working on a story about his relationship with Annie Laughlin, and let him know we had discovered what had happened to her, he said he would talk during the reunion weekend for the 1968 Cascade University football team in Cascade. The team featured Hall of Fame quarterback Rick Winslow, future NFL star and broadcaster Timmy Hilton, plus several other future NFL players, including linebacker Alex Tolliver and receiver Keith Oldham. Its coaching staff included future NFL coaches Howie Hallstrom, Carl Steele, and Klaus Rockwell, plus Pete Salisbury, who went on to great success as a college head coach himself. That weekend, the team received the university's Pioneer Award en masse. Powell said both the reunion and the visit might help put things in context. And as we have seen, he was right. Then he sat down and talked about Annie Laughlin."

Jake Powell was in a plush chair in his Cascade hotel suite, talking with Flanagan.

"She wrote us pretty much once a month. Her letter would be in an envelope, stuffed in another envelope, and it always came from a different place and person. I'd always assumed it went through a few hands before it got to me, and it always would be about three weeks behind."

"If you didn't know where she was, how did you write her back?"

"We'd put the letter to her in an envelope, put that envelope in another envelope, and then mail it to the person who sent us the last letter. But we never got Annie's letters from the same person twice."

"When did this start?"

"I'd say the mid '70s."

"You weren't in politics then. Why didn't she want you to know where she was?"

"She didn't want to put us in that position. I guess you could say she wanted us to have plausible deniability. I was a lawyer. Kit was a journalist. Plus, let's face it, the less we knew, the less there was a chance of us inadvertently letting something slip to the wrong person or even the FBI following us to her. And then when I ran for office, that made it even more important."

Flanagan was shown each time he asked a question, or each time the editor felt a "knowing nod" from the reporter was good TV during one of Powell's answers.

"Did you ever see her?"

"No."

"Not even before you ran for office?"

"No. The last time we saw her was before she went underground."

"Did you turn her letters over to the FBI?"

"No."

"Why not?"

"I had no desire to. For one thing, we always knew she didn't have a hand in the bombings."

"What do you mean?"

"Some nuts went farther than she knew they were going to. They were mad at her for scuttling the plan to blow up the Air Force plane in 1968, so they lied and told the FBI that she had known what they were going to do."

"And how do you know that's true?"

"Because Annie told us."

"And you believed her?"

"Sure did."

"Did you tell that to the FBI?"

"No."

"Why not?"

"She asked us not to. She said it wouldn't go any good and she liked the way her life was."

"Did you talk to her on the phone?"

"Once, maybe twice a year. She'd always call us at a hotel when I was traveling, or both of us were traveling. When we knew a long time ahead of time where we'd be, we'd send her a hotel phone number. We did that even after we got cell phones. I never asked, but she probably I always thought she probably wouldn't be surprised if she was using a pre-paid phone card and a payphone."

"You ever try and talk her into turning herself in?"

"Sure. All the time. She said she was doing fine, she was contributing where she was and this was paying back her debt – if there was a debt to pay."

"When was the last time you heard from her?"

"Two months ago. She didn't even tell us she was sick." He choked up. "Then we got a call from someone in Colorado who said she was a friend of Annie's and she had promised Annie that she would call us after … after she was gone."

Suddenly, Bill Flanagan was standing outside a school, outlined against a mountain backdrop.

# THIRTY-EIGHT: "NIGHTS IN WHITE SATIN"

"Annie Laughlin was living here – in tiny Leonardo, Colorado, on the western slope of the Rocky Mountains. The popular high school teacher known as Sharon Kesey died of Hodgkin's Disease three weeks ago. Virtually the whole town, and hundreds of returned students, attended the funeral. So did U.S. Senator Jake Powell and Kit Powell, who officially were on a suddenly arranged Colorado mountain vacation. Several days later, when we arrived in Leonardo to trace this story, I spoke with principal Arthur Young."

Young, a chubby and bespectacled man in a sleeveless sweater, was at his school desk. The wall was filled with academic-oriented plaques.

"A couple of days after Sharon died, the FBI told me the story," he said. "They said they'd gotten a letter from her, a letter her friend promised to mail after she died, saying she was Annie Laughlin. I didn't know who Annie Laughlin was, and they had to tell me. She was Sharon to us, she was great here, and I'm convinced she hadn't done what they said she did. But I suppose this is terrible to say, I wouldn't much care now if she had. The kids and the town loved her."

Young laughed.

"You should have seen her coach the girls' basketball team. Sharon didn't know a damn thing about it. But we needed her, so she was out there. Every year, when basketball practice was about to start, she always said she had a jock friend she could call for advice if she had to. I guess I know who that was now."

Jake Powell was back on the screen.

"I want something on the record," he said. "We disagreed, passionately. But she was my best friend, except for my wife. I feel that way, now more than ever."

"Even if you didn't know where she was, don't these admissions make you more vulnerable in your next campaign?"

"No."

"Why not?"

"There won't be a next campaign. I'm not running again."

# CHAPTER BY CHAPTER: THE MUSICAL TITLES

All singles or albums were on the charts at the time of the chapters, with the exception of Chapter 38.

ONE (Aug. 26, 1968): "Waiting for the Sun"...Doors album.

TWO (Aug. 26, 1968): "Jumpin' Jack Flash"...Rolling Stones single.

THREE (Aug. 28, 1968): "Born To Be Wild"...Steppenwolf single.

FOUR (Sept. 12): "MacArthur Park"...Richard Harris single.

FIVE (Sept. 14): "Hey Jude"...Beatles single.

SIX (Sept. 16): "Bookends"...Simon and Garfunkel album.

SEVEN (Sept. 20): "Classical Gas"...Mason Williams single.

EIGHT (Sept. 23): "I've Just Gotta Get a Message to You"...Bee Gees single.

NINE (Sept. 26): "Hello, I Love You"...Doors single.

TEN (Sept. 30): "All Along the Watchtower"...Jimi Hendrix single.

ELEVEN (Oct. 8): "Scarborough Fair"...Simon and Garfunkel single.

TWELVE (Oct. 12): "Magic Carpet Ride"...Steppenwolf single.

THIRTEEN (Oct. 16): "People Got To Be Free"...Young Rascals single.

FOURTEEN (Oct. 24): "Abraham, Martin and John"...Dion single.

FIFTEEN (Oct. 27): "Hush"...Deep Purple single.

SIXTEEN (Oct. 31): "In-A-Gadda-Da-Vida"...Iron Butterfly single.

SEVENTEEN (Nov. 3): "Piece of My Heart"...Big Brother and The Holding Company single.

EIGHTTEEN (Nov. 5): "Crosstown Traffic"...Jimi Hendrix single.

NINETEEN (Nov. 6): "Crown of Creation"...Jefferson Airplane album.

TWENTY (Nov. 8): "Light My Fire"...Jose Feliciano single

TWENTY-ONE (Nov. 9): "Fire"...Arthur Brown single.

TWENTY-TWO (Nov. 10): "Think!"...Aretha Franklin single.

TWENTY-THREE (Nov. 15): "Revolution"...Beatles single.

TWENTY-FOUR (Nov. 21): "In Search of the Lost Chord"...Moody Blues album.

TWENTY-FIVE (Nov. 23): "Waiting for the Sun"...Doors album.

TWENTY-SIX (Nov. 26): "White Room"...Cream single.

TWENTY-SEVEN (Dec. 12): "Hair!"...Original cast album.

TWENTY-EIGHT (Dec. 17): "Tuesday Afternoon"...Moody Blues single.

TWENTY-NINE (Dec. 21): "Goin' up the Country"...Canned Heat single.

THIRTY (Dec. 27): "Jennifer Juniper"...Donovan single.

THIRTY-ONE (Jan. 7, 1969): "I Heard It Through the Grapevine"...Marvin Gaye single.

THIRTY-TWO (Jan. 10): "Crimson and Clover"...Everyday People single.

THIRTY-THREE (Jan. 14): "Wheels of Fire"...Cream album.

THIRTY-FOUR (Jan. 15): "Hurdy Gurdy Man"...Donovan single.

THIRTY-FIVE (Jan. 16): "Magic Bus"...The Who single.

THIRTY-SIX (Jan. 17): "While My Guitar Gently Weeps"...Beatles album cut.

THIRTY-SEVEN (Jan. 20): "The Weight"...The Band album cut.

THIRTY-EIGHT: "Nights in White Satin"...Moody Blues single.

Made in United States
North Haven, CT
28 November 2022

27476982R00152